The Legend of th

Book 3

Depths of

Darkness

MARGIT SANDEMO

Translated from the Swedish
by Gregory Herring and Angela Cook

Tanman

The Legend of the Ice People

Depths of Darkness

The original Norwegian version was published in 1982 under the title
Sagan om Isfolket 3: Avgrunnen by Bladkompaniet, Oslo, Norway

First published in Great Britain in paperback in September 2008
by Tagman Worldwide Ltd in The Tagman Press imprint.

Tagman Worldwide Ltd
Media House
Burrel Road, St Ives, Huntingdon,
Cambridgeshire, PE27 3LE
Tel: 0845 644 4186
Fax: 0845 644 4187
www.tagmanpress.co.uk
email: editorial@tagmanpress.co.uk

ISBN: Paperback 978-1-903571-79-8
A CIP catalogue record for this book is available from the British Library

Text & Cover Design: Richard Legg
Translation: Gregory Herring and Angela Cook

Printed by CLE Print Ltd, St Ives, Cambridgeshire, PE27 3LE, UK

Tagman www.tagmanpress.co.uk

This first English translation of *The Legend of the Ice People*
is dedicated with love and gratitude to the memory
of my dear late husband Asbjorn Sandemo,
who made my life a fairy tale

The Legend of the Ice People

Further titles to be published in 2008

Chapter 1

The wind wailed and moaned through the treetops of the dense pine forest, seeming to imitate the rhythmic chanting of monks performing a solemn liturgy of sorrow and anguish in a giant cathedral. As they bowed unwillingly before the wind, the branches of the pines were twisting and screaming in protest. Overhead, the pale autumn moon appeared only fleetingly between ragged clouds that were chasing each other in a wild frenzy across the heavens.

Sol laughed aloud as she ran beneath the trees. The fury of the weather was arousing all the deepest passions in her, making her feel alive and exhilarated. She was a woman now – as free and unfettered as the storm that tore at the trees above her. Clutched very tightly to her chest, she carried a small bundle of Hanna's possessions. Tengel had given them to her earlier that same day, before she had taken farewell of him and the rest of the family at their home, Linden Allée. This act symbolised for her a very important fact – her time had come at last!

Her younger brother Are had agreed to provide an escort for her along the road to the harbour at Oslo, where a ship lay ready to sail for Denmark. They had ridden together about half the distance, when Sol suddenly insisted on taking a shortcut alone through the trees. Despite his reluctance, Are had agreed to this and rode on, leading her horse and carrying her small trunk. Because he wanted to be sure that she got safely aboard the ship, he had resolved to meet her on the other side of the forest.

Charlotte Meiden had arranged Sol's trip to Denmark. She was to be the companion to an older noblewoman, who was frightened of making such a long sea journey on her own. The family had decided that Sol would be right for this role, because she had conducted herself so impeccably these past five years. Now, however, recognising that she was becoming restless and was eager to be gone, they felt unable to hold her back any longer.

Yes, she had behaved well – but only because she wanted to be allowed to devote herself to her beloved craft when she reached adulthood. How difficult it had been at times, too! There had been occasions when people had been unkind or insulting to those she loved and her fingers had tingled with the desire to do something.

On one occasion she had made a doll to represent a snooty highborn lady who made disparaging comments about Charlotte. Sol had managed to get a strand of the woman's hair and sew it into the doll. Just as she was about to pierce its 'heart' with a needle, she came to her senses, remembering that she had made Tengel a solemn faithful promise never to do such things. So she had destroyed the doll, allowing herself to feel virtuous – but she still felt a little fretful afterwards, wondering whether or not she still had the power.

In general Tengel was very pleased with her work among the sick and they had come to rely on her almost as much as on him. There had been one or two cases where her methods of healing had been a mite drastic perhaps, but she had been careful and no one had noticed! Neither had she killed anybody whom she thought should be spared a life of martyrdom to sickness and pain. Except perhaps a couple of times, she thought with regret. But they were merely trifles and couldn't really count against her. She had only acted that way to make sure her powers didn't completely stagnate. Now, at long last, her time of doing penance was over.

She had not wanted to ride through the forest. She needed to feel the wind against her face and the earth under her feet, in the knowledge that all this was hers. She wanted to listen to the storm as it engulfed her and to laugh at the moon.

'I'm free, Hanna,' she whispered. 'I'm free, and now our time begins.'

Her own plans for the journey to Denmark were markedly different from those of the family. With her schemes in mind, she had made some enquiries and been told that the authorities did indeed eagerly hunt down and capture witches almost continually in Denmark. However, most often these were just normal women with no knowledge of the black arts, whom spiteful neighbours had branded as witches. But Sol knew where the real witches and wizards were to be found. Hanna had once spoken the name of the place with deep reverence. That was where she wanted to go – that was where she *would* go!

Unsurprisingly, because of the vigour with which they were persecuted, true witches were now few in number. But those who had managed to survive were real enough. She was one of them, one of those few – together with Tengel. But Tengel had always been unwilling to practice the true craft, wasting his powers instead on 'good deeds'. How did he do it? She still found it difficult to understand. Five years of goodness and decency had been more than enough for her!

Sol stopped running suddenly. It was time to take stock of the precious objects she had been deprived of for so long. Laughing with gleeful anticipation, she opened the bundle she had been grasping so tightly to her chest. There was the skull of a child found buried under the floor of a barn one hundred years go, neither blessed with baptism nor burial; the finger of a hanged criminal; the heart of a black dog; earth from a graveyard; snakes tongues – and yes, there it was, the most prized of them all – the mandrake – an heirloom discovered in the lands of the Mediterranean long, long ago and plucked out of the earth beneath a gallows tree, where a murderer had spilled his seed at the moment of death. That was the place where the mandrake had grown and where the root, which so closely resembled a human form, had screamed so piercingly when pulled from the earth. As a result, the master sorcerer – who had performed the deed on a Thursday night under a full moon – had been driven insane.

That was the story as Hanna had told it to her and she knew she must take the utmost care of the mandrake – it was priceless. Sol felt the weight of the grotesque dried root in her hand. It was big – longer than her hand – and there were marks where someone had cut small pieces from the ends of the root. Could it have been her much feared ancestor, Tengel the Evil One, who had done this? It was said that the root had been handed down from him. Sol felt certain that the pieces would have been used in secret potions. She knew the power that mandrake possessed and how it could be used in so many ways – in a love potion or perhaps to destroy an enemy or even to create wealth for its keeper.

A thin leather strap was tied round it. She gave a satisfied nod. Now that it was hers she could use it for its true purpose! She untangled the strap and hung the mandrake around her neck, tucking it out of sight. It felt heavy and rough against the skin between her breasts, almost as if it was forming itself to her body. She shuddered; it seemed to be alive. But she would get used to it. Now the most powerful amulet of all, the greatest known talisman of good fortune, protected her. She felt safe in the world – and for her this was a solemn occasion.

Dag was already in Copenhagen. He had been studying law at the university there for a year and a half, and intended to find a good occupation for himself when he returned to Norway. The family trusted him to look after Sol, hoping that some good might come out of the trip – an offer of employment perhaps or useful new social contacts. By social contacts Silje, always the romantic one, had naturally thought first and foremost of a suitable marriage. Dag could introduce her to the right sort of people at Court and in the finest circles of society, because many of his academic friends were nobles or highly born. Nowadays he mixed with distinguished company and the plan was that she would stay with him for one month, before returning home.

Sol grinned as she hurried on through the screaming wind-torn forest. It would, of course, be comforting to have her foster brother at hand, but as far as she was concerned the 'right circles' would be those she chose for herself! Even so, she reflected, one should not discount the Court altogether – there might be a few handsome fellows there.

Sol had remained chaste and modest since the time, at the age of fourteen, when she had seduced the stable lad, Klaus. Now she felt quite ready to have another adventure of that kind. After all, the episode with Klaus had been somewhat unsatisfying and had been nothing more than a conquest for its own sake. She realised full well that there were many more exciting emotions to explore in a relationship between a man and a woman. As these thoughts tumbled through her mind, she ran her hands down the curves of her body, knowing how beautiful she was. A great many people had told her so, and countless men had also reached out with their lustful hands to grasp at her – even those lying in their sick beds.

Poor Hanna, she thought, with a sudden pang of regret. She had never had Sol's opportunities. She had been ugly, so hideous in fact that folk turned their backs on her. She had been lonely as well, shut away in a little mountain valley. Sol on the other hand had her whole life and the whole world at her feet – and she intended to use all her talents to their full.

Everyone at home had been sad when she left, but they also understood that she needed to have the freedom to spread her wings or she would be stifled by her surroundings. In truth, she knew that her fractious and impatient behaviour during the last six months had been painful for them all. Tengel and Silje had hugged her so tightly as they said farewell and little sister Liv had had tears in her eyes. Charlotte Meiden had come to see her off and to send good wishes to Dag – but at last, to her great relief, she and Are had ridden off down the avenue of linden trees, Silje's beloved allée.

There was a gap in the trees lining the allée, where one had withered and died. It was the Dowager Baroness's tree and Tengel had chopped it down after the old lady passed away. Her body now lay buried in the cemetery at Gråstensholm and Tengel had planted a new sapling in place of the old tree. Sol remembered when he had done it and also Silje's unusual outburst of anger, which had followed the event.

'You are not to enchant any more trees, Tengel,' she said, shaking visibly. 'I cannot cope with watching them all the time.'

'They have helped me many times,' he replied defensively. 'You know that, through them, I have been able to discover hidden sicknesses in you all.'

'Yes, I know. But it terrifies me so! As soon as I see a yellow leaf lying on the ground I fall into a fit of panic.'

'As you wish,' Tengel had said. 'I promise I won't put a hex on any more trees. Besides, we have no new family members to dedicate trees to.'

'No, but all four of our children are growing up, so we may expect grandchildren in a few years.'

'All right!' Tengel had smiled at her with loving eyes and given her his word that all the new trees from then on would just be ordinary trees.

Remembering these things, Sol slowed her pace a little. She had reached a clearing in the forest and was approaching a small cluster of cottages. The smell of salt in the air also told her that she was getting closer to the fjord. Far in the distance she saw the smoke from many houses. There, beyond the Akershus fortress, lies Oslo, she said to herself.

Dawn was just breaking and the glow of the moon was beginning to fade, as a curtain of light grew brighter and stronger along the horizon. After walking through the forest darkness for so long, the new grey light appeared to Sol to shimmer above the sleeping village, and the deep silence of the surrounding fields contrasted sharply with the deafening roar of the wind that had filled her ears among the trees.

She walked quietly past the low-roofed cottages, where no signs of life were yet to be seen. Only the wind whistling over the grass, the far off noises of the forest and the sound of cattle rustling in the straw of an unseen barn broke the silence. When she reached a lane leading up to a church, she stopped, brushing aside the locks of long black hair that the wind was blowing across her face.

She stood for a while without moving, looking about; then she turned slowly several times, taking in every detail of the silent scene. She saw the stocks, the whipping pole and the place alongside the churchyard wall where a vast number of stones lay on the ground, silently proclaiming that many people had been stoned to death there. A little further away stood the block, the place of execution where the condemned would bow their heads one last time to await the fall of an axe. An empty gallows could be seen some way off, but still close enough to be visible to the entire congregation.

These were the things her eyes could see; but, as she stood there, Sol realised she could also sense much more. Facing the wind to keep it from blowing her hair into her face, she was surprised by how much she could really feel – anguish and the fear of death from all those who had ended their days here; shame swirling like an invisible mist round the stocks; the sorrow and sadness of relatives; the curiosity of the crowds, mixed with bloodlust and a drooling desire to witness ultimate spectacles.

Sol had no fear of the dead. Once, when she was very young, she had laughed aloud at a hanged corpse twisting slowly on a gallows. Silje had believed it was just childish innocence, but it was not that at all. The black of night, darkness and death made up Sol's world. Her name, which meant 'the sun', had been given to her by Silje to protect her – but it had not helped in the least. The moon, not the sun, was the light she truly followed.

Sol had been truly afraid only once in her life – when Tengel had turned his rage upon her. On that occasion, she had killed a worthless wretch of a verger, who was intent on harming her family. Her love and respect for Tengel remained boundless, but it was because she had been anxious not to be the victim of his rage again that she had kept her composure for so long. That aside, nothing else on earth could frighten her.

Behind Sol, in the shadowy pine forest and unseen by her, the pale fluttering phosphorescent flame of a will-o'-the-wisp chased eerily back and forth among the trees. Flaring and diminishing in turns, the little-understood rural phenomenon cast its strange mysterious glow in all directions. Then abruptly it extinguished itself, as the dawn light grew stronger.

It was the year 1599, Sol was just twenty years old and her real life was about to begin.

* * * *

As expected, Are stood waiting on the other side of the forest. He was Tengel's only son, with the callow features of a thirteen-year-old, wide cheekbones and coal-black hair. While Tengel and Silje's other three children and foster children were creations of beauty, one could not rightly say this of Are. To make up for this, he did have a natural aura of invincibility that Sol considered was worth far more in the long term.

He accompanied her to the ship and made sure she and

the old noblewoman were properly settled on board. The old lady said she was pleasantly surprised to have such a 'beautiful and well brought up young lady' for an escort. Sol in her turn responded with her 'be nice to old ladies' manner. Her voice became soft and reverent and her demeanour showed nothing but respect.

They stood on deck for a long time, waving to Are, who waited on the quayside waving back at them. The ship weighed anchor and eased away from the quay. The adventure had begun.

The crossing to Denmark was quite arduous and unpleasant, as the ship was buffeted by heavy seas, first from one side then the other. Sol had prepared a potion to prevent seasickness, for which the old lady was very grateful. She boasted bravely to Sol that, indeed, they seemed to be the only passengers who were not suffering from the discomfort of that unpleasant malady.

If Sol, however, had been hoping for her first small adventure during the voyage, she was to be sadly disappointed. Most of the male passengers hung over the rail or lay curled up in some cubby-hole, while the crew was a collection of grumpy fat old matelots with no appeal at all. Of course, the voyage in itself was unbelievably exciting for a young woman eager for new experiences. She took every opportunity to go out on deck and whenever the waves crashed over the bows, showering her with water, she would scream with joy. As the ship dived down headlong between giant waves, she let out an ecstatic yell and when it pulled itself up again, heavy and awash with salt water, she cheered from the bottom of her heart. At last she understood how dreary life at Linden Allée had been all these years.

A carriage was waiting for the old lady when they docked in Copenhagen and once she had settled her comfortably inside it, Sol had discharged her responsibilities. The lady had been so pleased with her onboard companion that she presented Sol with a small purse that jingled with the sound of coins. Making a conscious effort to stop herself from counting it there and then, Sol curtseyed and waved a cheery farewell as the carriage drew away.

She was not going to be left to her fate, however, because Dag was already there on the quayside waiting for her. On catching sight of him, she ran full tilt and threw herself into his arms. 'Dag! My, how handsome you've become – and you've grown too, little brother!'

She pushed him away from her to arm's length and looked him up and down. He now had the face of a grown man. Although his nose was still long and straight, and his face narrow, all his features had become better proportioned and more in balance. His metal-grey eyes were defined by thick brown eyebrows, which contrasted with his blond hair. The elegant clothes he wore were the height of fashion. Gone was the everyday padded doublet with a patterned front, high neck and cuffs and there was no sign of the baggy breeches he had always worn at home.

Now that Dag was living in Copenhagen, he had adopted the ways of the city. He sported a hat with a wide brim, one side held up with a clasp and a long sweeping feather. His shirt collar was wide, turned down and had long points. Trousers and jacket were more close-fitting than she had been used to seeing on him at home, showing off his manliness to advantage. Finally, he wore black and tan boots that she found really impressive. Oh, how handsome, so very handsome he was!

Almost before she had completed her inspection of Dag, her womanly eye started to take note of the few ladies she saw on the quayside. 'Is this the way all people dress here?' she exclaimed. 'I must look so old fashioned! I'm going to find somewhere to hide, Dag.'

He chuckled – their admiration was mutual, despite her simple older Norwegian garb. 'There is no need for that, I'm sure. My, this is going to be difficult!'

'What is?'

'Keeping all the admirers away from you.'

'Why would you want to keep them away?' laughed Sol.

Dag took this as a joke – but it wasn't.

'We can walk to my lodgings; it's not very far. Let me take your trunk – I don't think it's too heavy – and your bundle too.'

'No, I'll carry that.'

Dag gave her a questioning look, but didn't insist. 'So tell me, how are things at home?' he asked eagerly, as they left the harbour and began walking along a busy street.

Sol found it nearly impossible to take her eyes off all the extraordinary and wonderful new things that surrounded her, with folk swarming everywhere and even animals in the street. There were the cries of moneylenders and pungent smells of fish, tar, oil, smoke and waste, as well as the aromas of fruit and vegetables. Although she had travelled to Akershus and Oslo with Tengel a few times, this was different in every way. This was the great wide world she longed for!

'At home? All is well. They all send their best, especially Charlotte, of course. I have brought letters, lots of letters – and money.'

'That's wonderful,' murmured Dag.

'And Are wondered if you could get him one of those modern Snaphaunce muskets.' She broke off again, gazing around excitedly. 'Oh Dag! This is all so exciting! Look at that house – it's so big!' She chattered on and on, bubbling over with eagerness to see everything.

'I expect Mama Charlotte is feeling alone now?' said Dag thoughtfully.

'Yes, and she is impatient for you to complete your studies and come home. But she and Silje spend a lot of time together.'

'And the others. What of them?'

'Tengel works hard with the sick – but he tries to do no more than a few days each week. It is not easy when people still come just to feel his healing touch. Some have travelled a very long way – and he has never been able to refuse anyone. We had a horrible outbreak of plague last winter and he forbade the sick to come to our home, not wanting us to be infected, but, to Tengel's dismay, they still came like swarms of flies. The Ice People, though, are strong folk, as you know and we all survived, except for your poor Grand-mama, the Dowager Baroness, who could not fight off the sickness.'

'Yes, I know – and I still miss her terribly.'

'As do I,' said Sol quietly. 'She was a fine old lady. Tengel was downhearted at the time because they were very close. Yet it is strange that time does not seem to show on Tengel.'

'You remember Hanna?' said Dag. 'She lived to a great age.'

'Do I remember Hanna?' she asked, with a note of pain in her voice. She punched him and swore at him jokingly in her peasant Norwegian dialect. 'I'm telling you little brother that I too will be an ancient! I shall outlive all of you!'

'That's as maybe,' said Dag, suddenly ill at ease. 'And Silje, how are things with her?'

'Silje is the same as ever. Happy and confident, as long as she has her Tengel. She paints and does so many other things – she is perhaps a little more matronly than she was, but it suits her. Oh, yes! I haven't told you yet – Liv has found a suitor.'

Dag stopped dead on the crest of the road, causing a horse and cart to brake sharply behind them. Then they stepped smartly to one side, between a cooper's forge and a coppersmith's workshop.

'What did you say?' he exclaimed. 'Liv has a suitor? But, good God, she is just a child!'

'Sixteen, nearly seventeen. And more gentle and sweet than you would believe. Silje was not any older when she fell for Tengel's charms.'

Dag was no longer listening; his face was rigid.

'My little sister has a suitor. What sort of man is he, may I ask?'

'Don't get so angry! Well, what can I say? His name is Laurents and he is from a good family, though not of noble birth – but then Liv herself is a commoner. His parents were very wealthy merchants. The father is dead and Laurents is carrying on the business.'

'And do you like him?'

Sol shrugged her shoulders. 'He's not really my sort,' she answered evasively.

They carried on walking, but Dag was silent for a long time. He put great faith in Sol's opinion about people – nobody was as perceptive as her, in his experience.

'And Liv? What does she say?' He broke off, raising his voice. 'Sol! Don't lift your skirts so high! It's not that filthy here!'

'Well, Liv doesn't speak much about it, so in truth I can't say how she feels.' Sol paused and looked carefully at Dag. 'But we have heard that *you* are to be wed! Will it be soon?'

'I? Who has told you this?'

'Charlotte. We understand it is a certain Mistress Trolle.'

'Has Mama said this? And to Liv as well?'

'To all of us – she was overjoyed.'

'Oh dear, oh dear,' laughed Dag, but with a hint of irritation. 'I mentioned in one or two letters that she is among my circle of friends and that she is a sweet and pleasant girl. Yes, I was interested, but she was not the one and only for me. I haven't seen her in weeks! Mother is such a matchmaker!'

He seemed disinclined to say more, so Sol just nodded and they walked in silence for a while.

'Are is a very good lad,' she added after an interval. 'He is so self-assured and friendly, with both feet on the ground; not like the rest of us at all. He will do well.'

'I'm sure he will. You cannot imagine how much I miss them all. But what about you, Sol? Have you found an admirer?'

'Me?' She laughed as they turned down a genteel-looking side street. 'No! Where would I find an admirer?'

'Don't hide your light under a bushel, Sol! I'm sure you already have many admirers.'

She suddenly became more serious. 'That may be so, but I do not pay them any heed – though it frightens me sometimes, Dag, because I don't seem to be able to fall in love with anyone.'

He looked at her thoughtfully, mulling over what she had just said.

'You just haven't found the right man for you yet,' he said gently. 'And anyway, I know how fond you can be of people.'

'Oh of my closest family, yes! But, for me, Tengel overshadows all other men. Not that I am in love with him. Of course I'm not – that would be sick! But, you see, he is my ideal. Nobody can measure up to him. I compare all young men to him and they all fall hopelessly short of the mark.'

'Of course they do! There is only one Tengel.'

'Yes, and that is what makes it so confusing.'

Dag pondered this. 'One might say something about how you could be looking for a father figure because you never knew your own father. But I sense that would not be true. You are not seeking a man with Tengel's virtues, Sol, but one with his power and demonic ways!'

'In truth I think it is as you say,' she replied, crestfallen.

'But let me tell you one thing, dear friend,' Dag continued quietly. 'The power Tengel has does not come from within himself. He draws his strength from Silje!'

Sol was quiet for some time; then she said, 'Yes, but her strength depends on her having his love.'

'That is also true.'

'Then neither one is complete without the other.'

'No. We have been very fortunate you and I, to have grown up in such a home. Anyhow, here we are! This door here.'

'My, what a fine house,' said Sol admiring the timber-framed walls of the house and a fan-shaped decoration painted in blue and gold above the door.

'Yes and the people I live with are decent folk. You shall have your own room while you are here. Unfortunately you have arrived at a difficult time. They have just lost their little son.'

'Is he dead?'

'No, as I said, he is lost. He disappeared three days ago.'

'Oh! That's terrible,' said Sol. 'Worse than anything else.'

'Not knowing? Yes it is. The poor mother is almost insane with worry. They dragged the river near here, but found nothing. Now they believe that someone stole the child. There is no trace of him.'

They had entered the house and could not discuss the matter further. The master and mistress rose from their chairs in the parlour and came to greet them. Dag had not exaggerated – the young mother's hands were shaking visibly and her face bore the traces of too many tears.

In a solemn voice, Dag introduced them to Sol. 'May I present my foster sister, Sol Angelica – and these are my good hosts, the Count and Countess Strahlenhelm.'

Sol made a low curtsey. 'Your sister is delightful,' said the Count, taking her hand. 'Henriette, have you ever seen such lovely eyes? I declare I have never seen eyes with such a colour. Amber!'

His wife could do no more than nod in their direction and offer a wan smile.

Sol was secretly admiring her clothing. She wore a ruff as big as a mill wheel, a pearl-embroidered bonnet and, beneath her brocade skirts she must have been wearing an enormous farthingale, because her hips were so wide she could comfortably rest her arms on them.

The Count said, 'Perhaps Dag, you will show young Sol to her room. We shall have a simple meal shortly, but you must excuse my wife, she will retire. She cannot cope with too much at the moment.'

'Of course, I quite understand,' answered Sol quietly. As she spoke a violent unfamiliar feeling came over her. There was an invisible presence that disturbed her intensely and made her feel restless.

The Countess left the room, covering her face with a handkerchief. Sol waited until she had gone, then turned to the Count.

'The room can wait. I think, perhaps, I can help you to find your child.'

'Sol!' exclaimed Dag, with a warning glance.

His host raised his hand, bidding him to be silent. 'What do you mean by that, young lady?'

'I know that I should say nothing, Dag, but you must understand that this is urgent!'

'What are you talking about?' asked the Count. 'Do you know something?'

Dag intervened. 'This can be very dangerous for my sister. I have no doubt that she can help – but she could pay for it with her life. Everything depends on your discretion.'

'Explain yourself!'

'You have already noticed my sister's eyes, Count Strahlenhelm. She has been blessed with them for a purpose. When Sol says that it is urgent, it means that she senses that the child still lives – for now. That Sol waited until your wife left the room was because she knows that your wife would not be able to stay silent.'

The Count looked blankly from one to the other.

'My child's life means everything to me.'

'Will you swear never to speak of that which you will witness here?' asked Sol, fretful and bursting with impatience. 'And never denounce me?'

'I so swear.'

'Good. Now give me something belonging to the child – a piece of clothing worn lately will do, so long as it has not been washed since he wore it. But remember: I cannot promise to find him – I can only try. It may just indicate his whereabouts.'

The tall distinguished man let out a deep sigh. 'I beg you, Mistress Sol. For even the merest suggestion, I will thank you on bended knee.'

'And I can trust you to be discreet?'

'I understand well what may happen to you should the authorities get word of your – abilities. In fact my wife had already expressed a wish for us to use the services of a so-called 'wise woman', but we knew of none and did not dare enquire. I urge you, let my gratitude stand guarantee for my silence!'

'And if I should not succeed?'

'Then you will have my gratitude for trying. But what if my wife or one of the servants should find out about your involvement?'

Sol felt inside the fold of her skirts. 'Give your wife this sleeping draught at once. It is not strong. Mix it with something for her to drink. You must order your servants not to disturb us.'

The Count gave Dag a curious look. 'You have kept this to yourself, Dag.'

Dag winced. 'These are not the sorts of talents that one speaks of in company, Your Grace.'

'No, no, quite right.'

He hurried from the room, carrying the powder in his hand.

'You shouldn't have done that, Sol,' muttered Dag.

'Should I not?'

He sighed. 'Well, perhaps. Should you prevail, then you will have earned his friendship for life. He is a powerful man, Sol. More powerful than you know.'

'Really? Who is he, then?'

'A judge – one of the highest in the Danish judiciary.'

'Oh dear!' said Sol, putting her hand to her mouth. 'So I seem to have got myself into a fine muddle.'

'Indeed. It's hardly surprising that he knows of no wise women, because he has been sending them to their deaths. That is why I implored you to say nothing.'

'But Dag, I could not stay silent. I could sense that the child lives and suffers. The feeling is everywhere in this room. It cried out to me from every inch of this house.'

'Then, for all our sakes,' said Dag, with a note of worry in his voice, 'let us hope you find the boy.'

Chapter 2

Before many minutes had passed the Count returned. 'I have given my wife the potion,' he said hesitantly. 'I have also told the servants that we are not to be disturbed.'

'Thank you,' replied Sol. 'That's very important to me.'

The Count nodded. 'Yes and you are right about Henriette's emotional condition. She would very likely speak too quickly and too loudly of things that are best kept quiet. Now, I have brought this small plaything that my son always cradled in his arms while he slept. Everything else has been laundered.'

Sol took the soft rag-doll. 'It is made from cloth. It will be fine. May I sit down?'

'But, of course, please forgive my lack of courtesy.'

As she sat, Sol said, 'Now I must ask that you make no sound.'

The room was as silent as a grave. Not even the sounds from the street outside could be heard. The two men remained standing motionless for what seemed like a very long time, while Sol sat very still, holding the doll to her face, with her eyes closed. Finally, in a voice almost devoid of expression, she whispered, 'Dark – cold – not much room.'

The Count wanted to ask, 'Is he alive?' but restrained himself.

'He is sleeping,' said Sol in her normal voice. 'Or he may be unconscious, I cannot tell. I sense fear and loneliness, now passed. He feels nothing at the moment.'

'Oh, dear God!' thought Count Strahlenhelm, his mind in turmoil. All this was hard for him to believe. This woman, on whom he should be passing judgement, had brought him hope in his desperation. What should he do? Nothing! He was now a father first and foremost and his profession had no place here. In an instant it had ceased to exist. Nevertheless, in the back of his mind, a thought troubled him, pricking at his conscience. What of all the other 'wise women' he had sentenced, showing no mercy and invoking the full fury of the law? Then he realised that Sol was talking again, mostly to herself, but wanting confirmation.

'He has blond downy hair. Between one and two years – closer to two, I think. He is dressed in velvet – purple velvet. A wide lace collar.'

The Count cast a surprised, questioning glance at Dag.

'I have told her nothing,' whispered Dag.

The unfortunate father seemed to take new courage from these words. He stood taller and new hope shone in his tired face. Although much older than his wife, he was a handsome man in his way; ascetically slim and well dressed, with a sharp eye. He looked excitedly now at his unusual guest.

Sol was savouring the moment. She had been able to use her powers and she was being acknowledged. But still the fate of the child tormented her, setting her nerves on edge.

'We must hurry,' she said impatiently. 'It is urgent, terribly urgent.'

'But where is he?' shouted the Count.

'I do not know!' hissed Sol, suddenly no longer in control of her temper.

'Has someone taken him?'

'No! There is no evil anywhere. Now, keep quiet! I feel something!'

As a judge, the Count had learned much about human nature and did not allow her reprimand to anger him.

Dag was immensely proud of his sister, but equally concerned about how these unfolding events would end. He had grown up with Sol and Tengel's remarkable gifts, but he had never really felt comfortable with them. They were far too removed from his own personality. He had noticed that his fists were tightly clenched. What had Sol got them into? He could only pray that this would all end happily!

'I see a hasp,' said Sol, her fingers playing nervously with the doll. 'A locked hasp.'

'Has someone locked him away?' asked the child's father anxiously.

'No, the hasp is in the darkness.'

He wanted to ask how she could see these things if it was dark, but realised that the question would be too naïve.

'He has locked himself in somewhere,' she announced, 'and is not able to set himself free.'

The Count paced back and forth, agitated, like one obsessed. 'Here in this house?' he demanded.

Sol was uncertain. 'I do not believe so. He does not feel close. But he cannot have gone very far – he is so young. How did you lose him?'

'I was sitting in the next room – it is my office – with Dag, as he studied. My wife was entertaining one or two of her friends. They were sitting talking here in the parlour, while the boy played on the floor. His maid was in the nursery preparing to change him and when she returned to the room to ask after him, the ladies discovered that he was gone.'

'How long?'

'They thought it had been about a quarter of an hour since they had noticed him. He is a very quiet boy who plays a lot by himself. Mistress Sol, find him! I beg you to do all you can.'

She nodded. 'Where was he sitting?'

The Count pointed. 'There on the floor beside the hearth.'

Sol rose and walked over to the fireplace, knelt down and pressed the palm of her hand to the floorboards. She looked perplexed.

'Something must have happened. Something you have forgotten.'

'That is impossible. We have searched everywhere a thousand times – every corner of the house.'

'He is not in this house.'

The Count sighed. 'But we cannot have missed anything.'

'How did he leave the room? Could he have opened a door without help?'

'No, but as you can see, all the inside doors to the rooms remain open. He could never have opened the street door and the door to the garden was closed. That is why we believed that someone had taken him, but you think otherwise?'

Sol stood up, shaking with confusion and irritation. 'There is something here. Do you have a dog?'

'A watchdog – a large Ulmer hound, yes.'

'And can it open doors?'

'The door to the garden – yes. But it was closed when the boy disappeared.'

Dag got up and went into the adjoining room. There was a door that would not have been in view from where the ladies had been sitting. Sol and the Count followed him.

'But the dog was not indoors,' objected the Count. 'It was tied up in its pound beneath the kitchen window.'

'Outside in the garden?'

'Yes – well, not really – round the corner beside the kitchen garden.'

'And had you tied it there?'

'No, I cannot say who had done so. One of the servants, perhaps.'

'So no one asked about this at the time?'

'No, the dog was never discussed, because it had been tied in its usual place.'

They looked at the door leading to the garden. The handle was too high for a child to reach. But Sol's words were making them think anew.

Dag placed his hands upon the handle as a large dog might rest its paws, and then removed them. At that moment the latch released itself. Dag pushed the door and it swung outward into the garden. It was easy to imagine a large dog pressing its weight against it. Slowly and silently it swung back on its hinges and the latch engaged with a click. The door was locked once more.

'Yes, but the dog was tied up in its pound,' insisted the Count again.

'The question is, when was it tied up?' said Dag. 'It could have been after your son went missing, but before the ladies noticed he had gone.'

'I shall find out at once who tethered the dog and when,' said their host. 'You must understand that all this time we were sure somebody had entered the house in an unguarded moment and abducted the boy – because we had searched the house, you see. Now wait while I go and speak to the servants.'

'Not now,' said Sol quickly. 'We shouldn't waste time on things that are of little importance. I've found out that the dog is involved and that is enough. Let us go into the garden.'

The garden was not very large. A thick hedge and the wall of a large neighbouring house bordered it on two sides, while on their right were old sheds that formed a boundary to the next property. They walked towards the sheds, passing the kitchen garden as they went. The dog had been lying beside its kennel, but stood up as they walked by, wagging its tail in greeting. Dag patted it absent-mindedly as he passed. Sol had already walked the length of the sheds. A perpetual cackling told her that one was a hen house and a pig snorted at her from another.

'We have searched all of these sheds,' said the Count. 'Every single one.'

Sol nodded, 'He is not here. Have you tried using the dog to track him?'

'Of course, but ours is no tracker and even had I borrowed one from a friend, the trail was old – and it rained all night after the boy disappeared.'

The wall to the house next door was impenetrable – which only left the hedge. Sol crept on all fours along its whole length, stopping occasionally to lie flat on her stomach.

'Your clothes!' said the Count. 'They will be ruined!'

'Forget them!' Sol retorted. 'A child's life is more important. Start searching here!'

Both men began looking in the bushy hedge.

'It is very thick and we have already looked here.'

'You can't believe what a child can do,' said Sol.

Dag, who had squeezed his hand under a prickly hawthorn, asked, 'Do you think this gap is too narrow?'

The others came to see. Sol lay down flat and pulled herself halfway through the hedge.

'It looks impossible,' she said, 'but if he left the garden, then this must have been the place. We would not get through, but perhaps a two-year-old could? Is he small for his age, Your Grace?'

'Yes, I would have to say that he is – and he is only nineteen months. But surely he would not be able to get through this. It's not possible!'

'Well he did!' said Sol, backing out from the hedge again. 'Look what was caught in the thorns!' She opened her hand and revealed some fine strands of blond hair.

'Albrekt!' shouted the Count. 'This is the first sign of him!'

'Look under there,' said Sol. 'You will see that, if he crawled to the right inside the bushes, he would come out somewhere else.'

The Count did as he was asked. 'It might be possible – but it is unbelievable!'

'Children are unbelievable. What is on the other side?'

'A shop – it is their backyard.'

'And what day of the week did he go missing?'

'It was a Sunday. But we have searched in there as well. The whole neighbourhood has tried to find the boy. Even the constables and soldiers of the guard – everybody!'

Sol sat on the ground. She was unkempt, dirty and her face bore scratches from her encounter with the hawthorn bushes – but she still looked devastatingly beautiful.

'He crawled through here. I will stake my blessed soul upon it,' she declared.

That's easy for you to say, thought Dag. Sol, he knew, had never much cared for the blessedness of her soul.

'Can you not describe his whereabouts a little better?' asked Count Strahlenhelm.

'No. There was a smell, but I cannot say what it was. It is a smell I have come across before, but just now I can't recall where or what it is.'

'Can you see his surroundings?' wondered Dag out loud. 'Can you see what lies outside?'

'No, I saw nothing outside, and inside was too small for there to be many objects. There was something big and black in one corner, I seem to remember. I forget, because I cannot see anything at the moment. I was only able to see things when I was holding the doll in the house.'

'I shall fetch the doll,' said the Count.

'You do not need to. I have seen all I am able to see. It is the big black thing that smells. I think it is made of wood. It is stupid, but the word "thumbscrew" keeps coming to me.'

The two men looked at one another.

'Some sort of press?' asked Dag.

'We–ell, yes perhaps,' she replied, hesitating. 'It might be, but I am not sure.'

'One thing I don't understand,' said Dag, 'is how the little chap managed to lock himself in? How could he reach?'

Slowly Sol rubbed her brow. 'I believe I saw something beside the door that he may have stood on.'

'And not been able to open it again once inside?'

'Probably not.'

'What sort of small shed would have a hasp on the inside?' wondered the Count, who obviously by now had completely accepted Sol's unusual abilities.

'Only one that I know of,' said Dag dryly.

'No, not a privy,' decided Sol. 'I wonder if it is a corridor.'

'With another door?'

'Possibly, but I could not see one.'

'Sunday,' said Dag thoughtfully. 'The boy could have been screaming for a long time without being heard.

28

Especially in the merchants' quarter.'

Sol turned back to the hedge. 'We must get through here.'

'Not necessary,' said the judge. 'We can go round.' And he set off eagerly, tramping through the house.

'Sol, you look terrible,' mumbled Dag.

Count Strahlenhelm heard him and stopped. Together they helped to tidy her up and brushed off their own attire.

It did not take many minutes to walk round the block and into the backyard on the other side of the hedge. There they saw a maze of sheds and workshops, surrounded by untold numbers of empty casks, boxes and crates. Several rats retreated hurriedly to their hiding-places and the Count gave a shiver.

As they walked through the house, Sol had picked up the doll again. Now she stood with her eyes closed, grasping it tightly to her, taking no notice of a young lad who ran across the yard. He gave her an inquisitive glance, just as the servants had done while they watched from the windows, when Sol and the two men were in the garden. The lad hurried out into the street and they were alone once more.

'I have sensed all that I am able to. There is no more,' she told them.

'Try again!' urged Dag.

He had often made light of Sol's strange abilities when they were younger, but now that he was showing confidence in them, Sol allowed herself to relax completely. Banishing all thoughts from her head, she made her mind an empty shell and quickly found that new impressions were beginning to form.

'No, the child is not close to us,' she said excitedly. 'Count Strahlenhelm, his breathing is very weak! I fear we must hurry and I don't know where he is.'

'If he came through the bushes,' said Dag, 'and is not in this yard …'

'Then he must have gone out into the street!' finished the Count.

'Do you think the gate would have been open?' asked Sol. 'On a Sunday?'

'It must have been. There is no time to enquire,' replied the judge.

They hurried through the archway and back out onto the street. This was not the main street, but a side alley leading to it.

'Someone should have seen him out here,' commented Dag.

'Not if he went straight into another yard, without stopping,' answered Sol.

Then she stopped abruptly. 'That smell … if only I could remember what it was – a sort of acrid, metallic, oily smell. It stung the nostrils.'

Almost whispering, the Count asked, 'Is he nearby?'

'I cannot sense him.'

The boy's father let out a deep sigh of unbearable anxiety.

'If I were a very small boy who had just come out onto a strange street, what would I do?' wondered Dag. 'I would look about me – should I turn and retrace my steps? No, he cannot have done that, because we know he is not there.'

A horse-drawn carriage rumbled past on the main street.

'He is a timid lad,' the Count added quickly. 'The noise from the street would have frightened him.'

'So we should go in the other direction,' decided Sol.

They hurried down the narrow street, little more than an alley, examining all the gates and doors, checking to see if they were locked.

'Look!' shouted Dag, pointing suddenly. 'There is a wide gap under this gate. He may have crept through here!'

'And this gateway looks very much like our own,' added the Count.

Sol noticed how the older man showed signs of nervousness, like a hunting dog that has found a spoor but is not let off the leash. He led the way forward and they pushed open the door, which led into an arched entrance with a second door at the other side. This in turn led onto another street and, like the gate they had just opened, it too had a large gap below it. This was a shortcut between two streets, nothing more.

'No, we are too far from home here,' declared the Count as they stood together looking up and down the second street. 'This must be wrong.'

'At this point the youngster would be panicking,' said Dag calmly. 'Now he begins to run around helplessly, unable to find his mother or his father. Perhaps something caught his attention – an animal maybe. It was a Sunday, so there would be few people about.'

'Look! Look there!' shouted the Count suddenly. 'There is a sign hanging above a workshop! Look – along the street – on the right. Can that be something, Mistress Sol?'

The sign said 'Bookbinder – Printer' and Sol nodded quickly. 'Yes, of course! Printer's ink – that was the smell!'

It almost became a race to see which of them could get there first and they all burst into the printing-room at the same moment.

'Good day to you,' said the Count breathlessly, addressing two men who were working at the presses, surrounded by drawers of type and trays. 'I am Count Strahlenhelm. Have you heard that my young son went missing three days ago?'

'Oh, was that you?' replied the older of the two. 'Yes, we heard, but me and my son here live way down at the end of the street, by the rose tree, don't we?' He looked at his son for confirmation and the younger man nodded.

'Indeed,' the Count continued. 'But we have indications that have led us here. Do you have a small room, a cupboard, which contains an old press?'

'We have only recently taken on this workshop,' said the younger man. 'But we haven't found anything like that.'

'Do you have a backyard?'

'Yes, of course we do.'

'May we look around it?'

'Naturally.' They made as if to open a door at the back of the shop.

'No,' said Sol. 'The child must have entered from the street, otherwise it would have been impossible.'

Doubtfully the printer said, 'There is a gate from the street, but it is locked.'

Dag had already rushed out into the street, closely followed by the other four.

'There is a gap underneath, look! He could have got through there.'

The printer produced a large key and unlocked the gate. They walked through into the yard at the rear of the workshop and found it to be tidy and well kept. Several doors, when opened, revealed a privy and woodsheds that they quickly searched without success.

'Oh no,' said the dejected Count. 'This was just a dead end.'

Sol stood perfectly still and closed her eyes, breathing deeply. 'Quiet! He is here! Very close. I can feel it, yes, I can. You must look quickly!'

Both the printers were taken aback by her expression of anxiety. They did not understand what was going on.

'But there are no more doors here,' said Dag.

'Only the back door to the print-shop,' said the older of the two men.

'He could never have opened that!' said the Count.

The man turned to his son. 'Were you not here last Sunday?'

'I was, yes.'

'Was the door open at any time?' snapped Dag.

The younger man pondered.

'Yes, it probably was. When I was in the ...' He broke off and made an embarrassed gesture in the direction of the privy and began fidgeting with the front of his leather apron.

Dag shivered. He knew what these privies were like. They were nothing but a dark trench dug into the earth, where one looked for an unoccupied space on the ground to do what was necessary. They were usually quite unpleasant places.

'And you heard nothing then?' asked the Count. 'A child's cry, anything?'

'Not that I remember, but there may have been something that I didn't notice.'

Sol had already walked over to the door to the workshop, waiting while the older man opened it for them. Passing through it, they found themselves back inside the print-room, this time at the rear.

'That smell of the ink,' whispered Sol. 'Yes, here it is!'

'How can my little boy have got here?' moaned the Count, 'so incredibly far from home. No, I cannot believe this. Where would he be? There is nowhere he could hide.'

'And the printer who was here on Sunday would have been able to see him in here,' added Dag in a disappointed voice. 'Sol, I think you may be on a false trail.'

Sol shook her head furiously. Tormented by all the emotions and intuitions raging inside her, she turned impatiently to the younger printer and demanded, 'When you came back in here from the yard, what did you do? Think carefully, man! This is important!'

He looked at her with confusion showing on his face. 'It was the last thing I did before I went home. After that I locked up and left.'

'That's too simple! Please go out into the yard and come in again through the open door!' she commanded him.

Reluctantly he obeyed. 'First I closed the yard door and locked it, like this. Then I made sure all was in order for the Monday's work. After that I tidied away some bits and pieces and then left by the street door – and locked it.'

'And was that all?'

'Aye, that were all. Oh, except that I shut and locked the storeroom door.'

Almost with one voice, they all yelled, 'Storeroom door? What storeroom door?'

'Aye, behind yon dresser – beside the yard door. I never thought of it. We hardly ever go in there.'

The Count had already found it. In the wall behind the shelves, nearly out of sight, was a low door. He tugged at it, but it was locked.

'Was this open on Sunday?'

'I had fetched some things from there, yes.'

'But where does it lead?' urged Dag, as the older printer turned the key.

'It runs along the back of the house. We put everything we don't use in there – and a lot of old stuff was left there before we came. As yet we haven't got round to clearing it out.'

The door opened, giving entry to a narrow passage, stacked with jumbled pieces of equipment.

'Let Sol go first,' said Dag.

They waited for her to go in.

'Is there a small cubby-hole in here?' she called.

'No, this is just a passageway to the wheelwright's store in the next house. You will see it ...'

The older man broke off abruptly and stared open-mouthed.

'What is it?' demanded the Count.

'That old door in the passage is closed – it's usually always open. There is only a single door between us and the wheelwright's, but there is an old second door this side that's never been closed.'

Nodding suddenly, his son asked, 'And ain't there an old press in the passage behind that door?'

'What isn't behind that door! We haven't had time to look through every last piece of scrap, have we? Oh, it's locked – from inside!'

The Count threw himself, shoulder first, at the door. Because the door opened outwards, it would not break open easily and all he got for his trouble was a very painful shoulder. Dag squeezed his fingers over the top of the door and tugged at something. It felt like a hasp.

'Some help here, please.'

The men eased their fingers along the top edge, prising the door open. The young printer found an iron bar lying close by which he slid into the gap and, with a mighty heave, the hasp gave way and the door flew open.

Before them was a tiny dark room with another similar door facing them. Inside, in one corner, they could see an old wooden-screw printing press, stacked high with junk. On the floor in front of their feet there was a clutter of timber plank off-cuts. And there, with his cheek resting against one plank, lay a little boy in purple velvet – with very wet breeches.

The Count gave a heartfelt groan as he bent and lifted up the tiny limp body.

'Oh God!' he whispered. 'Dear God!'

'Well now,' said the older printer. 'To think he was here all the time! But how did you know?'

Before either of them had time to ponder the day's strange episode, Dag said quickly, 'We followed a trail of clues – but how is it that you didn't hear him?'

'Wouldn't have heard hardly anything from here back in the shop. And it's right noisy there too. We're never in here, neither. Oh dear, oh dear, what a terrible thing! That little mite getting lost this so far from home and nobody to see it.'

Shaking their heads in dismay, the two printers led the way back into the main print shop.

'Is he alive?' asked the Count in a trembling voice. 'Albrekt! Albrekt! Answer your Papa. We must take him to a healer at once.'

'That will not be necessary,' said Dag calmly. 'Sol has been my foster father's assistant for five years now and she is as practised in the healing arts as he is.'

'More!' said Sol, not in the least bit coy. 'In my own way, at least – I just do not have his healing hands. Let me see the child.'

After a moment of doubt, the Count handed Sol the tiny bundle he had been cradling.

'Yes, as I thought, we would have done better with Tengel's healing touch,' she conceded. 'But the boy is alive, Judge, of that there is no doubt, even though his time was beginning to run out.'

Now there you go again, thought Dag. The lad wasn't that bad and could probably have lasted a couple of days more, but Sol always had to over-dramatise just a little to make life more exciting!

'We must get him to drink some water, because thirst is a greater threat to his life,' she continued.

'The water here tastes bad,' said the printer. 'We only use it for our work. But we've got some wine.'

'Is it fully fermented and matured?' asked the judge.

'First class!' replied the printer.

'Then we'll try it,' said Sol, even though she doubted its provenance.

While the men fetched the wine and poured a measure, she gently shook the boy.

'We can do no more until he is awake,' she told them. 'Come on, wake up you adventurous little tyke!'

The Count forgave her the ill-chosen words, because her manner and tone was so gentle – but when she began to slap the child's face, it was too much for him.

'Now then – please don't do that!' he protested.

'There can be no rules of etiquette here,' said Sol, 'and look! He's waking up.'

The boy blinked and looked up at them.

'Thank you, dear Lord,' whispered the Count.

Sol was not fully in agreement with him about who should be thanked, but she simply said, 'The wine! Be quick! Before he fades again.'

Eager hands held the mug to the boy's lips. Instinctively the boy tried to drink and swallowed a sip or two before he choked, catching his breath and beginning to cry loudly.

'There, there – your Papa is here,' soothed the father and relieved Sol of him. 'Now, now – everything will be all right.'

The boy fell asleep – or fainted – against his father's shoulder. The Count's eyes were brimming with tears and he made no attempt to hide them. They thanked the printers for all their help and hurried homewards.

'We must give him medicines to bring his strength back as quickly as we can,' Sol explained as she ran to stay abreast of the Count. 'Will you allow me to treat him?'

'Why, yes! Of course, if you would be so kind,' replied the Count. 'But please say nothing of this to my wife as yet, in case something should go awry. Let us hope she is still sleeping.'

Feverish activity ensued as soon as they stepped back inside the house. Amazed and excited, the servants rushed back and forth, heeding Sol's every command. The child's soiled clothing was removed and he was placed in a tub of relaxing warm water spiced with switches of juniper. This certainly brought him back to life and Sol managed to get him to take sips of a warm potion containing all the strength-giving herbs she owned.

Dag could see that she was enjoying every moment that she was the centre of attention. She even made the whole procedure a little bit more impressive than it needed to be, by looking thoughtful and raising her eyebrows dramatically as she produced each small bag of herbs. Almost in pantomime fashion, she acted out the impression that each time she was making a momentous medical decision. When he caught her eye, Dag gave her a knowing look – he understood his foster sister only too well!

The boy cried weakly and was lifted out of the tub by impatient hands, waiting to dry him. He was quickly wrapped in a warmed towel, then the nursery maid attended to his sore bottom and dressed him in clean dry clothes.

Everybody was happy, very happy, that he had returned safely.

'Will he survive?' the Count asked Sol.

'There's no doubt about that! Just keep him from getting cold and give him the healing potions, as I tell you. You must let me know at once if he starts a fever or begins to cough. Gradually give him a little more to eat each day.'

You're playing this for all it's worth, thought Dag, with an amused grin – almost too much really. But with everything that's been happening no one else has noticed. Still, he couldn't help but feel very proud of her!

'That's good,' said the Count with a sigh of satisfaction. 'Will somebody go and wake my wife?'

One of the older women left the room. A short while later a muffled scream could be heard, followed at once by rapid noisy footsteps on the stairs, the sound of which echoed through the house.

'Albrekt?' shrieked the Countess from a distance. 'Can it be true? I cannot believe it. I don't believe it, I don't believe it!'

She stood in the doorway, pale-faced and swaying on her feet. Her husband held up the little boy for her to see and with a cry she rushed forward and snatched the child from his arms. She held him so close and so tightly that after a few moments the boy began to protest tearfully.

Sol understood now why the Count had not wanted to wake his wife as soon as they returned. They would never have been able to treat the child in peace, because of her overwhelming maternal feelings, and it was obvious they would need to act with great care when the time came to remove the poor little lad from his mother's loving arms. Finally the Countess sat down, stopped her sobbing and began to regain her composure.

'Where was he? How did you find him? Who found him?' she asked.

'Our little Sol here, she found him,' answered her husband softly.

'Oh, no! I think we all helped. I found the trail, but you men had the power of logic,' said Sol, exuding false modesty.

39

'What trail?' wondered the Countess.

The others exchanged knowing looks and Dag cut in quickly, 'A lock of hair caught in the hedge – after that there was only one course of action.'

Although it was a simple explanation, no one wanted to dwell further on the details.

'We must arrange a thanksgiving service in the church,' said the Countess.

Hearing this, Dag was not surprised to see a look of disdain flicker across his sister's features. He grimaced a quick warning to her and was relieved when she nodded and smiled wryly in acknowledgement. At long last Sol was shown to her room and made comfortable. An extravagant dinner was given in her honour and became a fitting celebration of the day's events.

During the dinner she looked flushed and happy, thought Dag – as happy as he had ever seen her. Her visit to Denmark had begun in the best way possible. Sol was the heroine of the hour – and how she loved it!

Chapter 3

It was some while before Dag found time to open the letters that Sol had brought with her from Linden Allée. He picked up Liv's first and, with weary fingers, opened it and began to read.

'My Dearest Brother,' she had written. 'Oh, how I miss you! Gråstensholm is so empty without you. I go up and visit Aunt Charlotte sometimes and that always gladdens her, because she can then talk about you, as do I. But I do pine for our walks around the castle. I look up at the tower and think of the times we stood up there and talked about life down below in the countryside and how people were no bigger than ants as they scurried about.

'Why must we grow up, Dag? I really wish we didn't have to.

'I heard that you are intending to marry a Mistress Trolle. It warms my heart to know that you have found a person to share your life. I hope that she will be kind to you. If she isn't, she will have to answer to me! I will not allow my little brother to be ill-treated!

'For my part, I have now said "yes" to Laurents Berenius and I do not believe I shall have any regrets. You

41

have yet to make his acquaintance, but he is all one could wish for – although I shall never be able to tell him of our lives of poverty in the Valley of the Ice People. He is a man who has everything. He has recently inherited his father's successful trading business and has German and Dutch ships arriving in Oslo all the time from foreign lands, carrying goods to load and unload.

'There are other things he owns too and all this Laurents now manages with pride. He is very handsome and knows the art of conversation. He can be a little too self-assured and overbearing sometimes perhaps – he is the "I always know best" sort, if you know what I mean. But that may well be because he is older than we are and probably does know best. It would never occur to him to discuss affairs of business with me, which is why I know so little of such things. Nonetheless, he has always been wonderful to me and I am so overcome by his attentiveness that it is embarrassing. I am not worthy of it all! Everyone said that I would be a fool if I did not say "yes", and I do like him. So I am sure that I shall have a good life with him. I have to say that it is not easy to resist such kindness.

'Our wedding will take place one week after the first day of winter. We all hope that you and Sol will be home by then.

'My regards to your Mistress Trolle – and live well my dear brother!

'Your devoted sister, Liv.'

Dag put the letter down. An uneasy feeling had come over him that felt like the onset of a cold or the sensation that comes with having eaten something disagreeable. For a while he sat in silent contemplation, before opening the next letter. It was from Mama Charlotte and contained all the usual warnings, snatches of familiar gossip, lots of

42

'Oh!'s and 'Ah!'s and her usual, and often expressed, feelings of loneliness and regret.

'Liv's husband-to-be is so delightful,' wrote Charlotte. 'It was I who brought them together. They met here and he fell instantly in love with her – not surprisingly, as Liv must be every man's dream of a wife. I am so pleased for her.'

Silje, with her impossible spelling, had written all about the coming wedding, including long passages with details of what was planned.

'Tengel an me we wer a little worryed, for Liv is so yong. But the boy cannit wate to hav her for hiz owen. He iz a extrodinry match for ower little girl. She cannit find bettr. Well boy iz the rong word – he iz a growen man. She moven to Osslo an that be good also that she be not so farr awey.

'Bothe you an Sol must komm home to the weddin. I worri so for Sol – you nowe why. Look after her well pleeze Dag! She haz bin wunderfol these last five yeers, but now she iz so orkward and testy that I thingk her ansestry iz shewing iself again. But we coodint keep her back eny longer.'

Tengel, unaccustomed to writing, had added a few short lines with heavy, ponderous strokes, saying how well everything was going at home and that they were all missing Dag. Then there was a letter from Are. Little brother Are – he was growing up fast as well. It wasn't a proper letter, just a sketched plan of Linden Allée, showing how he was going to enlarge and improve the outhouses – big plans, or so it would seem. But Are would be the one to do it. He knew what he wanted and always saw things through.

Suddenly as he finished his reading, Dag felt very homesick. He sat thumbing the letters, thinking how he could not wait to get back home again. He had already realised that he would not be able to travel back for the wedding, because it would be the middle of the term.

But what about Sol? He knew very well that he would not be able to get her to leave until she had experienced everything that this new life had to offer. Indeed Dag shared Silje's anxiety – Sol was not one who could be trusted on her own. He had arranged to take her to a party that coming Saturday and introduce her to some of his student friends. On reflection, he shuddered to think how things might turn out. But in spite of everything, she had made an excellent first impression on the Strahlenhelm household.

Then he found himself wondering about Laurents Berenius. What did Liv really feel about him? And what sort of an 'I know best' scoundrel was he really?

* * * *

Sol's eyes lit up when she arrived at the brightly lit inn that Dag's friends had chosen as the place for their party. They were seated round a long narrow table that showed signs of age in its blackened and worn surface. The people were all intellectual young men, accompanied by their sisters or cousins – to bring a woman to whom one was not related was not permitted and would be considered immoral. Such a woman would be thought of as very low class.

The ladies' eyes, like their pearls, glistened in the lamplight. The wooden tankards were filled to the brim and large plates of meat and bread were passed round the table. As the jollity increased, Sol could tell that she was being noticed. Countess Strahlenhelm had let her borrow one of her old gowns, a little out of date for the Countess's taste, but to Sol it was a marvel. She had never felt prettier than she did this evening and the admiring glances she was receiving from the young men were telling her in no uncertain terms that she was attractive. However, these boys did not interest her very much – except for one who had caught her attention for other reasons.

'Dag,' she whispered to her brother, 'what was it they said about that man over there? The one they called Preben.'

'Forget it,' Dag replied shortly, biting into a chicken drumstick.

'No, I want to know! They said something about the black arts.'

'Sol!' He turned to face her, his face very serious. '*Must* you always live so dangerously?'

'No, I think of it as perfectly normal. Oh well, I'll find out for myself.'

'You cannot go around asking people such pointed questions!' Then he paused, considering her question again. 'Oh, if you really wish to know – he is a member of an esoteric society here in Copenhagen.'

'Esoteric society, eh? Secret – members only, I suppose?'

'Yes, probably – but you must stay away from them. Do you understand?'

'Yes, little brother,' she said piously, as her eyes sought contact with Preben's over Dag's shoulder. 'I understand.'

Preben was nothing special to look at; in fact he had the kind of face that was instantly forgettable. He had noticed, however, that Sol was showing an interest in him and later in the evening, after they had exchanged numerous glances across the table, he approached her. By this time Dag was engaged elsewhere in the room in a discreet flirtation with a young girl.

'I hear it said that you are Dag's half sister,' said Preben.

'Something like that,' replied Sol. 'We grew up together.'

'I have observed your interest in my humble self. To what do I owe such pleasure?'

Sol's green eyes sparkled at him. 'Well, it's not because of your golden curls, for you have none!' she answered quickly. 'Can you not guess?'

'Yes – I notice your remarkable eyes! Something tells me that you have the same interests as I do.'

She nodded. 'Take me to one of your meetings.'

'We are afraid of spies and traitors.'

'Do I look like one?'

'No,' he answered. 'You look as though you are drawn to mysticism.'

'Indeed I am – in any case what *you* know as mysticism. For me it is merely what is obvious – but I am starved of contact with those who share my feelings. My whole life has been spent isolated in Norway and now I need to meet someone to talk to and to learn more!'

He nodded self-importantly. 'You will certainly learn things! I have to tell you that some quite frightening things can occur.'

Sol smiled and spoke in a low throaty voice. 'I am unlikely to be afraid.'

'As you will. I shall propose you at our next visit. If you are accepted, you may attend the time after that. But I warn you; these people are not to be trifled with. Do you have any references?'

'Only myself and I think that says quite a lot. You could ask Dag, of course, but I don't think I would want you to do that. He should not be made aware of everything I do here in Copenhagen.'

'That's true,' he said. 'A very sensible point of view.'

* * * *

The wedding between Liv and Laurents Berenius went as planned, but neither Dag nor Sol were able to make the journey home to be there. The reason was quite simply that there were no berths available at the right time. This was not unusual, because ships sailed between Denmark and Norway only very sporadically and even then the times and routes were unreliable.

Liv was the gentlest of Tengel and Silje's four children – more gentle even than Silje herself, whom she resembled most in all other respects. It was exactly as Charlotte had written: she was the dream of a wife and daughter-in-law. She was quick to accommodate and would ignore her own needs if need be. She was very clever and accomplished in almost everything – just how clever and accomplished was something that Laurents Berenius had not reckoned with.

Liv had, until then, been living an indifferent existence. She listened to the discussions of others, often agreeing politely, but without saying much herself. She told herself that everything would be well – Laurents is good-hearted and handsome and I have been very lucky, she reasoned, and now Dag is to marry Mistress Trolle. The whole family is happy for our sake, so I am doubly lucky.

Charlotte had spared no expense on the wedding. Naturally Silje wanted it to be held at Linden Allée, as was her right, but Charlotte arranged for great wagonloads of provisions to be delivered there and organised a procession of the most magnificent coaches to and from the church. She had insisted that, on the last day, they should have the great banquet at Gråstensholm and everyone agreed to this, so long as most of the celebrations took place at Linden Allée.

'We must impress the Berenius family,' she had told Tengel and Silje in finally talking them round to her way of thinking. 'The boy must not be allowed to think that he is marrying beneath himself. Indeed he is not! Nothing is too good for Dag's best friend.'

Liv looked wonderful, dressed in the rural wedding costume of the district. Over the years, her hair had darkened and now had the colour and sheen of unburnished copper. Her complexion was as soft as a petal and her eyes of deep blue were so trusting that one was moved just looking into them. Everyone could see how much Laurents was in love with her.

She smiled coyly at him and did her best to hide her nervousness. She was scared and uncertain and her heart still felt the ache of emptiness. This must be the way all brides feel, she consoled herself. Laurents looked very elegant: tall with short shiny brown hair and grey-brown eyes. He had a straight well formed nose and resolute mouth. She liked the possessive way he looked at her and she promised herself that she would make him happy.

The only cloud in her heaven was that Dag and Sol were not there. These last few weeks she would dearly have liked to talk to them, if for no other reason than to ask their opinion of Laurents. Sol had seen him and remained unusually passive. She had always found other things to do whenever Laurents came to visit, so Liv still did not know what Sol thought of him. But Dag had always been the one to whom Liv had taken her troubles and concerns and he was so far away. Now that he had Mistress Trolle to consider, how would he have time to be concerned, simply because she felt restless and at a loss? A sister could never be as interesting as a beloved.

So, overall, if she was going to be really honest, the

absence of her brother and sister had left Liv feeling even more than usually unsure of herself. Then there was a minor mishap following the ride from the church down to the garden that was decked out for the wedding feast.

The road was lined all the way on both sides by people from the estate, the village and the surrounding countryside, all of whom would be invited to attend the main celebrations after they had been well fed in the large barn. Young Are and some of the maids had decorated the barn and it looked truly splendid, inside and out. In the event the journey from the church was frantic, as it should have been on such an occasion. The bride's horse was pursued with wild shouts and the sound of musket fire to discourage bad magic or evil spirits from taking hold on her last day of chastity – but Liv was a good horsewoman and she had come back home safely.

In the yard she was presented with a large bowl of ale that she was to drink in full view of the crowd, before throwing the empty bowl over the roof of the house. If it landed on the other side of the house, then this was seen as the sign of a good marriage. Liv, however, did not grip the bowl well enough and as she pulled back her arm, it slipped. Flying sideways out of her hand, it landed on the front of the roof and fell back again on the same side. Although everyone made light of her mistake, Liv took it to heart. She wanted so badly to make Laurents happy.

The little accident, however, was soon forgotten. Indeed the wedding celebrations, lasting the customary three full days, were an astounding success and people in the region spoke about them admiringly for years afterwards. It was not until Liv was alone with her new husband in the imposing merchant's house in Oslo that it dawned on her that there could be no going back. Her childhood years with Tengel and Silje at last were over and from now on she would only return to Linden Allée as a guest. This left her with an uneasy sadness that she found difficult to put behind her. But once again she told herself that this was just a feeling that all brides suffered.

They were not entirely alone in the house; Laurents' mother lived there as well. She had attended the wedding, of course, but remained aloof the whole time and had spoken hardly a word to anyone. She had just seemed to sit looking for something to criticise, largely without success, except for one word that Liv had heard her muttering over and over to herself, 'Extravagance!' Liv felt sure that if the wedding had not been as magnificent as it had, then the old woman would have complained about poverty and miserliness.

Laurents had not wanted to 'make her a woman' during the wedding feast itself as was often customary. He wanted to wait until they were truly alone. 'I know what they are like,' he had said, 'those drunken asses who wander into the wedding chamber, as if by mistake, after everyone has left the couple alone. I will let nothing spoil our first time together, Liv.'

So during the period of feasting he had lain very quietly beside her, looking at her in the candlelight, caressing her slowly and gently, kissing her so carefully until they had fallen asleep with their honour and virtue intact. But now they found themselves together at last in this great house, the house that she would oversee from now on.

Carefully Liv folded her bridal gown, or more correctly, her 'woman's gown' that she had worn on the morning after the wedding ceremony. Now she would have to wear a headscarf, as a sign that she was a married woman. She smiled to herself. Silje, with Tengel's support, had always refused to wear one. She had suffered some harsh words because of it, but the two of them were more than able to resist people's idle gossip.

It was almost dark in the room that was now to be her real wedding chamber; only a single small candle burned dimly beside the bed. How strange it was to be alone here with Laurents! She suddenly realised that she hardly knew him and was gripped by anxiety. No, she must put aside such thoughts – especially now! She was very fond of him – such a mature man, so good-looking, as he stood there slowly removing his long wide-shouldered jacket in the half-light. She must endow him with all the love he deserved.

Mama Silje had given her some sound advice. 'Liv, men also need love. They need to feel they are loved. Give all your heart will allow, my child! This is the secret to Tengel's happiness and mine. Be completely open with each other. Dare to show how much it means to have him close to you.'

Yes, thought Liv, Laurents was very worthy of her love.

* * * *

Back home at Linden Allée, Tengel and Silje lay staring idly into the darkness.

'It was a wonderful wedding,' said Silje with a happy grin. 'Now I feel like a cloth that has been well and truly wrung dry.'

'Yes, you worked hard,' replied Tengel. 'I saw how busy you were all the time. And these three days were just the end of many months of preparation.'

Silje took his hand in hers. 'Have we done the right thing, Tengel? She is so young!'

He sighed. 'I have had the same thoughts. But you were the same age and you certainly knew what you wanted. Have you ever had any regrets?'

She rubbed her head on his shoulder and smiled. 'Are you fishing for something? I was just thinking how small and forsaken Liv seemed to be. She looked vulnerable and perplexed, as if she was at a loss for something. I don't know what – I can't really find the words.'

'I understand what you mean. Had it not been for the lad's eagerness and persistence, I would not have agreed to it. But he is a good man – reliable. And he is desperately in love with her.'

'Yes, and it was what she wanted. Oh well, we are just normal worried parents who do not want to let our children slip away from us. Our love child, Tengel.'

'Indeed. You were the stubborn one that time! You wanted to have that baby at any cost. Now I thank you for your stubbornness.'

'They are leaving us, Tengel! First Dag, then Sol – although she will be back, I hope – and now Liv. We have only Are left.'

'Yes, and he will stay.'

'Thank goodness for that!'

'It hurts to lose one's children.'

'We are not losing them,' she said. 'There are still there but we cannot see them.'

'That is true,' said Tengel. 'Linden Allée is a part of them, something they take with them out into the world. Likewise they have left something of themselves behind. They are still here, my Silje. Their laughter is on the breeze, their footsteps on the floor. They have been part of making this house and the whole farm what it is today.'

'Yes, and I think they have been happy here.'

'Of course they have!'

He wrapped his arms around her and they snuggled closer together.

* * * *

Inside the merchant's house, the candle was snuffed out. In the bed Liv lay in Laurents' arms, as he whispered sweet words to her and softly stroked her body; but she could not avoid feeling that this wasn't happening to her. In her mind she was somewhere else completely. Remembering Silje's words, she placed her arm across his neck and his caresses instantly grew bolder. Almost at once Liv felt a new sensation, a pleasant awakening, slow and throbbing, that began to burn inside her. With a murmur of delight she wriggled closer to him.

'Laurents,' she whispered ecstatically in his ear. 'This moment is so beautiful.'

His hand stopped. For a while there was not a sound in the room.

'Lie still,' he said in a strangled voice. 'Relax, Liv. You do not need to say or do anything. It is the duty of a woman to welcome her husband's cravings. He is the hunter and she is his prey.'

Taken aback, Liv tried to put her point of view and said, unhappily, 'I only wanted to show you how fond I am of you. My love for you is …'

'You can show your love in a thousand other ways,' he said tight-lipped, 'by being my help and support. In the marriage bed it is the man who shall be the active one; the woman will be passive, a source of rejuvenation for him. It is not for her to show her feelings. That is what one has harlots and street girls for.'

Liv stared wide-eyed into the darkness of the room. She was confused and filled suddenly with utter despair – and in that instant everything died; the flame that had been kindled inside her was extinguished and replaced by the deepest feelings of shame. As she submitted herself passively to her husband's desire, his embrace and his body, she found herself wishing she were dead. After he had slaked himself, he fell asleep with one arm stretched possessively across her breasts. But Liv could not sleep – for a very long time she lay awake, hearing only the sound of her own quiet and helpless sobbing.

* * * *

Sol followed the secretive Preben, as he cautiously made his way to a small dilapidated house on the outskirts of Copenhagen. She had managed to sneak out of the Strahlenhelm house, without Dag or anybody else knowing, to keep her previously arranged assignation with him. Full of his own importance, Preben had said to her at the outset, 'It was with great reluctance that they have allowed you to join in, so do not disturb their sacred black mass with worldly trivia! Remember, Satan will be with us tonight!'

Sol nodded perfunctorily. This would be exciting, she thought, as they descended a narrow stairway that led to a cellar. At the foot of the steps, Preben announced their arrival with a heavy drama-laden knock on the door. A voice from inside asked for the password.

'By the gravedigger's bones,' declared Preben solemnly and Sol almost burst out laughing.

A man wearing a black cloak opened the door. They entered without a word and went through a second door leading to a vaulted cellar, where about ten young people, also dressed in black cloaks, were standing. They regarded the newcomers in dismal silence.

One of the men was much older than the others. His cloak was lined with red and he wore a mask to hide the upper part of his face. The mask, however, could not conceal the look in his eyes when Sol entered the room. She had seen that look before and knew exactly what it meant.

To get her bearings, she glanced quickly around the room. A vast number of black candles lit up the vaulted ceiling and in front of her stood a long altar, over which a cross was hanging, upside down. The lime-washed walls had been covered with magic runes and the names of demons.

After a short period of silence a young woman stood up. She lowered her voice dramatically to give weight to her fateful words. 'We have permitted a novice from the province of Norway to join our secret meeting tonight. We shall decide among ourselves whether or not she will be admitted again. As we are all very advanced in our worship of the Devil and all his secrets, we expect the Norwegian ignoramus to abide by our edicts and do no more than learn from our skills. You have already sworn an oath to Apollyon – that's Preben – never to denounce us, have you not? That's good!'

Another girl said, 'You were allowed to come here because our friend described your strange eyes – but a pair of eyes do not make a real witch. You will have many trials before you are truly proficient.'

Sol said nothing. The masked man whispered something to the first woman, whose expression changed to one of distaste. Finally she nodded and turned grudgingly towards Sol.

'Our warlock, who is the incarnation of Satan himself, wishes to initiate you himself this very evening. This is highly unusual and a great honour. So that you may understand what is expected of you, our warlock will first perform the ritual with one of the other women present.'

Sol nodded. All the women – there were five of them – rushed towards the warlock to offer their services, but he waved them away with a dismissive gesture. Then one of the young men ran up to the altar, carrying a small bowl. Dipping his finger into the bowl, he drew a complicated design in blood on the altar.

The warlock walked over and stood in front of the motif and raised his arms. Everyone fell to their knees and began to chant their individual songs of ecstasy. The room was filled with an awful cacophony, as the congregation continued to work themselves into a rapturous frenzy. All the while, the warlock performed rites that were meaningless and impossible to understand, lighting different candles and rearranging a variety of items on the altar. Sol could make no sense of anything he was doing. To her it all seemed to be a combination of gibberish and self-invented ritual.

She began to feel uneasy; Sol had always been sensitive to her environment and here she sensed nothing but exertion and the reek of sweat, surrounded by meaningless emptiness. Suddenly the man raised his arms again and at once the noise ceased. In the strained silence they all waited.

The women were full of hungry expectation. Then, with great drama, the man moved one arm slowly down until it pointed directly at one of the girls and she obediently took a few steps closer to him. Her cloak fell from her shoulders and she stood before him completely naked.

The warlock pointed towards the altar and the girl, who seemed to be in a state of exaltation at being the chosen one, walked over to it and lay down. The others began chanting again, while their bodies began to sway rhythmically. One by one their cloaks fell to the floor. They were all naked, except for the warlock, who now started to draw patterns on the girl's body.

'What blasphemy!' thought Sol, when she saw that the design was similar to an archer's target. Perhaps he was afraid he would miss?

The warlock climbed up and lay on top of the girl. His large cloak draped over the pair of them and hung down over both sides of the altar, but nobody could be in any doubt as to what rite was being performed beneath the mantle. With loud exclamations of delight, the congregation began to fondle one another lustfully, their new incantations again consisting of jumbled moaning and wailing.

As soon as the warlock began to reach a peak of excitement, he stopped abruptly and stood up. With his cloak once more concealing his body, he turned to face Sol, as the girl on the altar quickly returned to her place with the others. Events seemed to have left her disappointed and unsatisfied.

The woman who was evidently the warlock's mouthpiece, or his priestess, pointed commandingly at Sol, 'Take the girl's place! Satan is ready to initiate you now!'

Sol frowned, but did not move.

'Remove your clothes!' repeated the woman impatiently, evidently annoyed that this newcomer was being treated with special consideration.

Still Sol stood her ground – but now the disappointment and anger that she had been suppressing since entering the room reached a peak and exploded. Her eyes flashed yellow like a cat's.

'Do you honestly expect me to let that ridiculous peddler of balderdash have a few moments of cheap excitement at my expense?' she demanded scornfully. 'Well not in this life!'

Sol saw the expressions on the ring of faces watching her start to harden. 'You have sworn the oath,' warned the woman. Beside her, Preben looked afraid.

'How do you dare to call our warlock a peddler of nonsense?' screamed the girl who had been lying on the altar.

'I call you all unenlightened fools!' hissed Sol angrily. 'What do you really know of the black arts? You are nothing but an ignorant pack of simpletons, lacking talent, trying to act dangerously and demonically. If you had looked upon yourselves with some humour and humility, I might have been prepared to stay and teach you one or two things. But you are too self-obsessed, too sombre! And you believe yourselves to be of great importance. Has this man really convinced you that he has come into contact with Satan – that he might be his chosen one – or perhaps even Satan himself?'

The warlock, realising that his prestige was being called into question, now drew himself up straight and spoke aloud for the first time. But his voice, when it emerged, was high-pitched and weak.

'Teach us one or two things?' he asked, mocking her. 'I will not be challenged by a slut of a girl from Norway. You question my powers, do you? Watch this!'

He flourished one hand and surreptitiously took a handful of powder from a pocket in his cloak and threw it on the fire. His cowed followers did not see this sleight of hand and the powder ignited with what seemed to be a series of small spontaneous explosions.

'Is that your sorcery? Throwing black powder on a fire?' asked Sol. 'Any child can do that!'

'I can bewitch you, destroy you!'

'Then do so, if you can!'

He took a deep breath. The hostility among his disciples towards Sol had become more open as their master fought for his position. Although still kneeling, they began murmuring threateningly and this clearly emboldened him. Walking up to Sol and mustering all his authority, he mumbled between clenched teeth, 'I order you to kiss my hand!'

Sol looked straight into his eyes with unconcealed contempt. Her savage beauty was a thing to see – her wild dark hair, the warm colour of her skin and her wide flashing eyes.

He stretched out his hand. 'Satan says, kiss it!'

There was not a sound within those four walls and nobody moved; Sol's eyes had suddenly become half-closed slits. 'Do you really believe that I will do your bidding?' she asked tonelessly. 'I order you to get down on your knees yourself!'

The warlock's eyes widened in utter surprise and helplessness. Then, unable to resist, he fell to his knees.

'Remove your cloak,' ordered Sol.

He meekly did as he was told and this drew a gasp from his congregation. Their hero, their god was obeying the commands of stranger!

'Look at him!' breathed Sol, pointing dismissively at the man, who stared dumbly up at her as though in a trance. 'See this wrinkled weakling with his sloping shoulders and torpid belly. Look at him now!'

Her hands reached quickly up to her neck and she pulled the leather strap holding the mandrake over her head. As the master caught sight of the grotesque talisman, he flinched backwards in horror, gasping for breath. Sol held the gnarled root in both hands, pointing it directly at him.

'Crawl in the dirt, little man! Crawl to the altar and turn the cross the right way up, for you have nothing to do with Satanism! There is nothing demonic in this room.'

To his followers' unending shame, their 'Great One' wriggled across the floor like a snake and, on reaching the altar, got to his feet then stretched up to grasp the cross and turn it the right way round. Then he sat down and gazed at Sol with the cowed expression of a dutiful dog.

Sol's fury had greatly expanded her powers. For many years she had practised and experimented on her own – but now, in front of an audience, she wanted to try one of the most difficult tricks that Hanna had described to her. So she closed her eyes and took a deep breath. Everyone sat staring at her, seemingly numbed by what they had just witnessed. When she had gathered her energy again, she opened her eyes and walked slowly up to the altar to take her place on the right-hand side of the cowering 'warlock'.

'Weakling!' she commanded in a monotone. 'Weakling, look to your left!'

A hushed and fearful cry immediately rose from the congregation. Sol smiled scornfully. She knew at once that she had succeeded.

'She's – standing on both sides of him in the same moment!' a jabbering voice cried out.

Sol heard the 'Master's' teeth chattering in fear, as his horrified gaze switched back and forth between the two images of Sol. She was unable to see her alter ego herself, because she needed to stand completely still, facing forward, to concentrate all her power. In this state her conscious mind seemed to leave her body and transfer itself to the other side of the altar. Slowly she relaxed, her mind returned to her body and the image disappeared. She felt the sweat on her brow, her heart was beating furiously and her legs were growing weak.

Tucking the mandrake carefully back into its hiding place inside her clothes, she strode up to the closest of the 'warlock's' disciples. Without warning, she grabbed hold of a leather pouch that hung at his side.

'You,' she said thoughtfully, feeling its weight, 'you have in this pouch two silver coins, a dried rose and a letter.'

The youth could do no more than nod frantically.

'And you,' she said, turning to a woman and touching her gently, 'you are expecting a child by that deformed excuse for a man at the altar. You have not dared to tell anyone, but it is true. You will suffer for this child and you will get no consideration from him!'

She then turned to another man and put her hands on his shoulders.

'Your only thought at this moment is how you will get home to your wife, to whom you have said nothing of this delightful little gathering. You are having a relationship with this girl beside you and she believes you will marry her.'

'Stop!' shouted the priestess, as Sol turned to face her. 'Stop! Say no more! Stop!'

'She's a real witch,' whispered one of the men, 'a proper witch! I did not think they existed.'

'Oh, yes, they exist,' said Sol, suddenly feeling weary. 'But they are very few and far between. And you are sick, my good man. You cannot hold down your food.'

'That's quite right.' he agreed plaintively.

'Here, take this powder,' ordered Sol. 'Drink an infusion of it every morning and free yourself of your debts. Then your body will be cured!'

She swung round to face the man who had brought her to the meeting.

'Farewell, Preben, I am sorry to have destroyed your dreams. But you must believe me when I say that witchcraft is not to be meddled with. I could not let that impostor take advantage of you in any way he saw fit. I shall not denounce you and I am going to trust that you will remain silent about me.'

With those words she turned on her heel and walked out of the room, leaving behind a smell of sweat and a group of people stripped of all honour and prestige. Not one of them would ever fully understand what had happened to them that evening – or remotely comprehend Sol and her secrets.

* * * *

In the great house where she lived in Oslo, Liv toiled endlessly to make everything perfect – but her face no longer radiated that special warmth that had always been part of her personality. Nowadays there was always an anxious look in her eyes, a discernible fear that all would not be exactly as it should. She wanted so badly to please her husband and make him happy, but she had learned a painful lesson: everything had to be on his terms.

With distress, she recalled the repeated attempts she had made to surprise him. There was the small picture of flowers that she had painted secretly and given him on his birthday. He had held it in his hands, turning it this way and that for a long time. 'It is very sweet of you, Liv,' he had said, 'and it is pretty. Very proficient even but …'

'But what?' she asked apprehensively, when he paused.

'I think you should concentrate on your embroidery, my child. It does not suit a woman to paint pictures. It is the job of great, well known artists. I want my little wife to do that for which she is best suited. Now, is there any sign that you are with child?'

Liv shook her head. She felt completely worthless. She couldn't even get pregnant! Poor Laurents, she thought, how discontented he must be with her. She was never in any doubt that he loved her. Every day he made her aware of this in so many ways. Unfortunately he insisted on treating her as a chattel.

She remembered how, on one occasion when they had been entertaining guests, she had begun a conversation with an older man. The lively discussion had covered current affairs, the latest social developments among the people of the city and what the King had done for Norway. Liv had been delighted to find the man intelligent and interested and several others had been drawn into the debate. Then suddenly she had seen Laurents staring at her. His thunderous face indicated that he was furious.

A sharp movement of his head was sufficient to order her to leave the group, whereupon she made her excuses and withdrew from the conversation. Later that evening he had been merciless – in a patronising voice he had scolded her, saying that he saw women who dared to involve themselves in the world of men's affairs as an abomination.

'Under no circumstances are you ever to make a fool of yourself like that again,' he had said. 'Do not presume to compare yourself with any man. I will not have such an unwomanly wife! Oh Liv, I can see that you have a lot to learn! You have deceived me, for I did not believe that you were so unruly and of such a poor background! You are too precious and adorable, you are my greatest treasure, and we shall soon rid you of your shortcomings, just you wait and see! But do not be fretful, because I am your big strong bear and will take care of you and do your thinking for you!'

Yes, she was starting to learn that, as long as she served him within the acceptable bounds of convention, he would be happy. But, oh, how difficult it was at times to suppress the impulsiveness that was part of her character. Why only last week she had forgotten herself yet again. They had been visiting one of Laurents' colleagues and, as they were leaving his home, the man had remarked on how brightly Sirius was shining.

Without thinking, she had corrected him, saying, 'That is not Sirius, it is Deneb in the constellation Cygnus, the Swan.'

That evening when they reached home Laurents had struck her. Without any warning, he had slapped her face twice, because she had exposed him 'to such grave humiliation in front of a colleague and his wife'. They all knew very well that the star in question was Sirius, he said angrily. Who did she think she was?

Liv felt certain that none of them knew the name of any other star, but she had been unable to defend herself and remained tearfully silent. Afterwards he had been full of regret and begged her forgiveness before taking her to bed and making impassioned and eager love to her. However, from that moment onward something vital had been lost forever. What little trust and intimacy that they had begun to share, despite the bad start to their marriage, had been trampled in the dust.

Although Liv was obviously a talented artist, like her mother, she was destined never again to pick up a brush in that household. Her husband's harsh criticisms had affected her confidence very badly and she dared not defy him, even secretly.

Neither did Laurents' mother do anything to make life easier for the young girl. She was a crotchety old lady, demanding and envious of Liv. She had wanted to keep her son for herself and would never have been able to tolerate any daughter-in-law, no matter how perfect. But the woman had soon discovered that the gentle and mild-mannered Liv was easy to dominate and this was something she did with relish.

Of course, Laurents saw none of this and believed that there was perfect harmony in the house. If ever there was the slightest controversy, he would side with his mother – after all, Liv was only an uneducated child. Her letters home, on the rare occasions she wrote them, contained only short encouraging reports to Mama Silje that told how good things were. But Liv, in fact, always wrote holding the paper at arm's length, because she was afraid that her constant tears would fall on the pages and smudge the ink.

Chapter 4

Although she should have travelled home some time ago, Sol had achieved such high status in the Strahlenhelm's household that they had invited her to stay through the winter as nursemaid for little Albrekt. They had apologised for offering her such a lowly position, but they felt strongly that their child would benefit from her exuberance and love of life.

Sol had thought about the offer at length. She had not travelled this far just to become a nursemaid, but the alternative was to return home. Until now she had not seen much of life in the wider world and she did need somewhere to live. Here was as good as anywhere, she thought. Only one thing troubled her. She was eager to visit Brösarps Backar, a place where she knew true witches could be found. She had asked Dag about it, but he had not heard of the place. After some thought, he had said that the latter part of the name made it sound as though it might be in Skåne.

'Is that the land on the other side of the Öresund strait?' she had asked.

'Yes,' he nodded. 'You know, the land that borders Sweden.'

In fact she did know of it. When thinking about this, she realised that crossing the straits during winter would be far too long and difficult a journey for her, so she had accepted the Strahlenhelm's offer to be Albrekt's nursemaid. As a compromise, she was to be known as his governess because, despite the boy being too young to learn very much, Sol was intelligent and educated enough to warrant the title. Furthermore, the Countess was expecting her second child; this meant she would not be able to take care of the boy herself, as she had done when their previous nursery maid had left and returned to her family.

Everything went well and the Count and Countess were most satisfied. Sol performed her duties in an exemplary fashion and everyone in the household became very fond of her. Whatever she did in her room during the evenings were things no one ever considered or even cared about.

It was during these evenings alone that she opened her small pouch and practised her craft. She allowed herself then to reflect on how eagerly she was looking forward to two things: the first was the journey to Brösarps Backar and the second was her determination to take part in a witches' ride to Blåkulla to meet the Evil One himself. Both these ambitions had been planted in her mind by Hanna during her childhood – but to fulfil them properly she would need a herb that she did not yet possess, which was another reason to stay until spring.

Tengel and Silje wrote to say that they were very pleased with the position she had been offered and that she could stay as long as Dag remained. On the subject of Liv, although they did not mention it in their letters, Sol understood from 'reading between the lines' that they were surprised and hurt that she seemed never to have the time to visit Linden Allée or allow them to visit her in Oslo.

Evidently they had never seen the inside of Liv's new home and this struck Sol as petty and not at all like her little sister.

What none of them could know was that Laurents always found a reason not to receive his wife's family. Similarly, using carefully chosen words, so as not to cause dismay, he would forbid her from travelling home to visit them. So Silje would despatch packages to her daughter, containing fine food and beautiful gifts, and this would send Laurents into a rage. He would rant and rave, and demand to know if they thought he was unable to support his own wife. Although Liv became acutely worried by this, she refused to throw the gifts away. Knowing how much love and care lay behind them, she hid them well away from Laurents' prying eyes. Sol knew none of this, but could not rid herself of an uneasy feeling over the strange way in which Liv had distanced herself from everyone.

* * * *

Although Sol had met many of the young men in Dag's circle of student friends, she did not want to make the acquaintance of adolescent intellectuals. Unconsciously she sought out men of high authority, combined with primitive virility. Matters were not made easier by the fact that most of the men attending the university were studying for the priesthood. This was considered to be the supreme vocation and other faculties, such as Law and the Sciences, were looked down on by the students of Theology because they were thought to be of lesser importance. Sol had heaved many a sigh of desperation over this state of affairs.

Primitive virile men of stature and authority – where did she find even one of those, she asked herself? They certainly did not grow on trees! Indeed she had often thought that the only individual capable of satisfying her might be Satan himself!

The year 1600 began with great religious ceremony and feasting. Sol did not take any part in this. She had managed to find the perfect excuse for never attending church. She 'sacrificed herself' by staying at home to care for little Albrekt, so that all the God-fearing servants could say their prayers. The Countess was concerned, but Sol explained casually that she visited the church once every week to receive a blessing. The truth was that Sol had not come anywhere close to a priest since her own fateful baptism; then she had spat in the face of His Reverence and kicked his pious shins!

In the spring the Count and Countess invited Sol to attend a royal ball with Dag. They were both extremely proud of this incredibly beautiful young girl and were keen to present her at court. Consequently the Countess chose a gown that matched with perfection the colour of Sol's eyes. It was made of thick green silk and, as she moved, the gold lamé petticoat showed through long slits in the skirt. They had tried to tame her wild locks in an artistic coiffure, but very quickly discovered that her hair was best left to hang freely. Once ready for the ball, she was such a vision of beauty that she took their breath away.

On the way to the castle in a carriage, Dag whispered fiercely to her, 'The men will flock to you like flies round a honey pot. Don't latch on to any one gentleman in particular – I forbid it!'

Sol whispered back with sneering disdain, 'I have no use for a decadent court jester! I want somebody who can bite!'

69

'God help us all,' mumbled Dag weakly. 'The coarse inheritance of the Ice People is still with us! There is far too much of Hanna in you.'

'And that is something I am very proud of,' replied Sol. 'But don't concern yourself overmuch, Little Brother. I shall conduct myself with such ladylike decorum it will make you choke!'

Dag could not help but laugh out loud at this – and sure enough when her turn came, Sol curtseyed deeply and formally to King Christian, a portly twenty-three-year-old who definitely had a twinkle in his eye as he looked at her. Not content with being in the third year of his marriage, he was currently engaged in a little extra-marital romance in the Court and was therefore under close scrutiny from two sides. Nonetheless, he quietly made a note of Sol's name and address.

As Dag had expected, the King was not alone in being attracted to her. Indeed a great many noblemen of all ages also showed intense interest. A certain Christian Friis proposed to her on the spot, as soon as he met her, and two youngsters, one a Gyldenstierne and the other a Bille, both old aristocratic families, began a fight over which of them was worthy of Sol's favour.

Sol had never enjoyed herself as much as she did at that ball. She behaved with great modesty, but all the time allowed her eyes to flirt wildly under the cover of a maidenly smile. The dance steps that Charlotte had taught her proved to be sorely outdated, but every admirer was eager to teach her new ones and she proved to be a fast learner. She also received several direct propositions of varying degrees of decency – but it was not difficult to demonstrate her integrity, for the simple reason that nobody there held any interest for her at all.

Then something happened that put an abrupt end to her grand life in Copenhagen.

There were very many guests and she had only made the acquaintance of a few of them, when she suddenly felt she was being watched. More than that, she sensed that harsh and vicious thoughts were being directed at her. Glancing about, she quickly singled out the source of this unrelenting animosity – although dressed very differently on this occasion, she was able to recognise the woman who had been the 'warlock's' priestess at the secret 'demonic' meeting in the cellar.

'Who would have guessed that she ranked so highly in the social hierarchy of the capital?' thought Sol. Not so surprising, then, that she had wanted to be rid of her, before too many secrets might be revealed! It was very clear that this woman had evil in mind and Sol realised she needed to remain very much on her guard.

Before too long the King retired – he had drunk so much that he fell asleep where he sat and had to be carried out! Sol was no stranger to rural parties and had often seen the excessive eating and drinking that took place, but this Court ball was beyond her wildest imaginings. As was the custom, when people had eaten their fill they would go outside and put their fingers down their throats to make room for more. Some did not make it to the door, but relied on the servants to clean up after them. 'What pigs they are!' thought Sol, wishing she were safely back in the Count's house again.

As she was watching these proceedings, a man she had not seen before approached her and bowed deeply. 'Mistress Sol?' he enquired politely. 'Your brother wishes to speak with you. He waits in the stateroom downstairs across the main hall.'

Somewhat bemused, Sol thanked the stranger, walked down the wide staircase and entered the stateroom – but it was empty and she stood uncertainly for some moments in the centre of the broad carpet, wondering what she should do next. Gilded decoration adorned everything possible in the large chamber – cornices, mirrors and wall panels. There were several doors leading off the stateroom, but all were closed and she had no wish to blunder into a bedroom or other private boudoir. After she had waited for some time and Dag had not shown himself, she went back out into the hall. Could she have gone to the wrong room by mistake? No, she did not think so. Slightly put out, she went back upstairs to the ballroom to ask the man for an explanation, but he was nowhere to be seen – and neither was Dag.

The Count and his wife were there, but they had not seen Dag for some time. On learning this, Sol began to worry in earnest. The 'devil' woman was not in the room either and Sol's uneasiness quickly turned into a growing certainty that something was badly wrong.

She did not have to wait long for her fears to be confirmed. Suddenly the 'devil' woman came running into the room screaming, 'My husband! My husband is dead.'

A crowd immediately gathered around her, asking questions and interrupting one another, so it was impossible to understand what was being said. Judge Strahlenhelm raised his hand for silence and asked for a calm explanation of events. Although her account could hardly be called calm and was punctuated with fainting fits, the woman managed to explain that her husband lay dead in one of the chambers leading off the stateroom downstairs.

'So *that's* it!' thought Sol. Thank you very much!

'And he's been poisoned,' screamed the woman. 'It's not hard to guess who did it either. There's only one witch here able to mix powders!'

At that moment the man who had falsely summoned Sol to the downstairs stateroom reappeared, pointing an accusing finger at her. 'I saw that young woman enter the stateroom,' he shouted, 'only a short time ago.'

'After you had requested that I should go there,' said Sol calmly, hiding the turmoil she felt inside.

'What do you mean?' asked the man belligerently.

'You brought a false message from my brother that he wished to speak with me in the stateroom, but he was not there. Where is my brother now?'

'That's her!' screamed the woman. 'She's the witch I spoke of!'

At that moment Dag pushed through the throng.

'Where have you been?' asked Sol, her eyes showing the anxiety her voice was managing to keep in check.

'I was detained by a woman who wished to discuss a legal matter with me.'

'Which woman?' demanded the Count at once.

Dag pointed to the woman who had been yelling about the death of her husband.

'He is lying!' she cried. 'It is a conspiracy – these two siblings are working together.'

For a while there was confusion, and the atmosphere became extremely unpleasant. Then the Count, after reminding all present that he was a senior judge, asserted his authority and led the way downstairs to inspect the body, followed by the parties involved.

The corpse lay on the floor in one of the small rooms adjoining the stateroom and it was not difficult to see that the man had been poisoned. Sol asked to speak with the

Count in private and immediately told him every detail of her visit to the sect in the cellar. When she had finished, he drew a deep breath.

'That was extremely careless of you, Sol,' he said. 'I have lived close to you all winter and we have grown very fond of you. It has become quite apparent that you have been granted more talents than others, but I have chosen to ignore this because you have kept them in check and behaved well. Now we both find ourselves in an awkward situation. You must tell me the names of everyone in that cellar.'

'I can't do that, because I don't know who they are,' she replied. 'Besides, the younger ones were probably quite innocent. I should think they were so shocked that they stopped having any further interest in such childish practices.'

She decided not to mention Preben. He was after all one of Dag's student friends and she had more or less forced him to take her with him.

'But the head man, the warlock? What about him?' insisted the judge.

'Oh, yes, I'd like to see him get his comeuppance. He was a slimy little worm, deceiving other people for his own ends – but I don't know his name either.'

As she was trying to give the Count a good description of the man, a servant entered the room, interrupting her. He whispered something urgently to the Count and then turned and left.

'You're safe, Sol,' said Count Strahlenhelm. 'One of the guests has said that he was standing close enough to you to hear when you were asked to go down to the stateroom – by the man who is thought to be the lover of that "devil" woman. So it was indeed obviously a conspiracy. Only it was perpetrated *by* them – not *against* them.'

The Count called to Dag, who immediately walked over to join them.

'Sol is no longer under suspicion,' he said to the young man in a low voice, 'and of course, neither are you. I will take care of that woman and her lover. Nonetheless, Sol's predicament is dire. She has been denounced as a witch at a royal gathering. It's an accusation she can hardly deny and I could not neglect my duty to sentence her. But she saved the life of our son and has been loving and caring to us all since she came to our home. For this reason I will now repay the debt and save her life. I can only do this in one way, Dag. You must take your sister back to my house at once. In a few hours, while most people are still sleeping, two riders will be leaving for Glimmingehus on an errand for the King. I will ensure that they fetch Sol from our house before sunrise. She must go with them.'

Dag nodded his agreement.

After a moment the Count turned to Sol with a rueful smile, 'You Sol, will have to find passage by boat from Skåne to Norway. But being young and beautiful, that should not be too difficult. Do you understand?'

Sol nodded, hiding a smile. One wonderful thought had occurred to her as soon as the Count had mentioned Skåne. That was where Brösarp lay – and she wanted to go there more than anything else in the world!

But Dag protested strongly, 'My sister cannot make the long journey to Norway alone!'

The Count gave Dag another rueful smile. 'I believe your sister will manage exceedingly well on her own. She will have the military escort to help her find a ship sailing for Norway – and besides, what choice do we have?'

'None,' said Sol. 'Dag, don't worry. All will be well.' She

turned back to the Count. 'Your Excellency I owe you a great debt of gratitude.'

'You must hurry, both of you!' said the Count, waving away her thanks. 'Leave this way. We will collect your capes and bring them home. Meanwhile I shall say that Sol has eluded me. Go at once. Be quick!'

Without further ado, they left by a back door. Dag berated Sol continuously all the way home, but she wasn't listening. Her heart was already full of anticipation – she would be going to Brösarps Backar! Nothing else mattered at that moment. She promised Dag faithfully that she would be back home in Norway by the time he returned after finishing his studies. This was a promise she fully intended to keep, if for no other reason than to avoid causing more trouble for her brother.

* * * *

In the darkness of the pre-dawn hours, Sol's royal escort waited for her outside the Count's house. They sat stolidly astride their mounts in total silence, the horses' breath enveloping them in clouds of steam. Only after long farewells to little Albrekt and his parents, and once more promising Dag that she would take good care of herself, did she take a good look at her unexpected travelling companions.

They were two imposing men, dressed in uniform leather jerkins and high boots. They carried big wheel-lock muskets and both had powder cartridges strapped across their chests. One of them was a youngster – typically Danish, blond and pale skinned. She could see at once that he was very shy and she could imagine his face changing to bright pink and back again like the shifting colours on a windswept field of corn at sunset.

'Oh my!' thought Sol, with some delight. Such a sweet boy! He will have to be seduced and shown the mysteries of love. If only the other one wasn't keeping such a close eye on the lad!

The other escort, in fact, was a giant of a man, who appeared to regard Sol as a punishment and an inconvenience. She put his age at about forty and could tell he was a seasoned warrior. Sol suspected she would be having many bitter altercations with him on this journey.

Although unaware of Sol's thoughts, Dag was decidedly unhappy with the arrangements. 'I ought to be going with you,' he said agitatedly. 'But I am studying so hard at the moment. The final examinations are taking all my time and effort.'

'Do you think you will do well?' she asked.

'I believe I shall have an excellent result – but naturally I am very nervous.'

'Good luck, Little Brother! I will soon be on a ship bound for Norway.'

'Yes I know, but you should have had a chaperone with you – an older woman who could safeguard your honour.'

'That won't be necessary!' said the older of the two escorts sharply. 'She will come to no harm from either of us!' He managed to make his assertion sound like an insult.

'But what is this?' said the Countess. 'Sol's horse has no side-saddle!'

'We must ride fast, Your Ladyship. The young lady will have to sit astride.'

Sol's eyes sparkled. 'That will be much better. I have never liked those uncomfortable ladies' saddles.'

'So you know how to use a man's saddle, then?' queried the older man, sounding innocent. 'I'm very glad to hear it.'

Sol understood now that he had arranged this riding method deliberately, because he hated the idea of having a woman along to slow him down. 'You can be sure I will have no difficulties,' she replied, mounting the horse easily.

Without further ado, still in darkness, they set off. As they rode down towards the harbour they could hear nothing but the sound of their horses' hooves on the cobbles. Within minutes the first light of dawn began to show in the sky and Sol rode forward alongside the two men.

'What are your names?' she asked brightly, her expression showing that she was thrilled at the thought of the adventurous journey that lay ahead. 'It would be good to know, especially as we shall be travelling together for some time.'

Both men turned and looked more closely at her, noticing now in the growing light her rosy cheeks, her bright eyes and the gleaming smile. The younger man, who was riding closer to her, answered shyly. 'I am Jörgen and my commander here is Jacob Skille.'

'And I am Sol. I am very grateful to you for letting me journey with you.'

Jacob Skille, a soldier in King Christian's personal bodyguard, sniffed loudly as they rode on, but added no embellishment to his subordinate's introduction. It had been arranged that they would sail across Öresund strait on a barge-like vessel, taking their horses and baggage with them and once they were under way, Sol went and stood at the rail to enjoy the smell of the fresh sea air. In the morning mist she could see an island in the middle of the straits rising up spectre-like out of the water and the mysterious sight made her pulse quicken.

This was the island of Ven, Jörgen had told her and Sol wondered idly what possibilities for mysterious deeds might exist out there in the fastness of the sea. Then her thoughts ran on again into the immediate future and she turned her gaze to look towards the distant landfall of the far side of the strait, where she might meet people like herself at last. Hopefully they would be wiser and more knowledgeable – beings she could learn from. She had already been disappointed once, in Preben's shabby little cellar, and she no longer dared to have many great hopes or expectations.

'Witches gather each Thursday of the full moon during summer at Brösarps Backar,' Hanna had told her. The old woman had said she always dreamed that she might go there one day herself. But that was so many years ago now and who could say whether the witches still gathered at this notorious site? Who even, would know if there were any witches left in any of the Nordic countries? What if she, Sol Angelica, was the only one?

These thoughts made her feel suddenly very alone! But this did not daunt her in the least. In fact, it quickened the elation and excitement she felt, that she was at last really pursuing her true destiny.

'Each Thursday of the full moon' had been Hanna's precise words. In that case, she was going to be a little early. There were some days to go yet, but the moon was waxing – and she still had some distance to travel. At least she was finished with Copenhagen. As far as she could tell, she would be unwelcome there forever, unless she faded from people's memories. Still, she had no great yearning to return to that particular city – there were many other adventures waiting ahead of her!

As the barge ploughed on across the strait, Jacob Skille stood holding the horses to keep them calm. Young Jörgen was standing in the bow, alone. Sol went over to him and, just as she had expected, the boy's cheeks turned bright red, like a pair of ripe apples, even before she spoke.

'What are you going to do in Glimmingehus?' she wondered, her warm eyes bathing him in their glow.

With an effort, he shifted his eyes away from her gaze. 'We are couriers with messages from His Majesty, King Christian, to Sire Rosencrantz, the incumbent of Glimmingehus Manor. There has been unrest in Sweden, and Skåne is a part of Denmark that is under threat. As you know, Mistress, the Swedes want to take Skåne. They regard it as a natural part of Sweden.'

'What sort of unrest?' asked Sol.

The youth had to overcome his awkwardness in order to answer her in a matter-of-fact way. But however much he tried to look unconcerned, she noticed that he kept nervously twisting the end of a thin rope round and round his index finger.

'You've heard tell of the Linköping Bloodbath?' he asked.

'The Stockholm Bloodbath is something I know of, but not Linköping.'

'It happened last March. The great Gustav Banér and his brother Sten, together with noblemen from the Sparre and Bielke families, were beheaded during Duke Karl's purge on those sworn to Sigismund. Many Swedish noblemen fled the country; most of them to Poland, but some also went to Skåne. Our Danish King is afraid of conflict. The Duke now has plans to be crowned King of Sweden – and he is as cruel and hard as his father, Gustav Wasa.'

'But Gustav Wasa died a long time ago – more than forty years since!'

'Yes, but do not forget that his son, Erik XIV, followed

him. His fate was a dreadful one – imprisoned, and probably murdered at the hand of his brother Johan III. Sigismund, the Polish son of Johan, followed him. Now we have Duke Karl, brother of Erik and Johan.'

'I see,' said Sol. 'A battle for power, just as there is in so many other places. Are the folk in Skåne faithful to the Danish King? I would not want to risk a dagger in the back while I'm there, would you?'

'It is quite safe. He has much support amongst the Göinge.'

Sol could see that Jörgen was an educated young man from the upper classes. She had never interested herself much in the Swedes and their kings, but she asked who the Göinge were. Blushing and twisting his piece of tar-soaked rope continuously, Jörgen explained that the Göinge were a nomadic warrior folk, who lived mostly in the northeastern part of Skåne which bordered Sweden; they were also known as 'Snaphauncers', after the Snaphaunce musket, the type of firearm they preferred to use.

'And the Göinge are friendly towards the Danes?'

'Yes.'

'That is comforting to know,' said Sol with an artless smile. 'And where is Brösarp? Do you know?'

The bluntness of her question took him by surprise. Sol was sure that this young man, with the first down of manhood just visible on his soft cheeks, would still be scared of the bogeyman or the chimney sweep. He'd certainly have a fright if I showed him one or two of my better tricks, she thought. The prospect of doing that amused her, but she reined in her thoughts again as the youth struggled to frame his reply.

'B–Brösarp? I do not know where that is,' he mumbled at last.

Without their noticing, Jacob Skille had walked over to stand behind them. How long he had been there was not clear, but he made his presence felt by clearing his throat loudly.

'Brösarp lies on the east coast,' he said in a harsh voice. 'It is a good distance away.'

Sol turned to face this hardened giant of a man and found that she had to tilt her head backward in order to meet his gaze full on. 'Is it far from Glimmingehus?'

'No, not especially.'

He drew a rough map by running his finger across the damp surface of the dark wooden hull.

'Here is Skåne's south-easterly point, and Glimmingehus lies a short distance inland. Go further up the coast and one quickly reaches Simrishamn and Kivik – and just north of Kivik is Brösarp. But why do you ask?'

'I shall be going there.'

'What! No, you shall not! I will be putting you on a ship bound for Norway as soon as we reach Skåne.'

Sol decided to bluff it out. 'Did my brother say nothing to you about me travelling to Brösarp?'

'Not a word. What will you do there?'

'Visit friends,' she answered simply.

Skille's face expressed everything he felt about young ladies who went gallivanting about unaccompanied on such long expeditions.

'I will have none of it!'

'I shall manage on my own,' Sol insisted.

'I have given my word.' His answer was short and sharp. 'Don't make life awkward!'

Sol's lowered her eyelids slightly and her eyes shimmered with a green cat-like glow. Held by their gaze, Jacob Skille was disconcerted to find that, for no good reason he was changing his mind, feeling suddenly that he had acted foolishly and been unnecessarily hard on the girl.

'We return to Copenhagen on Sunday,' he said, ending on a more deferential note. 'Your visit ought to be over by then and you can join us again at Glimmingehus. I am honour bound to Judge Strahlenhelm to see you safely on board a Norwegian boat.'

'But of course,' Sol replied.

She had no intention whatsoever of leaving Brösarps Backar after such a short time, but wisely decided to keep that to herself. She had not forgotten either that Dag would soon complete his studies and that they had agreed to meet up again in Norway. But there were so many things that she wanted to get done before then – and somehow they would all have to be fitted in!

* * * *

When at last they disembarked in Skåne, they found themselves in wide rolling countryside. As they rode inland, the trees seemed to be growing almost horizontally, turning their backs on the harsh untamed winds from the sea. The sun was up and the sound of larks celebrating the day came from overhead. Spring had definitely arrived in this part of Denmark.

The beech trees were wearing their soft green mantle; the rich earth steamed gently from the furrows left by the plough and the ground underfoot was dry and warm from the sun. Sol felt ready to burst with the energy and feeling of freedom that every new spring brought with it. To her great pleasure they rode at a good pace through the quiet morning and Sol's hair flew in the wind and her skirts blew back, occasionally showing more of her legs than decency allowed. But nothing could stem her wild exhilaration.

She had been so restrained through the past winter – indeed over the whole of the past six years – and now wanted nothing more than to throw off these bonds. She knew she needed to release all the seething emotions that simmered within her and, as she rode, she tossed her head and laughed wildly at the wind. If King Christian's bodyguard or dragoon thought that she would be holding them back, then he would have to think again, she told herself. She would never find it hard to keep up with their pace.

They gradually left the plains, where all the small farms were identical, consisting of four squat buildings enclosing a courtyard. This was a rural style peculiar to Skåne and they noticed this changing as they reached the uplands and the welcoming shade of beech-woods, where flocks of small birds chirped and twittered their morning songs. Sol rode last as they filed along the narrow path, but her horse never lagged behind. She noticed that Skille pushed up the pace from time to time to try and embarrass her, but she would not give him that satisfaction! To spare the horses, he eventually had to reduce the pace to a quick trot.

The trees thinned and they came to a field where Skille called a halt. They had ridden a long way and both animals and humans needed rest and refreshment. Sol quickly lifted down her panniers onto the grass and laid out the food that the Strahlenhelms had given her to take on the journey. When the two men saw the sumptuous fare spread before them their eyes widened. Their own packs contained only meagre soldiers' rations.

'Help yourselves, please,' said Sol with a grin. 'I will never be able to eat all this!'

After exchanging doubtful glances, the pair politely took a few small bits of food.

'No, no! Take as much as you want,' urged Sol. 'Can't you see it's in my own best interests to feed the two of you. The way to a man's heart is through his belly and I intend to charm you both with my irresistible morning meal. And look here – wine to soften you up even more!'

All this was said so self-mockingly that young Jörgen could not resist a careful smile and even Skille allowed the corners of his mouth to twitch slightly. The men didn't seem inclined to say very much, so Sol chattered on while they ate. Her eyes twinkled as she flirted constantly with Jörgen, making him turn bright pink with embarrassment once again.

'Save yourself the effort,' said Skille at last in a dull dry voice. 'The lad only has eyes for a certain Mistress Ottilie.'

Jörgen turned indignantly to his comrade. 'No! That's not really true.'

'Oh! How wonderful!' interrupted Sol with delight. 'So you have a young lady? I'm sure it makes you very happy to have a friend. Tell me about her! Are you betrothed?'

'He dare not ask her,' said the older man with derision. 'He admires her from afar and then keeps everyone in the barrack awake at night with his sighs.'

'What does she look like?' asked Sol. 'Is she pretty?'

'Oh, yes!' whispered Jörgen breathlessly. 'But I do not know how to approach her. I have never courted a maiden before. Can you teach me what I should do, Mistress Sol?'

'Of course, but first I must know what sort of person she is.'

'Ah, she is as pure and virtuous as a rosebud – yet as timid as a fawn.'

'Then you must stay as chaste as a Knight of the Grail,' declared Sol. 'But you must show her that you are the stronger one – for maidens such as this need to look up admiringly to their beloved. Court her politely, but do not play at being coy – you are already shy enough by nature. Most of all, treat her truly like a lady!'

'Well, Mistress, you seem to have experience,' said Skille sourly.

Sol rounded on him, her eyes glaring.

'No, I do not!' she exclaimed, her voice cold and harsh. 'I was defiled while I was just fourteen. Since then I have let no man touch me.'

Forgive me, Klaus, she thought. I know I turned the truth about who defiled whom on its head. But this sounds far better, you must agree.

'You poor child,' said Skille gently. 'Only fourteen and violated.'

A sudden irrational fury overcame Sol and the sustained feeling became violent and wild. This man felt compassion for her! He felt *pity*! She did not want this – she didn't know how to handle tenderness. She wanted men to admire her, to desire her. That made her strong and superior, able to fend them off or indulge them – whatever she chose. But she wanted pity from no man!

Still angry, she got up and walked away to stop herself from slapping him. However, the two men misinterpreted her action, believing that their awakening the memory had been too much for her. They thought that now she simply wanted to spare them her tears and their sympathy grew even more. After taking a few deep breaths, Sol regained her self-control and walked back to sit down on the grass again. She remained silent for some minutes, while she recovered her spirits.

'So how far have you got with your courting?' she asked at last in her usual friendly tone.

Jörgen's cheeks coloured. 'I have been alone with her once in her father's garden. You must understand, Mistress, that she is a very distinguished young lady. My desire to kiss her almost made me faint. Yet I didn't dare try, because I don't know how to.'

'Neither do I!' Sol lied cheerfully. 'Perhaps we should practice on each other?'

'Oh, no! That would be too unseemly!'

'Then Skille can teach us,' she teased. 'He has both children and grandchildren.'

'Skille? No! He's has been a soldier ever since he learned to crawl.'

There was a thunderous expression on Skille's face. 'Grandchildren!' he snorted. 'How old do you believe me to be, Mistress Sol?' Then breaking off, he stood up abruptly. 'No matter, there's no need to answer that. Let us be on our way and waste no more time on such foolish chatter!'

Following this episode, the two soldiers each began to regard her in a new light. A young man's yearning showed in Jörgen's pensive gaze – he was wondering whether a lesson from her in the art of kissing might be desirable after all. Skille, on the other hand, thought of her as a poor vulnerable child whose life had been destroyed by a ruthless and violent man.

Poor, dear Klaus – a ruthless and violent man? Sol's conscience should have troubled her greatly for giving that impression. She hated Skille's new protective attitude towards her. If there was one thing she prided herself on, it was her independence. He was not pushing them at such a fast pace any more either and he brought them to an early stop on the slopes of Romeleåsen.

'I shall ride ahead to see if I can find quarters for the night,' he told them. 'Wait here.'

The sun lay on the horizon. They were in woodland, and the song of a thrush could be heard echoing through the trees. Sol and Jörgen dismounted and stretched their aching legs.

'You can certainly feel this journey in your arse!' announced Sol loudly to the whole world, causing Jörgen to blush again. She wondered whether he imagined that fine ladies didn't have a backside to sit on?

Jörgen wanted to carry on with the 'lesson' they had spoken of earlier in the day, but Sol had lost the desire to seduce him. He was just too much of a weakling, she thought; too innocent and wet behind the ears. Although in practice she did not have anyone with whom to compare him, she still found him wanting. She had always sought figures of authority – as she had crudely expressed it to Dag, 'Someone with a bit of bite!'

Nevertheless, in an indifferent frame of mind, she decided to allow herself to be used as an object for his experimentation. She let him caress her face and touch her lips fleetingly, guiding him when he was clumsy or inept. She explained things in words she thought a virtuous young maiden would delight in hearing and, with some trepidation, she allowed him to run his hands over her curvaceous form. She stopped him from going below her waist, however, and he agreed.

'That is a sacred area for her,' said Sol. 'You must not sully your hands by touching another woman.'

Sol could see he was perplexed and confused. His hands were trembling and he was moaning under his breath as he crossed his legs in an immature way. But Sol still found that she had no desire for him at all.

She turned away and began to adjust the girth on her horse, thereby hoping to put the youth out of his misery. I must be completely without feelings, she thought, with some concern. All his touching should have excited me greatly, but it was time-consuming and bothersome. At that moment Jacob Skille returned and removed any further opportunity for embarrassment.

'There's no settlement close by and the countryside beyond the slopes of Romeleåsen is deserted,' he told them. 'Shall we continue, or do you want to camp here for the night?'

'We should stay here,' said Jörgen. 'I think the horses need the rest.'

Once the decision had been made, Sol spread out her saddle blanket on the grass. She looked at Jacob Skille with some apprehension, sensing that a change had come over him. Then suddenly she understood what it was. *She* had changed her view of *him*.

It was probably a result of Jörgen's puppy-like prodding and touching. Skille was the strong one, the leader making decisions for all three of them. He was well built and muscular, an uncouth warrior with little interest in women. Close inspection revealed a curious attraction in his face. He could never be called an Adonis – far from it – but his eyes held a glow and clarity that Sol found appealing. He had fine strong white teeth and his skin was tanned and weather-beaten. He was a little unshaven and a splash or two of water on his face and hands would not go amiss, she thought, followed by a comb through his wild unruly hair. Also his body moved with a confident easy efficiency and there was something inviting about his bearing. Smiling to herself, Sol breathed a sigh of relief. I'm not without feelings after all, she thought.

During the years she had spent helping Tengel to attend the sick, she had suppressed her interest in men and all thoughts of things erotic. It was partly because she had been so shaken by Tengel's anger following the incident with Klaus that she had wanted to do all she could to placate him. But now the father figure of Tengel, the only man in the world whom she truly respected, was far away. Furthermore she was also free from the constraints of Judge Strahlenhelm, his family and Dag. No one would ever know what she did between leaving Copenhagen and arriving back in Norway. Yet whatever it was, she was determined to make the most of her liberty.

There was no opportunity for small talk during that evening. After eating a modest meal Skille wrapped himself immediately in his blanket, ordered the others to do likewise and bade them a curt goodnight.

Sol had been able to position herself so that it was impossible for Jörgen to reach her without disturbing his superior. She was glad of this; the last thing she wanted was more clumsy young hands fumbling over her, or breathless panting and moaning in her ear. She was of course pleased to see evidence of how much he desired her, but despite this, she had decided that the demure Ottilie could have him back untouched. Once she lay down she found that she was feeling extremely tired. Exhausted from the hard ride, she quickly fell into a deep sleep.

Chapter 5

The little band of brothers and sisters created by Silje and Tengel had by now mostly gone their separate ways. Are, the youngest, was still at home on the farm at Linden Allée, discussing with Tengel and Charlotte possible plans for developing forestry and other projects on the estate; Dag was studying hard in Copenhagen waiting for his exams to begin; while Sol was riding around Skåne, having been forced to leave the Danish capital because of her secret involvement in witchcraft.

These three, by and large, were happy and enjoying life. Unfortunately things were not going so well for poor Liv, who was the one who perhaps most deserved life's greatest rewards for her unfailing friendliness and unselfish love for her fellow man. In the prosperous but cold-hearted house in Oslo where she lived, young Liv was fighting a losing battle in trying to please her husband. During the day, while he was at his offices, her mother-in-law gave her not a moment of peace and in the evenings Liv had to cheer and gratify her husband.

On arriving home, Laurents would pat her idly on her head and ask how his 'little sugar lump' had been; but he

91

would never stop and listen when she tried to tell him about her day – not that there was ever much to tell. She had also learnt that it was best to remain silent about the humiliation she suffered at his mother's hands. On the one occasion when she had mentioned it, he had become aggressive and called her ungrateful. He told her that she would have to accept that his mother was old and helpless. Once, when she had asked to be allowed more independence to show how much she could do, he had said, 'Yes! Please do! Ask cook to let you make a cake, my dear!'

He continually pointed out that she was not thankful for all he did for her and, after the incident with the cook and the cake, she gave up. From her place on the chaise-longue, Liv's mother-in-law continued to blight her existence. Today, as on every other day, Liv was running about fetching and carrying – her bowl of confectionery, her mirror, her jug of ale – but, as a result of the woman's constant whining, Liv still felt that she never did enough.

'Nobody cares a jot about *my* aches and pains,' complained the old woman, clutching ostentatiously at her heart. (It was the wrong side of her chest, but Liv thought it best not to point this out.) 'My son is interested only in his business and my daughter-in-law is lazy and quite incapable of understanding my wishes.'

'And what is it you wish for now, dear Mother?' Liv enquired shyly.

'Oh, how will you ever be able to help me? You think of none but yourself, while I lie here alone and forgotten. As soon as you had gone down to eat, I suffered an attack. This poor little heart of mine cannot bear to see my dear son in such a miserable marriage. I have just been lying here helpless – alone – and so afraid.'

'I did not know.'

'I called,' gasped her mother-in-law, 'but nobody came. There was no one to help me.'

Liv was overcome with anxiety, because she had left her mother-in-law and gone down for breakfast. Now, with overwhelming feelings of guilt, she asked the old woman if she would like some food brought to her.

No, she replied, she wasn't hungry – not least because she had secretly just eaten fifteen sweet buns – and anyway could not manage a single thing. Indeed she hadn't felt like food at all for many, many days, she added. Obviously she was not long for this world, but who would care?

'It will be your fault should I die, Liv,' she said. 'I want you to know this and remember it well!'

Liv gazed down at her hands. 'So perhaps you need me to remain at home with you? As you well know, the wife of one of Laurents's colleagues has invited me to visit her today – but if you are feeling poorly, dear Mother …'

'So how can she invite you but not me!' snapped the mother-in-law. 'Well, just you go – typical that you should think of your own amusement. Go! Don't spare a thought for me!'

This was the first time Liv had been asked to visit anyone on her own and she had been looking forward to leaving the house, even for a short while. She was well aware that she had been invited purely for reasons of protocol. She would never genuinely be included in such an exalted circle of friends, because she simply did not belong to the Oslo bourgeoisie and consequently counted for little in this narrow local world.

'I can truly decline the invitation.'

'You must not do that. I shall manage well enough. I am so used to being abandoned now. It was all so different when there was just me and Laurents. He always had time to spend here then. It was so pleasant when it was just him and me. He always appreciated his little Mama. But now he has to work all the hours God sends just to satisfy a demanding wife. He, who could have had anyone from among the really distinguished people in this town. All the young ladies of the bourgeoisie were vying for his attentions. That he should have chosen a "Miss Nothing from a farmyard ..."'

She spat out the last words, but Liv tried not to listen. She knew that Laurents and his mother could not have lived alone in the house for very long, because his father had died only a short time before Liv's marriage to Laurents. Liv was also curious about the woman's illness. If something took her fancy – a new scandal or some juicy local gossip perhaps – then she would walk miles to hear more. Meanwhile, when nothing of note was happening, she lay stretched out across the chaise-longue and repeated the words to anyone who would listen. She was sick, so terribly sick.

'Well, Mother, if as you say, you can manage very well, I shall be on my way,' said Liv unconvinced. 'Do you have everything you need close by?'

'Just go,' said the woman, sounding exhausted.

Was Liv really going to be permitted to leave their home? If she did, she would no doubt receive a double dose of poison-tongued gibes later on. But she could put up with that. She felt that if she didn't get out of the house soon she would suffocate. Now, now at last it seemed she really was going to be allowed to be absent for a while!

But, oh no! That would not be happening today. Her mother-in-law had no intention of letting Liv get a breath of fresh air. When the girl had dressed and was about to leave, the old dowager threw back her head and clutched at her own throat.

'Uhh! I cannot breathe! I need air!'

Liv rushed to fetch the smelling salts. As soon as the woman had regained her composure, Liv asked, 'Shall I send for the healer?'

'No, no. We must not disturb such an important man with petty things. What would he say if my family were unable to care for me?'

Liv gazed down at the pale suffering face of her mother-in-law and resigned herself. Hurrying from the bedchamber, she sent word to her hostess that she very much regretted that she would have to decline the kind invitation. Shortly afterwards mother-in-law became remarkably healthy once more and resumed the ceaseless persecution of her daughter-in-law as a matter of priority.

* * * *

In their temporary overnight camp on the slopes of Romeleåsen, Sol awoke suddenly with a stifled cry of alarm. Jacob Skille sat up at the same moment. It was the middle of a shadowy pre-summer night and the moon lit up an eerie scene. The horses were whinnying and pulling at their traces in fear and Sol could see that two men were crouched over Jörgen, who was obviously fighting for his life. At the same moment Skille turned to ward off two more, who threw themselves upon him.

Sol reacted on instinct and with great speed. Grabbing a sharp-edged stone with both hands, she brought it down with full force on the head of one of Jörgen's attackers. Before the other had been able to do more than turn to look up at her, she smashed the same stone into his face.

Jörgen was fighting for breath, as they had clearly been trying to choke him to death. Blood from her two victims was pouring over him, but Sol did not stop to help him further at that moment. Instead she flung herself towards Skille, intent on going to his aid.

Her assistance, however, wasn't immediately needed, because he had drawn his knife and was in the process of slaughtering one of the men. He must have woken in time and been prepared for the attack. Now as she watched, he became embroiled in a violent rolling fight to the death with the fourth and last of the highwaymen. Suddenly, before she could decide whether or not to get involved, a fifth man rushed from the trees and grabbed her from behind. She struggled madly, but her assailant held her in an iron grip and swept her up onto the nearest horse. The next moment, with a wild shout, he spurred the animal forward into the trees.

Snatching a look over her shoulder, Sol saw that Skille had killed his second attacker and was running towards the horses. Sol's bitter curses at being carried off would have shocked the good dragoon, for no normal young lady would ever have expressed herself in such a manner – but in all likelihood he had not noticed them in the mêlée of noise and combat. Hearing the sound of his galloping horse thundering closer, Sol did all she could to make things difficult for her captor – twisting and turning in his grasp, throwing herself from side to side, biting and scratching.

Low branches were brushing against her face as they raced recklessly onward and then, above the pounding of the horse's hooves, she heard Skille's voice ring out in a sudden hoarse shout. 'Lean forward, out of the way!'

Instinctively she obeyed and the next instant a shot echoed across Romeleåsen. The robber holding her screamed and flung his arms wide. The horse swerved and Sol fell headlong to the ground, doing her best to roll away from the galloping hooves. Skille stopped and dismounted, calling to the other horse, which had bolted. When the animal returned, Sol realised that it was Skille's horse the highwayman had taken. That was probably why he gave chase so quickly, she thought bitterly. She had finished up sprawled in a prickly juniper bush but, to her surprise, the dragoon came to assist her first.

'I'm sorry for dawdling,' he said in an anxious voice. 'But it took time to load the musket on horseback. Are you feeling all right?'

Sol rose unsteadily to her feet. 'Yes I think so. That was a very good shot.'

She mumbled other words of admiration and thanks, and then promptly fell into his arms. Jacob Skille held her tightly, his concern for her wellbeing making his whole body tremble.

'Hmmm,' murmured Sol, savouring the moment, 'there is something to be said for being taken care of after all.'

'What d'you say?' he asked.

'Nothing – you are so big and strong, that's all. But you already know that.' She gently freed herself from his arms. 'We must go back and see how Jörgen is!'

'Of course.'

He let her go with a noticeable reluctance and they returned quickly to their camp. There they found Jörgen was still obviously shaken from his ordeal. He was unable to speak clearly at first and they saw he had cuts on one arm, but otherwise he did not, at first sight, seem badly hurt.

'Thank you very much,' he said to Sol at last in a hoarse whisper. 'You moved very quickly.'

'What! Did you do this?' asked Jacob Skille, pointing at the bloodied corpses of the two men lying at his feet with their skulls crushed.

Sol nodded vigorously.

'You poor child,' he said, 'to be forced to do something so brutal!'

Sol tried to demonstrate her distress by trembling, but she was not very successful.

'Well, you certainly had no regard for your own safety,' added Skille, 'and we are very much in your debt. What fools they were to tangle with the King's Dragoons! But of course they could not know that. How is it with you now, Jörgen?'

The young lad was still unsteady on his feet and he thought before answering.

'I – I think I'm losing blood …'

They examined him more closely. Until now, they had not realised that he had been stabbed several times.

'We need to take care of those wounds,' said Sol, unceremoniously tearing large strips from her petticoat. 'Lie down again and relax.' Turning to Skille she asked, 'Are there really no houses nearby?'

'No. But maybe if we ride further south towards the sea …'

'Yes, that's what we must do,' she said decisively, as she bound up Jörgen's injuries as best she could. 'He cannot ride very far in this condition.'

'But I …' the lad began to protest.

'She's right, my lad,' said Skille. 'You would never survive the journey to Glimmingehus as you are.'

Realising they spoke the truth, he nodded in agreement and they helped him gently up onto his horse. As they were leaving the clearing, Sol reigned in her mount.

'Wait one moment,' she said. 'May I go back – to say a prayer for their souls?'

Skille was about to say 'no', but thought better of it.

'Yes, you're a good girl. Shall we come with you? Are you afraid of spectres?'

'No, no,' she replied. 'That won't be necessary. I was simply worried that their souls might follow us.'

'I understand. We'll wait here,' said Skille.

She hurried back and jumped down from her horse. Making sure that her companions couldn't see what she was about to do, she walked over to the body of one of the robbers, an older man with greyish hair streaked with white. This was the one that Skille had stabbed to death, so his head and face had not been disfigured. Sol smiled while she cut off the dead man's hair, and rolled and knotted it before putting it away in her purse. Then she hurried back to where her companions were waiting.

'Now it's over,' she said devoutly. 'May their souls find peace!'

Skille mumbled something obscure as they urged their mounts on once more, heading south. They rode three abreast, with Jörgen in the middle, supported on each side. They had not ridden very far before they came upon a small farm settlement. They woke the people in the first cottage they reached and explained what had happened.

'Aha!' said the farmer, 'those five have been like a plague on us hereabouts for a long time. They died at the hands of King Christian's Dragoons, did they? I take my hat off to you lads! I hope they didn't threaten you, young Mistress?'

Sol and Skille exchanged knowing glances.

'It was this young mistress, in fact, who gave them a pasting,' said Skille, 'and that's putting it mildly, as well!'

Sol smiled graciously. 'With such a bold warrior as His

Majesty's Dragoon Jacob Skille nearby, any maiden would feel safe, would she not?' she asked demurely.

Skille turned away, muttering to himself in some embarrassment, and the farm folk promised to take good care of Jörgen. Sol noticed that the farmer had a sweet young daughter. That will be good for the lad, she thought, because the virtuous prim and proper Ottilie sounded so boring. He may well need to rest his head in the ample bosom of a down-to-earth peasant girl!

* * * *

Now there were just the two of them, as they set off again under the steely blue moonlit sky. But they had not travelled far before the moon disappeared and grey clouds darkened the heavens. Heavy rain came well before the first light of dawn, but by then they had reached the sea.

'Damnation,' hissed Skille, through clenched teeth. 'I cannot risk you catching a cold on top of everything else that's happened this night – you being so slender and frail. Looks like there's some fishers' huts yonder. We'll put up there a while.'

There were only two deserted fishermen's huts and both were old and dilapidated. They may once have belonged to a local farm, but if they did it certainly was not visible from where they stood. Skille entered one of the huts, followed by Sol – his shoulders were soaked and hunched against the night's chill air.

'Slender and frail', she thought to herself, smiling inwardly. Oh well, that was something she hadn't been called before. There was always something new to learn every day!

'These huts have not been used in many years,' said Skille, his voice echoing round the weathered grey timbers. 'We can put the horses in here and we'll take the other one.'

The rain was falling very heavily now, but it did not drown out the constant booming of the Baltic waves pounding the shore. The horses were evidently content to find a roof over their heads and Sol also felt relieved that they had found shelter from the downpour.

'You're frozen,' said Jacob Skille, as he made up a bed on the small sleeping platform in the other hut. 'If you sleep here, I'll go in with the horses.'

'No!' she replied quickly. 'There was nowhere for anyone to sleep in there. Anyway – I don't want to be left alone.'

'I understand.' His voice was full of compassion. 'You're frightened and cold. I shall stay here with you. And you can be sure I shall behave honourably towards you.'

He, in fact, treated Sol wonderfully. She was not accustomed to such consideration and unreasonably it angered her at first, making her morose and sullen. But as the warmth returned to her frozen limbs, she started to relax and appreciate his attentiveness. She allowed him to rub her dry with a rough soldier's towel and, in return, she poured him generous measures of wine from the jug the Count had supplied – but she drank only a modest amount herself.

In due course, he wrapped the saddle blankets around them both and they lay down side by side, his arm resting protectively across her body, so that she would feel safe and warm. A gentle trembling, which Skille thought had been brought on by the night's harrowing events, gradually subsided. However, Sol knew it was only a reaction to the cold and rain.

'Are you feeling better?' he whispered, pulling her closer.

'Wonderful, thank you,' she mumbled. Then without thinking she asked, 'Do you know where black nightshade grows?'

'Black nightshade? What on earth is that?'

No, thought Sol, she could have saved her breath; she should have known better than to ask. Both of them were finding the sound of the rain on the roof above their heads very soothing after the events of the night and before long they were fast asleep.

However, Jacob Skille, the common dragoon who until that day had always considered women to be a hindrance to his success as a soldier, now had an extraordinary dream. He lay floating, hovering, rising and falling slowly above a strange lake where the water was not water, but something else exquisitely soft and gentle. Peculiar creatures, ethereal and magical floated around him. One of them came close to him and he reached out and held on to her – he knew it was a female creature – and she came willingly to him, encircling his body. He could sense the tender warmth that radiated from her and he began to have those feelings that he recognised from his most secret dreams – but this time they were much deeper and much stronger.

Instinctively his hands reached out towards the lower parts of the wonderful creature's body, where he sensed all the temptations of the world were hidden. But his fumbling fingers tangled in her clothes until she helped him – and then she was free. Her skin felt soft against his hands as they sought out her secret places that were already warm and moist. Jacob pressed himself ardently against her, his body beginning to shake, and he felt an unbearable burning grow in his groin. His own clothes were now in the way, but small, nimble fingers quickly found what they wanted.

Sol had also been dreaming, but she woke quickly and

realised at once what was happening. She saw that her splendid warrior was unaware of his actions, as he moaned and writhed in his dream. Carefully easing herself into position, she took his hand and placed it where she knew he wanted it to be. She knew that she too had yearned for this and at once felt her body begin to tingle and ache with desire.

In the depths of his sleep, he nevertheless knew she was ready for him, and he tried to unfasten his trousers – but he was confused and panting heavily and did not succeed. Sol's hand moved at once to help and she gasped when she saw his size; very clearly now she could feel that her body was preparing itself to take him.

At that moment Jacob Skille woke up. Sol turned to him as if still dreaming herself and moaned softly in her throat, keeping her eyes closed. She heard his fearful gasp as he realised what he was about to do but, before he could recoil, she moved her whole body and thrust herself quickly down onto him.

As he entered her, she 'woke up' with a yelp of surprise, sounding like a young puppy. From above she looked straight down into his face, her eyes wide with surprise.

Skille was filled with alarm, but he was powerless to stop himself.

'Jacob!' she whispered in amazement. 'Oh, Jacob!'

She threw her arms around his neck and her body responded avidly to his urgent rhythm. Their passionate tempo increased irresistibly until, at last as one body, they reached the dizzying twin peaks of erotic ecstasy together.

* * * *

Some time afterwards, as they lay silently side by side on the sleeping platform, exhausted and sharing a deep feeling of peace, Skille turned wonderingly to look at her.

'I'm sorry,' he whispered. 'I dunno what happened to me. At first I was dreaming …'

'So was I, Jacob,' she murmured. 'So was I. But it was the power of nature itself that drove us. We have both lived with loneliness for too long.'

'Yes, you're right. I'm glad you feel that way.'

'Was it good for you?'

'I was in heaven, Sol. Purest heaven!'

'So now you might change your mind a little about what girls are like.'

He was shocked. 'But you are the only one for me now. You do understand that don't you? I cannot leave you on your own now!'

'Oh, dearest Jacob,' she replied with gentle sadness, 'you know I have to leave Denmark. What's more, I should lose my respect for you if you were to neglect your duty. Let us just enjoy our short time with each other to the full and remember one another fondly. I thought that I would never again be able to tolerate the touch of a man – but you have given me this wonderful irreplaceable moment. You've healed me, Jacob, and made me forget the awful things that happened to me when I was fourteen.'

'I have? Then truly I am gladdened.'

As dawn broke and before they prepared to journey onwards, they lay together once more. This time they played tender teasing games with each other, learning some of the mysteries of sensual love with complete candour and trust. So, when they parted at a crossroads near Glimmingehus – one going to the fortress that rose up majestically from the flat countryside around it and the other bound for Brösarps

Backar – they agreed they would meet again in a few days, and the prospect delighted them both.

Without looking back, Sol hurried northwards, following the Baltic coastline on her way to Brösarps Backar. Her horse seemed to enjoy pounding across the firm sand, as if it knew she was straining to reach the haze ahead of them and see what secrets it concealed. The sea had thrown up a soft mist that partly concealed its long torpid waves, but an occasional shaft of sunshine would break through to explode the dull grey-blue pastel colours into shards of shimmering brightness.

Having stopped earlier and asked directions from a fisherman as she travelled the coast road, Sol knew she must be nearing the end of her journey. She had broached the subject of Brösarps Backar with him very carefully and explained that she was a little frightened that she might meet witches there. His response, however, had left her feeling strongly disappointed.

'Witches? What witches?'

The man had simply laughed, then asked her what old yarns she had been listening to. He promised her that she could feel very safe in Brösarp today. Only the older folk, the very old, he assured her, still told tales of witches.

Her hopes had seemingly been dashed and she was instantly overcome by an empty feeling of despair. Nonetheless she wanted to know more – what did the old ones say? How disappointing, she thought. If only she had been here a hundred years ago, she would almost certainly have found herself belonging to a coven. She would have followed her spirit among the burial mounds, raised stones and cairns from the pagan times – but no longer it seemed, not in these times. A gentle peace apparently lay now upon Brösarps Backar.

Sol had squinted into the sun while talking to the man, in order to hide her unusual eyes. She had thanked him, said how relieved she was and made to leave. But she did not finally move on before she had cleverly got him to reveal where the oldest people in those parts were living.

She would not give up without trying. She had come this far to be close to her soul mates and she must carry on until she knew for certain that, in all the Nordic lands, no one other than she possessed such strange powers. Well, no one except Tengel, of course – but he didn't count.

Despite the sadness she felt at being a century too late, she took a certain melancholy delight in riding through this beautiful countryside. When she finally reached a point where she saw Brösarps Backar stretching out in front of her, she realised that this must be one of the most wonderful places in all the Nordic lands. From the picturesque village of Haväng on the coast, up to the soft rounded hills carpeted with cowslips and anemones, there were many small cottages with typical high-pitched roofs dotted all across the slopes of Linderödsåsen. Each new crest and bend revealed wonderful new vistas, and the sight of such beauty, so beyond compare, made Sol ache with joy.

As she rode on, intent on finding the cottages of the older people, she passed a *kummel*, an old burial mound, and could not help wondering – had *they* been here?

'Where are they all gone?' she complained aloud to the deserted world around her. Her desire to talk to other people who would understand had been made more intense than ever, because she now believed that she had been denied her last hope of finding them. But at last she arrived at a small cottage that resembled the description the fisherman had given her. She dismounted and tethered her horse beneath a crab-apple tree that stood in full blossom.

Sol was immediately made very welcome by a gaunt, gnarled old couple. They brought her some food, for which she was most thankful, because in her eagerness to reach Brösarps Backar she had not stopped to eat. She knew she would not be able to spin the yarn about being scared of witches with these people, because she needed to ask them more searching questions. A new strategy was needed, so she told them that her grandmother had told her stories of witches and how they met on the Thursday nights of the full moon throughout the summer. And now that she was here, she wanted to see if the stories were true.

As she listened, the old woman turned her full attention to the cooking pots on the hearth, rattling them for all she was worth. Her husband, however, stared curiously at Sol.

'Oh yes,' said the old man at last, his voice dropping to a whisper, 'they're true stories, you can be sure of that! I saw 'em myself once, as a lad, afore they were banished.'

Sol's heart skipped a beat. 'Banished? Then they didn't all die?'

'No, no. The Lord of the Manor of Glimmingehus brought his knights and all to seize them, but they were warned and had gone away. Aye and it were my own mother that warned 'em.'

Sol suddenly felt great sympathy for his mother. The old man's eyes had a rheumy faraway gaze and they became moist with tears of nostalgia as he continued his reminiscences.

'I remember seeing 'em as if it were just yesterday. I'd woke in the dead of night to a strange singin'. And, as it were a summer night, I crept out to see what it was – and then I saw 'em.'

Sol knew how old people could often recall events from their childhood clearly and in great detail, while things that had happened in more recent years were shrouded in mist. She saw how the old man was inspired by her interest and how he enjoyed the feeling of importance it gave him to recount this unexplained story after all this time. To make things clearer, he led Sol outside and the old woman followed behind them.

'Over there. Over by the *kummel* is where I saw 'em – and they were many. They came from far and wide to meet here. They couldn't meet in the wintertime – but you'd know that of course, young Mistress.'

They understood each other in spite of the differences in their languages. Sol spoke Danish quite well, having known Charlotte Meiden for so many years and also from the recent months she had spent in Copenhagen. These old peasant folk were speaking the Skåne dialect, a mixture of Danish, Swedish and Old Norse that was difficult for a Norwegian to master. When the old couple had difficulty understanding her Norwegian, Sol spoke as much Danish as she could, enunciating her words slowly and as clearly as possible.

'There was something lying on the *kummel* stones,' the old man continued, 'and they'd gathered round it. I tell ye, never in my life has I trembled so much as when I saw and heard 'em all.'

Sol thought back to the idiotic séance in the cellar in Copenhagen, where she had not been made to tremble in the slightest. Although there were some similarities with the description she had just heard, what had happened here sounded far more real. Should she begin to hope?

'You say that they all fled. Where did they go?'

There was a pause and the couple exchanged wary glances, hesitating to speak further.

'All this was a hundred years past, wasn't it?' said Sol quickly. 'Surely they are all long dead now? I just want to follow in their footsteps. I shall not cause anyone harm. The authorities are no friends of mine either.'

'What d'you mean a hundred years ago?' the old man joked. 'I aren't quite that old yet!'

'No of course not! I beg your pardon,' smiled Sol, but her lips were trembling with anticipation. 'How many years ago could it have been since you saw them, old Sir?'

He half closed his eyes to concentrate and started mentally to count.

'Oh well, it's gotta be round sixty or more years since. I am seventy and a few now and I'd be all of ten or twelve back then. Yes! Sixty-odd years. That'd be about right.'

Sixty years ago? Her hopes had just risen – risen by forty years!

'But then I don't suppose you'd know where they fled to?' Sol asked again.

'I heard one of them say a place to my mother,' he said hesitantly. 'But I don't know …'

'Asch, it don't make no matter this long after,' interrupted the old woman. 'Aren't going to be none of 'em living now! The Lord of the Manor and his soldiers did for them long since! You know it's so!'

The old man thought long and hard. 'That's as maybe, but I swore to my mother never to speak of it.'

Sol rummaged in her purse. She still had the silver coins she had been given by the lady she accompanied on the boat from Norway. She would never have the chance to put them to better use, she thought. Not only for her but for the old couple as well.

'Here, take these,' she said. 'One for each of you.'

Their eyes widened and, hands shaking, they took the

money. Never had they seen so much, they told her, and went straight into a small back room to hide away their new-found wealth. From outside by listening intently Sol was able to overhear their conversation.

'She's a kindly lady – an' right good lookin' too!' said the old man.

The woman muttered, but not quietly enough. 'Can't you see? She be one of them. I saw it straightaways. We must throw some iron after her when she rides off.'

'No!' he gasped. 'You can't mean that! One of 'em – oh dear God!'

Fear was showing in his eyes when they came out of the room so, making up her mind quickly, Sol decided to tell them the whole truth.

'Yes, I am one of them.' She beamed a smile at them. 'But you have nothing to fear from me – quite the contrary. I have medicines for your sore leg, dear Mother, and for your aches and pains, old Father, if you will accept them.'

They exchanged worried glances for long moments before they consented. Then Sol presented them with their potions and, in exchange, they were happy to provide her with the information she wanted. She was told she would have to ride inland, far into the dense woods to a place where deep ravines hid a river. They described the route in detail and, with shouts of gratitude ringing in her ears, she rode away from Brösarps Backar. Nonetheless, she still heard the dull thud of an iron axe hitting the ground as soon as she was out of sight. The old man threw it after her to ward off spirits. She allowed herself a wry smile at the old superstition – but did not look back!

I'll be seeing half of Skåne if things continue like this, she mused as she galloped onward. Settling into her stride, she made herself comfortable in the saddle and hoped the weather would remain fine – but she was prepared for any hardship, she told herself, as long as she found what she was searching for.

It was not difficult to follow the directions she had been given, but the trail was winding and long. She passed the huge awe-inspiring fortress at Vittskövle, crossed a great stretch of wide flat countryside beyond it, then rode on through woods and spinneys to a small settlement some way inland called Tollarp. From there she followed the river westwards and deep into thick green sun-dappled forests.

Sixty years ago, she pondered, as she rode. Am I mad to believe that there could still be anyone living from that time? In her heart she truly did not think so, but there was a part of her stubborn spirit that would force her to go on until she had exhausted every possibility.

Ansgar's Klyfta was the name of the ravine the witches had chosen as their gathering place for the future, according to the old couple. The covens had apparently vowed to meet under every full moon throughout all the summers and she wondered how many meetings there might have been over the years. As she reflected on these things, she realised it was taking a very long time to locate the right place.

She did not dare pursue enquiries in the small peasant villages and settlements she passed through, but luckily she had plenty of time to spare. While she made her way through those leafy woods, riding and sometimes on foot, she thought how different they were from the dark Norwegian pine forests she was used to. In the dappled sunlight she was hoping to catch sight of something else – black nightshade – the herb she still needed in order to make her ride to Blåkulla. She had already searched along the coast every time she had rested and was now looking under the tree roots and in the dark shadows of the forest, but she did not really know what it looked like. Hanna had never described the plant in detail, saying only that it was very hard to find in Tröndelag – which was why Sol had hoped to find it more easily in southern Skåne.

In the depths of the forest she stopped and stared straight ahead, her eyes focused on nothing in particular. It had been fourteen years since she had last seen Hanna, and although the image of the terrible old witch had faded to a dim memory, there remained a strong bond between them – the bond that exists between two people who understand one another in every way.

'Hanna,' she whispered, 'why did you leave me all on my own? Why did Heming the Bailiff-killer take your life – and with it the love and support we gave each other.'

She paused and breathed deeply for long moments, struggling to build up her courage. 'I wish you could help me, Hanna,' she murmured. 'I feel so alone here in this world now. So terribly alone.'

Chapter 6

While Sol was roaming beneath the green spring foliage of the beech woods in the region of Ansgar's Klyfta, Liv stood at the window of her fashionable merchant's house in Oslo looking out at the filthy streets of the city. The rain beat down endlessly and an ache in the pit of her stomach would not leave her; neither would the despondency that filled her heart.

Her fingers tapped restlessly and nervously on the windowsill. If only she had something to occupy her, but whenever she decided on something, the feelings of guilt and anxiety grew inside her. Would it be allowed? Should a dutiful wife be doing this or that?

However would she learn these new rules, brought up as she had been to help whenever and wherever needed in a loving and selfless home, where everyone had respect for the happiness of others and they all carried out the tasks to which they were best suited. But here she was scolded if she tried to help in the wrong way, and again if she did not help in the right way! What was the right way? What was the wrong way? Those things seemed to change from day to day.

And what was happening at Linden Allée right now? It

was probably raining there as well. It used to drop from the leaves of the linden trees and form small rivulets along the approach to the house. It made a pond in the yard just at the bottom of the steps. Papa had said he was going to do something about it for years, but as soon as the rain stopped, it was forgotten again. Young Are will probably be the one to put a drain in front of the steps, she thought.

The other two were in Denmark and would soon be home again, but *she* would not be going home – she had left Linden Allée and Gråstensholm forever, it seemed. Whenever she suggested that they should go back for a visit to her parents, Laurents would tell her that he did not have time. 'Anyway, you should not go there too often,' he would say. 'They are strange people! Charlotte Meiden is a disgrace for someone of her class. She is so radical – and an unwed mother to boot!'

Liv was aware that Laurents believed that Charlotte, in common with all unwed mothers, should have suffered punishment in the pillory. There the townsfolk, including the father of the child, would have thrown stones and spat at her. Charlotte had been spared this fate and Laurents was sorely displeased, because such leniency, he insisted, could only lead to general decline.

Liv could never imagine kind good-hearted Charlotte bound in the stocks. Laurents knew nothing about how Dag had once been left abandoned to die. Liv neither wanted – nor dared – to tell her husband about that.

'Yes, your father earns good money, so I can acknowledge him,' Laurents would say, always with contempt in his voice whenever he spoke of her family. 'But in everything else he is strange, you must agree. And, God help me, no one could call him handsome!'

Liv had always regarded her father as the most beautiful

person on earth. There was nobody anywhere in the world who had such loving eyes!

'Your brother, Are, is acceptable. At least he speaks in a way one can comprehend, despite being a farmer. But your mother is just too extreme by far – her head uncovered, as though she were living in sin with your father! It is from her that you have inherited your laziness in the home, is it not? As well as all these foolish notions about painting!'

Liv had never dared reveal to Laurents that Silje went by the artistic name of Master Arngrim – a person whose work he admired so much. He wanted Master Arngrim to weave him a tapestry, but had always been refused because the artist was too busy. Furthermore Liv could not understand why he thought she was lazy in the home. On the farm they had all said that she was the perfect housekeeper, unlike her mother. Things were not the same here, where she was expected to manage the household, take command of the servants and always be available when Laurents or his mother needed help.

Liv did not like giving orders to the servants. At home she had always spoken to them in a friendly manner, lending a hand in the kitchen whenever it was needed. It was all so different and difficult here.

She had seen how Laurents always became very unsure of himself in Sol's company. He was beguiled by her charm, yet fearful of her strong individuality and self-confidence. He was also aware of her complete lack of admiration for him and of interest in what he did. Consequently he had said many unpleasant things about Sol when she was out of earshot.

Her husband had never met Dag. What faults would Laurents find in him, she wondered? Did everybody regard her family in this way? She would be very downhearted if that were the case, but she refused to believe it because they had always had so many friends.

Mother-in-law was taking her afternoon nap. This was the best part of the day – Liv's own half-hour. But the tight knot of anxiety inside her meant she could no longer relax as she used to.

Outside, the rain poured down unceasingly onto the windowsill. A maid walked through the room and Liv stood back from the window and went over to rearrange the ornaments on the dresser. It was not at all necessary; she was simply making believe she had something to do.

* * * *

Far away, deep in Skåne at that moment, Sol stood still holding her horse. Tollarp? Where on earth was it? Surely she should arrive there soon? She had begun to get the horrible feeling that she was lost. Damnation! She did not have time for this.

She remounted and continued riding, on the off-chance that she would come across a cottage or village, or some sign of life, where she could ask directions. But there was nothing – and time was passing. The steep hilly terrain told her that she must be somewhere in the Linderödsåsen area, but that did her no good at all, as she knew nothing about Linderödsåsen. She needed to find Tollarp, or the river that flowed through it.

She had seen no sign of either. Did nobody live in this part of Skåne, she wondered? What if she had reached the territory of the Göinge Snaphauncers? Then she would not be far from the border with Sweden. Was she already in Sweden? No, surely not.

Then, just as she was cursing the emptiness of the place, she heard voices off in the distance. She urged her horse forward and the wood soon gave way to open fields dotted with oak trees. Some way off, by a fence, stood a group of foot soldiers and their coarse laughter carried easily to her on the still spring air. Sol was not frightened of them – besides they had no horses on which to pursue her. Yet still she waited on the edge of the wood, frowning.

What in all the world were they doing? Suddenly a wave of disgust swept over her and she pulled the horse back into the trees. She could see that they had tied a woman to the fence, bent forwards with her skirts thrown up over her head. Now each of them in turn was pleasuring himself on her from behind.

Sol swore through clenched teeth. There were a lot of them – perhaps twelve or fifteen. She saw only the pathetic naked backside of the woman and evidence that she had probably been a virgin when they began their defilement. Sol heard the girl's pained and hopeless sobbing and these same cries seemed to awaken new excitement in her tormentors.

Seeing that another ruffian was about to set upon her, Sol quickly took her two gold chains from her purse and placed them round her neck. Then she retrieved an impressive hat from her pack and straightened it into shape before putting it on her head with her hair twisted into a knot under it. Then she threw one leg over the pommel and sat side-saddle, as a lady would. In just a few moments, she had transformed herself from a carefree wild young girl to a worthy noblewoman. Straightening her back exaggeratedly, she prompted her horse forward.

'Stop!' she yelled at the top of her voice to the man who

had stepped forward, his manhood proud, to further defile the wretched woman on the fence.

On hearing her voice, the soldiers turned in total surprise to face her, their mouths agape at the unexpected interruption.

'Set the girl free, you worthless cowards!' shouted Sol vehemently, scarcely realising how important and impressive she had become.

The soldiers remained rooted to the spot, their faces still frozen in astonishment. After a long moment of silence, one of them plucked up the courage to speak.

'Ha! Our commanding officer, are ye? Can't even talk like us. Come down off that horse and you can have some of the same!'

'I shall do nothing of the sort,' she retorted scornfully. 'You are far too ugly and insignificant.'

Sol was wary of dismounting. She felt safer in the saddle, looking down from above them.

'If you do not release her at once it will go badly for you all,' she said slowly, her yellow-green eyes half closed.

Several of the men hesitated. She seemed to be a lady of class and influence, likely to report them – but the man about to take his turn with the unfortunate creature on the fence just grinned. 'Reckon you can stop me then?'

'Yes!'

That simple statement made him pause for a second; then he turned and moved determinedly towards the girl, his back to Sol.

'How'd that be?' he asked over his shoulder.

'Because you can't commit your dreadful deed now,' said Sol in a fierce undertone. 'You can't manage it because your manhood is deserting you in front of your ruffian friends!'

A chorus of coarse laughter began, led by the man with

his back to her as he pressed himself against the girl's naked flesh. Then he stopped abruptly and cursed.

'Satan's hellfire!'

The watching men continued to stare open-mouthed in the ensuing silence. Then the voice of the girl's assailant rose to a high-pitched screech of fear and dismay. 'Satan! Satan!'

Somebody laughed uneasily; then all the men fell silent and stood still, anxiety plain on all their faces. Sol decided to use this new silence to her advantage.

'That is what will happen to any of you who try to touch her now,' she told them.

'You damned witch!' screamed the afflicted man, almost in tears, taking a step towards Sol's horse. He had not understood that all Sol had done was to use psychology against him – together with a little bit of suggestion, of course.

'Don't you touch me, you pox-ridden worm,' she said in a hard clear voice. 'Any one of you who lays a hand on me or that girl will lose the power of their manhood for the rest of their life.'

Some of the others had had begun to move towards her, but now at these words they faltered. Seeing her sitting tall in the saddle, her eyes glittering and glowing with an unnatural yellow sheen, they felt their passions fade. Collectively they thought it would be sensible to avoid such a future.

'Now get out of here!' Sol ordered them impatiently. Her dispassionate voice conveyed that she had no more time to waste on such a gang of perverts. 'Go, and be grateful that I do not make you suffer worse!'

'The bailiff shall hear of this,' yelled one of them.

Sol's cat-like eyes turned full on him. 'I would be careful

119

if I were you,' she said ominously. 'Because if he does, I shall geld you instantly without even coming near you.'

'You don't scare me,' he replied belligerently, but there was an unmistakable tremor in his voice. He obviously did not want to lose face in front of his comrades.

'Crawl on the ground like a dog – now!' ordered Sol in an icy voice.

To the other soldiers' complete astonishment, the man sank to his knees, whining like a dog fearful of being beaten. Then he crawled away from her, whimpering and struggling along on his hands and knees.

All this was too much for the other men of this brave band of infantry. There was a moment's hesitation before one of them made the 'Devil's horns' gesture for protection with his index and little finger. Then someone cried, 'Come on lads!' and, like frightened rabbits, they scurried away over boulders and through bushes, chased by the now barking 'dog' soldier.

Focussing her powers at a distance, Sol released him from the trance. Instantly he fell headlong in a somersault before getting to his feet and stumbling after the others, as though the Devil himself was snapping at his heels. She waited until they were but dots in the distance, then dismounted and went over to the fence, where the young woman was still sobbing pathetically.

'Oh, dear God,' Sol muttered, as she pulled the skirts down to cover her bleeding body. 'Such animals!'

Then she bent down and loosened the straps that bound her. A mass of blond hair hid the face, but Sol saw by the skin and the outline of the body that this was no mature woman. Eventually she helped the poor lass to stand up straight.

'What is our world coming to?' gasped Sol. 'How old are you?'

Scarcely able to answer through her sobs, the girl replied, 'Thirteen years.'

'Oh, no! You poor child!'

Sol was almost moved to tears, completely forgetting that she had been only one year older when she seduced young Klaus – but those circumstances had been entirely different. She doubted she had ever seen such a vulnerable creature as this child. The tear-stained face should have been round and rosy cheeked – a typical peasant girl's face – but poverty and hunger had also left their mark. The girl's clothes were no better than rags and she was so riddled with lice that Sol could see them crawling in the clothes. They were probably in her beautiful hair as well.

'Jesus and Maria,' said Sol softly, wiping clean the inside of the girl's thighs with some grass. 'You need a good wash and scrub – but first we must leave this place. I need your help. I have lost my way and need to know how I get can to Tollarp – or better still to the land west of Tollarp. Can you help?'

The girl struggled to stop her hysterical sobbing. 'Y–you a–are already there, M–miss.'

'I am? But there should be a river that I am to follow west from Tollarp. Up to the higher lands beyond.'

'The r–river flows behind that little r–ridge o–over there.'

'Well, that's good to know. Now, let's get you on the horse. Up you go.'

'What me?'

'Yes. Hurry up.'

The girl tried to mount up, but then gave a loud shout of pain and stopped.

'I can't, Miss! It hurts too much.'

Sol insisted, but had to help her very carefully up onto the horse. Because of the pain, they found it easier to sit her sideways in the saddle. The child's courage and ability to think properly had obviously been drained by the shock of what had happened to her and she clung on to the animal in a stunned silence.

Because of this Sol preferred to walk alongside and lead the horse – and Mama Silje would never have forgiven her if she had caught lice. She had always been very strict about things like that and as children they had suffered all kinds of horrible cures designed to rid them of a variety of bugs that preyed on every one of them.

Luckily the soldiers had run off in the opposite direction from the river. The girl said they had gone towards Tollarp and Sol realised she did not need to go there now that she was already west of that little village.

'What's your name?' asked Sol as she walked along holding the horse's bridle.

'Meta.'

'Do you live nearby?'

'Yes. Well, no. Well, not any more.'

'What does that mean?' asked Sol.

The girl tried to dry her tears, rubbing her eyes with her hands. Her face became very smudged. 'I live nowhere now,' she sobbed. 'I walk the byways and beg for alms.'

'Do you not have parents then? Are you not in service on a farm?'

'No. Mother was called a harlot – you see, I was born out of wedlock. She died last spring. Since then I've just wandered, and never been back home again.'

'But you were still a virgin?'

'Oh, yes. Ma was particular I shouldn't go the same road she did.'

'And this happened to you!'

'They knew my Ma,' said the girl, ashamed. 'They were going to teach me to be like her.'

Sol clenched her teeth. 'I should have turned them into living cobblestones – then they would feel people walking all over them forever, slowly wearing them down with their shoes!'

Meta said nothing. Perhaps I've frightened her, thought Sol, and looked up at the child. 'Everything will be all right, you'll see,' she said with a kindly smile. 'So where did you and your mother live?'

'By the river. We're on the way there.'

'Wonderful.'

They travelled quite a long way before reaching the river. Although Meta's sobbing and sniffing finally stopped, she remained a wretched and deeply disturbed child, clinging tightly to the horse to avoid being sent sprawling to the ground. At last Meta pointed to a wattle and daub hut that Sol could barely see – it looked more like a pile of earth than a dwelling. When they reached it, Sol told Meta to get down, but the girl hesitated.

'I don't think ... We'd best not go in.'

'Why is that?'

'I ... don't want to.'

Foolishness, thought Sol, you need somewhere to live. Yet this was not a pleasant place. It was dark and foreboding beneath the overhang of the riverbank. Sol found an opening in the wall that might once have been an entrance, stooped down and crept gingerly into the darkness.

Inside she jerked to a sudden halt as she came face to face with a rotting corpse that lay staring up empty-eyed at her from a mattress on the floor. Deeply saddened, Sol thought how terrible that the girl was not even able to give her mother a decent burial. She evidently had no one to talk to and there was nobody she could ask for help. Well, they would take what they could and go, because the girl certainly could not stay here.

Sol found only a cooking pot – a shoddy iron thing with no handle – and then went outside again. Seeking a weak spot in the hut wall, she tugged at it sharply with both hands and brought the whole pile of sticks and earth crashing down upon the body inside.

'There! That will be her grave. May her memory be at peace,' muttered Sol.

From twisted straw she quickly fashioned a protective talisman to place on top of the pile. That would stop the spirit of the dead woman from pursuing them. Sol was not one for saying prayers; as far as she was concerned they were just superstition. For the girl's sake, however, she also quickly bound two sticks together with a strip of bark to form a burial cross and wedged it into the ground.

For the next hour they walked along the riverbank, with Meta still sobbing fitfully to herself. Eventually they came upon a quiet backwater and there Sol gathered some wood and built a fire. It was a beautiful place, a hollow where the river widened to a large pool that was surrounded by rocky outcrops and small hillocks. Sol filled the pot with water and placed it on the fire. While they waited for it to boil, she took some food from her pack and gave it to the girl – but she ate it with such ferocity that Sol had to force her to slow down.

'You'll make yourself ill, eating like that,' she warned. 'Now, if you've had enough, we can get started.'

Meta looked surprised. 'With what?'

'Getting you clean, of course. Out of those clothes and into the water!'

'Into the water!' the frightened girl exclaimed. 'No! It's a danger, for sure!'

'You're afraid of bathing? Well you do seem to have had

a strong dislike of washing and that's a fact. But bathing will do you no harm, quite the opposite in fact.'

'No, I daren't.'

Sol was left with no alternative but to pull off her own clothes and drag Meta into the water. But first she washed the girl's hair over the pot of water, which was by now quite hot, using some lye from her purse. Convinced she was going to die from this treatment, Meta screamed. Things were not made any better when Sol took a few leafy birch twigs and used them to scrub Meta's body from top to toe until the skin was almost red raw.

'Look,' yelled Sol, trying to make herself heard above the screams. 'Look in the pot – see all those dead lice and nits? And God only knows what else is floating in there? They have been living on you! Now, into the river with you and we'll rinse you clean!'

The screams that accompanied the battle to get Meta into the water must have been heard for miles around. But Sol's mind was made up and she was the stronger of the two. She had some sympathy for the girl, nonetheless, having suffered a cruel assault herself only a short time ago – but it could not be avoided.

When at last Meta began to discover how wonderful and cool the water felt against her well scrubbed body, she gave a few final gasps and then relaxed. From time to time a fleeting trembling smile lit up her face.

'Bäckahästen won't get me, will he?' she asked tentatively. 'Ma said never to go near to a river, as Bäckahästen lives there.'

Sol realised that Bäckahästen was the local name for a water sprite or satyr.

'Why are you scared of him?' she asked. 'To me he is a friend.'

Meta gave Sol a strange look, trying to understand what sort of person she was. Then she let her head fall back into the water, so that Sol could rinse off her hair properly. She laughed gleefully at how different everything sounded when her ears were under water.

'I can hear the stream bubbling over by the rocks,' she said, smiling. 'It sounds like a singing waterfall!'

At last Sol decided Meta was clean enough. 'You are so beautiful,' said Meta as they both stepped out of the water hand in hand.

'Yes,' replied Sol, 'and that is a great advantage for a girl, believe me! You'll not do badly either as long as you get some flesh on your bones and let those lice sores heal.'

'But I'll never be as lovely as you,' replied Meta admiringly.

No that would be asking too much, thought Sol, a shade more directly than modesty allowed.

Now the unfortunate girl was thoroughly clean, Sol dressed her in one of the two extra dresses she had brought with her – not her best one – and plaited her heavy, straw-coloured hair into long braids. Sol had also given her a potion to ensure there be no consequences following the ordeal she had suffered at the hands of the soldiers. Lastly she produced her small mirror to allow Meta to admire herself.

'There now,' she said. 'Cleanliness is not such a bad thing, is it?'

The girl's face lit up at the sight of her reflected image.

'I look so grand,' she gasped, blushing. 'And it feels so lovely being clean! Thank you, Mistress. I never thought such a fine lady as you could be so kind.'

Sol's laughter echoed around the rocky pool. 'Me – kind? Now I've heard everything! Remember this Meta – I only do things for my own sake. Nothing else.'

And she really believed she did.

'Now I want you to wait here until I return,' said Sol. 'I have some affairs to attend to and I cannot take you with me. I will be two or maybe three days, but if you build a shelter you will be all right here. Then we must see if we can find a place for you. Are there any manors or large farm estates nearby?'

'Yes, a few: the Gyllenstierna's at Fulltofta; Bosjökloster monastery on the island in the lake; oh, and Vittskövle – Ma was known at all of them.'

Too well known, probably, thought Sol to herself. 'I rode past Vittskövle – it's too far away. We'll see if Fulltofta or Bosjökloster can take you on as a maid. Would you like that?'

'Oh, yes and now that I look so grand, perhaps I won't be so afraid to ask,' she replied. 'But you must have your dress back.'

'What, that old rag!' Sol immediately regretted the arrogant tone of her reply. Compared to the girl's rags this new dress was the height of fashion. 'I'm sorry; I didn't mean it like that, Meta. It was said in jest – but you may keep the dress.'

The girl was almost about to burst into tears again, but this time from happiness. Sol felt quite noble! It wasn't a bad sensation all things considered!

Then Meta, her face falling, said quietly, 'Please don't leave me now, Mistress.'

'But I have to.'

'Promise to come back!'

'Are you frightened?'

'A little – of boars and ghosts and suchlike!'

'There are none here, I promise you. And I shall return. Here take this knife; I have another. You will feel safer. And give no more thought to what happened.'

'It's not easy to do, Mistress.'

'No, you are right, it is not.' Then on a whim she asked the girl, 'Do you know where Ansgar's Klyfta is?'

'Yes, more or less. But it's very dangerous there. They say it goes straight down into the depths and there lives the one whose name we dare not speak.'

How nice that would be, thought Sol, with a sigh. If only there were such a place, then she would have thrown herself into its darkness without a second thought. As she reflected on what the girl had said, she found the idea was incredibly appealing.

With a crooked smile she declared, 'Foolish drivel! Have I given you to believe that I am afraid?'

'No.'

Sol listened carefully, as Meta described how to get to Ansgar's Klyfta, although somewhat vaguely. From what she said it did not seem very far away. Then Sol asked, 'Do you know if there is any black nightshade growing around here by the river?'

'Black nightshade?' queried Meta with a frown. 'What is that?'

Sol sighed resignedly. A few moments later she said farewell and set off again on what was proving to be a long and erratic journey.

* * * *

In Oslo the rain had finally stopped and Liv stood once again at her window. She did this because there was nothing better with which to occupy her time – but neither did she dare to try and find something fulfilling to do. The house was quiet, because with a rare burst of energy her mother-in-law had gone out to visit neighbours and listen to gossip.

Liv heard someone open the street door; then she recognised the characteristic slam that announced the return of Laurents. She pulled back her shoulders, but felt the ache in her midriff worsening. Composing herself she went and greeted her husband with a smile.

'Good day, Berenius. You are home early today.'

He would not allow her to say Laurents – first names, he felt, were so vulgar. Liv did not agree, but as always kept her thoughts to herself. His expression brightened as soon as he saw her.

'There you are, dear heart!' he said embracing her. 'How well that dress suits you. Indeed, I thought it would when I chose the blue-grey silk. And how has my little angel been today, then?'

'Quite well,' she replied with a fixed smile. 'Indeed very well, thank you – except it can be dreary at times when you are not here.'

He turned away impatiently. 'I've heard all that before. I do everything for you, my very own hands work to support you and you need have no worries, no reason to be downcast. You do not have to lift a finger here, yet still you complain.'

'Forgive me,' she whispered. 'I shall not do so again. Can you not tell me something of what you do at your office, Berenius?'

'What!' He laughed, then said, 'do you think I should bore you with things that you have no likelihood of ever understanding? Don't be silly, Liv.'

'I only meant – well, a wife should share her man's life and tribulations. I should be pleased to do that.'

'I think not! We share our life here at home. That which is outside is my affair.'

'I am quite clever at counting,' she continued eagerly, 'and I am told that I write with a neat hand. Could I not be of help to you in your office? Then we should be together and I might come out ... Oh, no! I'm sorry! Forgive me!'

His face had taken on a thunderous look and with one swift movement he reached out and tore a riding crop from its place on the wall. Liv, who had been made to suffer it once before, whined like a little puppy and ran from him, fleeing from room to room, crying helplessly, with her husband at her heels.

'Stop!' he roared. 'Stop you ungrateful girl!'

Liv was forced into a corner in the furthest room. The crop whistled as he swung it through the air – it was not a heavy stroke, but it stung horribly.

'How dare you imply that you could be of any help to me in my business!' he hissed at her, foam dribbling from the corners of his mouth. 'Count? You, a mere wife! How dare you presume so much?'

Whimpering, Liv sank limply to the floor. Seeing her helplessness caused her husband's wrath to evaporate in an instant. He immediately dropped the riding crop and took her hand.

'Now look here. Oh! What have I done to my little turtledove.' He fussed her elaborately, showing his remorse. 'Dear me, her tiny hand is bleeding!'

He kissed her hand thoroughly to remove all traces of the blood, then squeezed it as he drew her to him.

'There, there. No more tears, my little pigeon. Your big strong husband is here to take care of everything, so you will know that I love you more than anything else in this world. I want only what is best for you. It pains me to discipline you, but we must rid you of these foolish notions, must we not?'

Liv had brought herself under control and stood up straight once again. She nodded her head in silent agreement, but her eyes held the glare of a damaged and wounded animal.

'There then,' he declared self-righteously, 'all is well again isn't it? And tonight my dearest, we shall have an amorous interlude together, shall we not? Little turtledove wouldn't want to deny her very own husband, would she?'

It took all her willpower to suppress a shiver. She knew all about these amorous interludes. They were only for his pleasure. All she had to do was remain completely passive and submit tamely to his selfish attentions with grateful admiration.

Chapter 7

Although the sun had gone down, there was still some daylight left when Sol at last stumbled upon the edge of a deep ravine. It lay deep in an area of wooded wilderness, far from any sign of human habitation. By the time she reached the top of this great cleft in the forest, she was tired, hungry and depressed, after searching and wandering back and forth all through the afternoon and evening. What exactly was she searching for, she asked herself a hundred times – a forgotten place without significance that had been deserted a great many years ago?

She shivered. Never had her spirit felt so alone as it did now. Was all this just because of an old tale of witches who used to meet in times past? Now she was the last of them. What exactly was the strange compulsion that had brought her here?

Heaving a deep, deep sigh, she looked down over the jagged cliff-top, pondering the darkness below her. Burnt out remains of logs in a disused fire pit were clearly visible far below. This must be Ansgar's Klyfta, she felt sure. But it would not have been named after Saint Ansgar, the Apostle of the North, who had brought Christianity to the

Nordic lands – of that she was certain. This was no bottomless chasm either. From where she stood, she could see the whole floor of the ravine and it was pleasantly flat and green with grass. Such were the stories that people managed to make up.

Was the fire pit still in use? Could that mean that there would still be some kind of meetings, rituals? No, she told herself, she should not start to assume anything; after all a woodcutter or a charcoal burner probably used it.

But in her loneliness deep in the woods of that foreign land, Sol made up her mind at that moment to return to this place the following night when the moon was full. Perhaps she would be able to communicate significantly in some way or sense the presence of the dead, the persecuted souls who had once congregated here nearly a century ago. She wanted to try and find just the smallest link of fellowship with their spirits, as a comfort to herself in this world of ordinary people where she did not belong. Still feeling downhearted, she turned away to find a place where she and her horse could rest and shelter for the night.

* * * *

Twenty-four hours later the full moon shone over a vast geographical area, flooding light simultaneously upon the sea, the burial mound at Brösarps Backar and Ansgar's Klyfta, deep in the mysterious woodland far inland. Among the trees close to the Ansgar ravine, a strengthening breeze caught Sol's hair. She was dressed all in black and the scalp of the dead highwayman was now tied securely to the top of a long stick that she carried. The hair of the dead man blew wildly in the wind, flapping against the stick and making an eerie humming sound as it did so.

It was Thursday night and she was making her way carefully towards the spot where she had stood the previous night. When she was still some distance away, the smell of smoke from a bonfire suddenly prickled her nostrils. As she drew nearer, she noticed a thick plume of smoke billowing up from the ravine and spreading lazily into the treetops. Seeing this, her heart began to race and knock against her ribs. Woodcutters, she thought – but why would they be about so late at night? Charcoal burners? She had seen no charcoal piles when she was last there.

Sol stopped at the edge of the ravine. She could now see a fire that was burning below. And three figures were seated around it! Yes, three people in all – but two of them were women. What would women be doing out at this hour of the night?

She could see that they were talking and poking the fire with sticks. As she watched them, her body began to tremble. Sol closed her eyes and took a deep breath. They were witches! There could be no other explanation. Opening her eyes again she stood where she was, not moving for a long while, just watching.

They will surely see me soon, she thought. What a dramatic figure I must seem with my hair and my skirts flailing in the wind and my seer-staff held aloft – and I am silhouetted by the moon as well!

Sol had always had a feeling for melodrama – but she had barely finished that thought when one of the women looked up. After a moment she pointed excitedly at her. She remained seated, but her two companions stood up warily and watched with anxious expressions, as Sol started to make her way down the steep slope.

Full of uncertainty she walked towards them, but stopped a short distance from the fire to give them an opportunity to weigh her up. For a long moment nobody uttered a word. In the lengthening silence Sol reflected on how much nicer it was to come down to the warmth of the fire and into the lee of the ravine. Then the woman who had remained seated spoke out in rasping tones.

'Be welcome, daughter of the Ice People!'

Taken by surprise Sol asked, 'You know me? You know the Ice People?'

With a wave of her hand, the woman indicated that Sol should sit down and the others returned to their places.

'No, you I do not know,' said the old woman with a twisted grin. 'But the name of the Ice People means much to those in our fellowship. Nobody can mistake the eyes. Yet I do know that they lived in Tröndelag until they were all killed about fifteen years ago. How can it be that you are here now?'

'Ah! It is a long story,' said Sol. 'I had heard about the witches of Brösarps Backar from Hanna, an old member of the family. Because I am nearly all that is left of the true Ice People, I have longed to visit this place my whole life.'

'Hanna?' muttered the old one. She was wrapped in a dark shawl and cowl, so that her face was barely visible. 'My grandmother, who was one of us, had heard tell of a young lass called Hanna of the Ice People who had great powers. Could it have been the same person, do you think?'

'It is quite possible. Everything I know, Hanna taught me.'

'How did you find your way here from Brösarp?' asked the other woman.

Sol smiled. 'She who has but one desire in life will make sure it is fulfilled! But no! I had help from an old couple.

They helped me because they knew what I am. The bailiff's soldiers will learn nothing from them.'

'Good,' said the woman.

Sol was so happy she could have cried. They shared their food with her, simple bread and water and she learned more about them while they talked, all of them eagerly asking and answering questions of each other.

The old woman's complexion was as smooth and tender as that of any maiden, but she was otherwise white-haired and toothless. The other woman was middle-aged and appeared to be in such poor health that Sol was afraid she might die at any moment. She was pale and emaciated, and neither the fire nor her several shawls seemed able to give her any warmth. Her blond hair, split and coarse, was turning grey; her cheeks were hollow and the skin around her eyes, mouth and jaw-line was drawn tight. Every few moments she was wracked by a dry rasping and persistent cough.

The man was strange, silent and hard for Sol to fathom. He was tall and lean, with limbs that seemed only loosely attached to his body. Tired eyes looked out from his long gaunt face and his wrists bore deep scars – evidence of the bailiff's shackles.

The three individuals seemed to liven up now that Sol had arrived. When she had finished telling them of her adventures, she waited eagerly to hear their stories – but what she heard was largely a tale of pitiful lives spent continually fleeing persecution and constantly seeking refuge and concealment. Above their heads the moon was no longer in view. Now the blackness of the night had closed in on them – and it felt much darker beyond the snug ring of light that enveloped them, close to the fire.

'Ah, we that are left are so few,' sighed the old woman. 'It should come as no surprise after the way the Church and the authorities have behaved. When they could not find those like us, they took anyone they could! I tell you child, they seized folk indiscriminately. Normal friendly women who had no connection with witchcraft were taken captive on no more than the evil word of a hateful neighbour. And my heart still bleeds for these unfortunate ones. The true ones, those of us who have been given these unwanted powers that we revere so highly, had to become ten times more cautious. Fifty years past we numbered many here in Denmark. Now only a handful of us remain – and most are here before you!'

That truly is not a great many, thought Sol. The two women were unlikely to survive the next winter and the man was not in good health either. When they had gone, what then? What and who would be left? Only a world of emptiness!

'I am most likely alone in Norway,' said Sol, 'except for my uncle. But he has lapsed. He will not use his powers except to heal.'

The old woman looked at her, the wisdom of the ages in her eyes.

'No, child you are not alone,' she said. 'You have companionship.'

Sol started. 'Where? Who is she?'

'Not she – but they.'

'There is more than one?'

The old woman nodded. 'The Finnish woodsmen have come from the east into Sweden. They work in the forests in the great shires of Ångermanland, Dalarna and Värmland. They have their own language and culture, and are largely ignored by the rest of the people. Slowly they have travelled further west and they are now to be found in the deepest forests of Solör in Norway. There they clear the timber and thicket, taking land for themselves. Among them are men and women who know much of the occult.'

Sol's eyes glowed. 'Then I must go to them at once. Despite the devotion of my family, whom I love so much, you cannot know how forlorn my life has been.'

The man nodded. 'We understand your emptiness – as it is ours also.'

She looked pointedly at his wrists. 'Have you suffered in the clutches of the bailiff's men?'

'Yes. For too long I languished in a dungeon. Oh, my dear child, you could never begin to know what such dungeons are like! Take care not to be taken! They have been known to 'forget' those of us they have seized for many a year. I have seen woman taken to the stake in clothes so rotten that they have fallen from their bodies!'

'How did you escape?'

He smiled, showing long canine teeth. 'With witchcraft. I imposed my will on one of the guards.'

'Wonderful!' said Sol slowly, filled with admiration.

'But it took time. Afterwards on the outside, I was so exhausted from my effort of willpower, over so many weeks, that I slept for several days in a barn. I shall never permit myself to be captured again.'

'That is plain to understand. Oh, I feel I have found such happiness here with you that I want to stay – for a long, long time.'

'No!' said the younger, sickly woman. She spoke Danish, while the others had only the local Skåne dialect. 'You must not stay. My consummate gift is to interpret the fate of people. You must go home. At once! Someone at home needs you very much!'

'Me? But who?'

'I cannot say. I only know that someone dear to you is suffering and only you can help.'

Sol's manner had become instantly solemn. 'Help? In what way?'

'You must use any means at your disposal. I know that you will have no hesitation.'

Sol waved aside a moth that was attempting suicide in the flames of the fire and spoke very slowly. 'You obviously know a lot.'

'Yes, I do know a great deal about you. I touched your hand a short while ago – do you remember? I saw then many things that would have made the bailiff turn pale and the executioner take his torch to your pyre. You are in truth a unique and peculiar creature – yet still one of us. Travel home, Sol! We should be overjoyed to have you among us, for you have given us new life, but now your place is there.'

Sol nodded fervently. 'Yes, if someone there is suffering I shall go – as soon as I am able.'

Unexpectedly the old woman said, 'You say you love your family? That is hard for me to believe.'

'Why?'

'Do you not know why you were called the Ice People?'

'Yes. It was because our valley was so well hidden and the only way to get to it was under a glacier.'

'You are wrong! You were so called, because you were born with ice in your hearts. You can never love anyone. You may give men your body – but they will never have your love. You, who are of the true kin, have none to give!'

Sol was confused. That must be wrong she thought – but could it be true? Being fond of people? Well yes, she was. But as for loving people, what was the truth of that? Then what about Tengel? If he did not love Silje, then there was no such thing as love in this world! But Tengel was not really of the *true kin*. He was a mix, a bastard, with both the best of humankind and also the worst of the evil tendencies seemingly carried in the blood of the Ice People. 'So what am *I*?' she asked herself, 'and what does the word *love* mean to me?'

Gloomily she looked behind her into the darkness below the sides of the ravine. She could see dim outlines of bushes keeping guard all around them and, as she watched, a chill passed through her like an icy wind probing her soul. The others sat in silence, watching her, waiting. But Sol did not want to talk about such things – not when there were other pressing matters to be discussed.

'Can you help me find black nightshade?' she asked instead.

They all smiled back at her, knowing why she wanted it.

The old woman said, 'We will show you a place where it grows on the bank of the river you passed, but until then you can take these. They are only the dried berries, of course, but they still hold the power.'

Sol took them, thanking the woman. They were curious about her powers, and were impressed when she told them of her talents and the things she had mastered. They in turn demonstrated some of their skills and all learned from each other as the night hours quickly passed.

Sol's eagerness and cheerfulness were infectious and some of these qualities quickly reflected themselves in the others' faces. Using her knowledge of healing herbs, she gave the sick woman some of her supply, although she doubted that they would save her. A pot that is crushed can never be made whole again. Nevertheless the woman was very grateful.

They showed great interest in Sol's mandrake. She saw in their eyes that they would willingly have sold their souls to possess it. But mandrake cannot be acquired by paying the highest price in the normal way – it can only change hands for a price lower than that paid by the present owner. Eventually the price is so low that the owner cannot sell it and his soul belongs to Satan. They had all heard the forlorn tale of the mandrake that had been bought for a grain of sand on the road – and there is nothing with less worth. The owner could not pass it on to anyone else and he went straight to hell.

No one knew what Sol's mandrake might be worth. But they all knew she would never sell it. She had already told them of her fatal attraction for the underworld.

The sick woman coughed again, but less severely. Sol's youthful exuberance and the herbs she had been given had obviously reinvigorated her. When she had calmed herself again, she said, 'Now Sol, you will be able to experience something that I believe is unknown to you. You have seen the cauldron over our fire?'

'Yes. Is it your evening meal?'

'No,' they laughed. 'It is something very different to that.'

Becoming serious again, the man said, 'It is an intoxicating potion. It is our custom to brew it to enrapture ourselves. The herbs and plants we use are secret. Now, let us take our places around the cauldron and draw this cape over us. You will then experience things you would not have imagined.'

'Will it be something special?'

'Oh yes,' said the sick woman. 'Something very special.'

'A flight to Blåkulla?'

'No, not at all. A flight to Blåkulla ought to be taken when you are completely alone and have plenty of time. This potion will awaken a knowledge of life that lies slumbering within. It is knowledge that lies within every human, but we have forgotten that we possess it.'

Sol nodded eagerly. 'Then bring the cauldron!'

* * * *

All around and above them on the cliff top the forest lay still and peaceful. The fire was slowly dying, but the night remained warm. All four sat huddled under the cover, deliberately allowing their senses to be assailed by the fumes from the special witches' brew.

Sol's world began to reel gently and she felt curiously light-headed, as visions floated by. Most of them were short and disjointed, making it impossible for her to grasp their meaning. It may also have been her joy at being with people like herself, people who understood her without the need for words, which stopped her gathering her thoughts.

Suddenly the man pulled aside the cover and moved the cauldron away. Sol realised then that they had all reached the necessary state of trance and with a sigh she sank back against the steep grassy slope rising behind her and rested her head against the earth. The old woman had done likewise, while the sick woman had simply sagged backwards to lie prostrate on the ground. The man had slumped forward where he sat and Sol watched him roll himself into a ball, as though he was trying to shut out the world around him completely.

Sol felt dizzy and the ravine's deep sides seemed to sway and swirl about her. Slowly she let her eyes fall closed. Gradually all her senses steadied again and seemed to become clearer.

The moon was shining again, but Sol was vaguely aware that this was another cycle in another time. She found herself on her knees, pulling and tearing at a woman who lay on the ground in front of her. It was cold and she must have been very young, because her hands seemed so small against the larger woman. Then, when she raised her eyes, in this same vision she saw a young maiden who said simply, 'Your mother is dead, you need to come with me.' This girl must be Silje, thought Sol in amazement. Yet how young she looked! No more than a child.

The vision disappeared, only to be replaced with another. In this one, Sol was sitting on somebody's knee. It was the woman she had just seen lying dead – her mother, Sunniva. How beautiful she was, with her dark sad eyes; there was a man there as well, but he was less distinct.

Abruptly the vision changed again and one face filled her entire view – Hanna! Sol writhed and moaned; she wanted so much to speak with her. But Hanna disappeared as quickly as she had come, without speaking, and new grotesque faces, trawled from the unknown depths of Sol's mind, rose up to take her place.

All the faces, Sol realised with a shock, shared certain things in common – they were all born from evil, loneliness and sorrow. Many among them were repulsive, some were beautiful and others were blurred. Although she could not say how or why, she knew with total certainty that the faces before her had been gathered together specially from many different generations. She knew that effectively she was looking back in time!

Among those she could see were all the accursed ones of the Ice People – her own kin, her forefathers! Although Hanna was not strictly speaking one of her line, it was not surprising that she had seen her image, because she had known her in life. These people she saw now, all of them long dead, were the ancestors from whom she was directly descended.

Sol sighed deeply as she lay in her trance. Although totally engrossed and enraptured by what was happening, she still could not repress a fear of something unknown – and this was not like her. As she fell deeper into her trance, she ceased to see her visions as dreams induced by a potion and began to experience the images as real.

Folk appeared in diffused settings that were less clear to her than the people themselves. The surroundings were little more than impressions of the harsh fight to survive in the hostile Valley of the Ice People; there were strong feelings of desperation, adversity, hopelessness and an intense yearning to be free. So Tengel and Silje had not been alone in their desire to leave the valley and live as a normal part of humanity.

Some of these nameless faces from times past were hideously disfigured. Fortunately *they* seemed to be few and far between and their repulsive tendencies only asserted themselves sporadically, as she had been told; on average one in every generation, according to Tengel. She did see some normal pleasant-looking people as well, but their images flashed by very quickly, as if she were meant to focus on her afflicted ancestors. Or was it just that she herself wanted to see more of those sorts of people?

Then a clear vision came to her of a truly handsome man carrying something. Thank goodness: the image of someone attractive at last! He had a thoroughly demonic appearance and the yellow cat-like eyes she knew so well – and an evil grin. Even though she remained unruffled by many other things, this image made her draw an excited breath.

This could have been the man for me, she thought. If she had met him or somebody like him, would she have fallen in love? She did not know and perhaps it was only then she began to comprehend just how divided her personality was. How hard it was to endure living with strands of humanity woven into the black mantle of her existence. The beautiful endlessly fascinating man into whose eyes she had just been staring was perhaps one of the few lucky ones among her forefathers: he seemed to be pure, unadulterated evil and for the first time she understood the unending tragedy that blighted the lives of those who were like her. This applied to nobody more than Tengel perhaps; but he had been strong enough to choose on which side he would stand. As indeed had Hanna – on the other side from Tengel!

But was Hanna entirely evil? Well, was she? Sol pondered this deeply, but was not able to reach any conclusion. Then, just as the image of the handsome man was floating out of the picture, Sol saw what he had been holding. It was the severed head of a woman with sightless eyes that were open wide and staring. Sol knew instinctively that he was the man who had killed her. Then another pair of unpleasant figures from the distant past came to her, a woman and a man, dressed in the simplest of smocks and leg bindings, the like of which she had never seen. Witnessing them, Sol shuddered violently and dug her fingers into the grass and moss, clenching her fists.

Now something was growing out of the darkness – something to which all the other images had been leading. When the darkness finally melted, a pair of piercing eyes full of hatred appeared, staring straight at her. She instantly felt as though she was drowning – she could never endure this scrutiny!

She shut her own eyes, but this did not stop her anguish, because she knew immediately that the images came from a long-buried fragment of her inner self that until now had remained undisturbed, preserved and passed on from one generation to the next. She found she was gasping for air and trying to scream; she felt as if something was strangling her.

The others heard her cries, but were too deep in their own reveries to offer help. Even if they had been more alert, however, there would have been little they could have done. The visions, once started, could not be stopped.

They had realised at the outset that this young girl would find the visions more difficult than normal folk. All three of them had already experienced similar visions of their own ancestors and they had learnt that, although they could not communicate directly with them, they could gain courage, strength and inspiration from their existence. But Sol was of the Ice People! Anyone of that clan who looked into the past was sure to suffer great torment!

If only she had known how the brew would affect her, Sol might have refused to join the others; but probably not – she was much too inquisitive to resist such an opportunity. Then a sudden wave of nausea flooded over her and she instinctively pulled away from the eyes of the awful being, who by now was almost touching her.

This could not be anything else but the original evil spirit of the Ice People. This must be Tengel the Evil One! He was neither human nor beast and although he may once have had the features of a man, it was difficult to see them now.

In stature he was short, squat – much smaller than Sol – and large ears protruded level with the flattened crown of his head. Half hidden beneath a heavy brow, the treacherous eyes continued to glare ferociously, separated by a twisted beak-like nose. His mouth was open in a bestial grin, his lips drawn back, so that she could see his short pointed teeth. Sol was relieved to see that a large cape engulfed the stunted body. She had already caught sight of the long bony claw-like fingers of one hand poking out from the front of the cape and did not want to see more.

But although he was physically repugnant, the worst thing by far was the overpowering aura of evil that surrounded him. Sol did not doubt for a single second that this creature had sworn himself to Satan. No human could have been born like this – this was a creature formed from the darkness of the underworld!

Sol was desperate to leave her trance-like state, to rid herself of this ogre. What did he want of her? Why did he stare at her with such hatred? Was he trying to tell her something? Suddenly a distant memory awoke – she had seen him before – only once, a long time ago – but where? Although her thoughts were in turmoil, she sensed that he hated her because of that previous meeting and that somehow he was afraid of her. But why? If only she could remember when and where.

She started to scream and scream, yelling at him to disappear, but still the vision remained. She was not destined to see further back in time. Only the Ice People's past would appear to her – or so it seemed – and that began with Tengel the Evil One. Everything before that was shrouded in darkness.

Sol was by now writhing like a snake across the grassy slope. She was not easily frightened, but this was too ghastly, too sickening even for her. With great strength of will, both the man and the sick woman had managed to crawl over to Sol. Still barely conscious themselves, they knelt unsteadily at her side, trying their best to waken her.

But Sol's eyes continued to stare, wild and empty, out into the darkness and her despairing cries grew ever louder, drowning out their pleas.

'Father!' she screamed again and again. 'Father! Father! … Father!'

* * * *

Back at home in Linden Allée, Tengel woke startled from a dream and sat up straight in his bed. His breathing was ragged and he was moaning involuntarily, as he stared unseeing into the darkness.

'Sol,' he whispered in a haunted voice.

Silje, woken by his movements, also sat up at once and gazed at him in alarm.

'Sol is in trouble,' he said, with fear in his voice. 'She wants my help.'

'But how?'

'I do not know. This has never happened before. I didn't know she had such a gift – or that I was able to sense her. Oh! My God, what am I to do? Sol! Sol! Sol!' he whispered again and again.

'Is she near to death?' asked Silje, frightened out of her wits.

'No, no, that is not what I feel. There is something else. I must try to join with her.'

Silje lay her hand gently on his arm. 'Give her my love too.'

'I shall,' he said tensely. 'Now keep very still and I shall try to – I do not know if I can do this.'

Silje lay back, watching Tengel, who was sitting with his

legs drawn up to his chest and his face pressed hard against his knees. Her hand still rested lovingly on his arm, but otherwise she did not move a muscle. Minutes passed like this and in her own inadequate human way Silje tried to concentrate all her thoughts and love on Sol. She had an endless bounty of love to give and she hoped it would help, even if only a little.

Tengel had begun to sweat profusely from his intense concentration. He shivered violently once, but did not say why. After what seemed to her a lifetime of anxious waiting, he raised his head and wiped the sweat from his brow.

'You knew exactly what to do as usual, Silje,' he said in an exhausted voice. 'To feel love was all she needed.'

'So what was the matter?'

'I cannot be sure. My God, I don't know what she has got involved in. It was nothing of this world, I can tell you that. It was a terror so great it defies description. Evil, Silje, base malignant evil was directed at our young Sol. Yet it was not real. I wonder – she would never – no, I have no idea what it might have been.'

'Is it over now?'

'Yes, yes, I think so. At the end everything felt calm and peaceful. The resistance has gone.'

'Resistance?'

'Yes, there was a power, an immense power and she was trying to fight it. I believe Sol has experimented with something forbidden and dangerous.'

'I can't help thinking of her as the sorcerer's apprentice,' whispered Silje. 'I told her many years ago that she should be careful.'

Tengel lay back in the bed. 'Sol has never been careful. But this time she was afraid, in fear of her life. She of all people! I had never expected that!'

Silje contemplated this. 'You know what she has done. I can feel it.'

He placed his arm under her head. 'I don't know, I only suspect.'

'Well – what?'

'There is magic that I have only heard tell of in occult legends. It gives the power to brew a potion from mystical herbs. It gives a person apparitions and illusions of their ancestors.'

Silje turned her head towards him. 'Do you mean that she saw the Ice People? Those who have been afflicted and accursed?'

'No, of course she did not really see them, but she was expecting to and therefore she created her own images of them. It was nothing more than the workings of her imagination – and Sol, as we well know, has a very active imagination!'

Silje lay quiet for a while.

'Imaginary spectres can be as frightening as real ones – I know that to be true,' she said warily, suddenly remembering her own youth. 'Why do you think that she encountered the Ice People?'

Tengel hesitated for a moment. 'Because I could sense them too, although only very weakly. In fact there was only one image. Truly Sol has macabre fantasies!'

'You shuddered once.'

'Did I? I am not surprised – I have never seen anything quite so grotesque. He hated her, Silje, with all the power of death!'

'Tengel the Evil One?'

He shivered again. 'Don't say that name, not here!'

'Then it was she alone who imagined that he hated her?'

'It must be so. There is no other explanation.'

They were silent for a while; then Tengel pulled Silje gently to himself.

'Thank you for helping,' he said.

'You could tell?' she asked with surprise.

'Only too well! I believe that together we managed to see her through something horrible.'

Silje was taken aback by this – just to think that she, homespun Silje might have been able to assist in such ways. She shivered suddenly, heaved a sigh and said a silent prayer.

* * * *

In the remote wooded ravine, Sol was aware of a sudden feeling of peace flowing through her body. The man and woman, shaken from watching her battle with a deadly unknown foe, lay her gently back on the grass. The old woman was still slumped some distance away in her own private world of illusions and now the other two, still muddled and not fully aware, returned to their fantasy state.

The horrific figure who had so shocked Sol had withdrawn into the pitch darkness. Other lesser apparitions continued to float through her consciousness, but Sol was so wearied by her extreme trauma that she no longer noticed them. The images themselves were also becoming less distinct and finally the last of them melted away into a blurry mist.

In the aftermath of the experience, she had a new but vague awareness that her ancestors before the time of Tengel the Evil One had a foreign appearance. She had glimpsed people trekking across open landscapes covered deep in snow. Something told her that, many generations ago, her forbears had roamed from far away in long-forgotten migrations and eventually settled in Norway. At that moment she recalled the old woman's words about the 'Finnish woodsmen' from the east.

The Evil Tengel's ancestors could have been the last of an unknown tribe from far off in the east, a tribe long dead and forgotten and whose people had special supernatural powers. Long dead and forgotten, that is, except for Sol and her family. Liv, Are and herself, she felt sure, were the only three people able to pass on the characteristics. I will do my best she thought; indeed she had made such a promise to Hanna. But she would not hurry – first she was going to live life to the full!

The Ice People? Was there indeed a third explanation for the name? Was it because they were a tribe who had come trekking across ice and snow countless centuries ago? It was certainly not impossible.

Suddenly she realised that she was wide awake and had been for some time. She was alone in the woods beside the dying embers of the fire – alone because her other three companions around the fire were still deep in their dreams and in no condition to provide further companionship. Sol there and then vowed that never again would she take part in an experiment like this one! The others' faces all had peaceful expressions – undoubtedly their ancestors were kind harmless folk. She had been made to suffer the grotesque terrible images of the Ice People. Now she had seen them – and once was enough!

She shivered again at the very thought – to face the evil of the Ice People again would be an extreme form of self-torture and that was something in which she did not indulge! Sitting up, she threw some fresh wood on the fire. What was it, she wondered, that had saved her and driven away that awful vision? She tried to cast her mind back, but she found everything was obscure.

Someone, she recalled, had shaken her and tried to talk to her, but that had not helped at all. No, there was something else. Might it have been Tengel? She remembered suddenly that she had called out to him in her desperation – but surely he was so far away and could not have helped. Had there perhaps been someone like him? After a few moments she shook her head in bewilderment – she simply could not remember.

Love? What about love? Hadn't she felt the embrace of warm unselfish love that had wrapped itself around her and protected her? Might that have been from Tengel – and Silje?

Silje? No, that was impossible, for she had no supernatural powers. Yet whatever had caused her to feel it, the passion of her foster parents' joint love had declared itself and touched her very deeply. Inside herself Sol was crying silently – but her tears were soft and tender and she was cherishing every one of them as they rolled unashamedly down her cheeks.

Chapter 8

Once they had all recovered from the effects of their experiences at Ansgar's Klyfta, the four companions sat and talked animatedly until morning. Gradually the night-time shadows faded and, as dawn approached, dew formed on the grass and birdsong welcomed the new day. Sol had considered staying with her three new-found friends for a few days, but because they had told her repeatedly that she was needed back in Norway, she had begun to have doubts.

Also she reminded herself that she must not forget Meta, who would be waiting for her. It had briefly slipped her mind that she wanted to see the poor child properly placed in work, with a roof over her head, preferably at Fulltofta. Then, after that she would meet again up with Jacob Skille, as they had planned – and she was really looking forward to that.

Before she did any of these things, however, she was determined to take her ride to Blåkulla. Now at last she had all the herbs she needed to mix the anointing unction that would allow her to travel great distances over dales and hills. So she decided very firmly that she was not prepared to wait any longer; she had already waited a lifetime.

If she went back first for Meta, there would not be enough time for the ride. Finding Meta a place would take time and, as soon as that was done she would need to go and meet Jacob. That meant she would have to wait until she was back at home in Norway again before taking the ride – and she was not prepared to delay any longer. For the next few days she would be alone and undisturbed, as they had said she must be. Meta would not be worried, because Sol had told her she would be gone for two or three days. That meant there would be plenty of time.

It crossed Sol's mind that she should feel guilty about leaving the poor abused girl alone in the woods, but she told herself with no remorse that, as the child had been alone since her mother died, she was by now very used to being on her own. So having thought all these things through carefully, Sol said a reluctant farewell to her three remarkable companions and returned to the place where she had left her horse hidden. She found it grazing contentedly and quickly mounted up.

The area around Linderödsåsen, she could see, was unbelievably deserted. From her vantage-point on the horse, she had an uninterrupted view all around as far as the eye could see. There was a house far in the distance, but otherwise the whole place appeared desolate and forsaken.

Her three companions were travelling south, heading back to the old woman's home, where they would stay for a few days. She could see them now; three small specks a long way off, making their way along the winding path down into the valley. They had asked her to join them, but when she explained that she wanted to look for the nightshade they knew that she would not want company.

'Will you have the strength, after all you went through last night?' enquired the old man.

'It cannot be any worse,' replied Sol.

'No indeed, it won't be worse,' said the sick woman, laughing. 'In fact it will be just the opposite! You have never been there before, you say? Well then, it will be a nice surprise!'

'But rest well first before you go,' advised the old woman. 'And remember also that the journey to Blåkulla takes quite a long time.'

'How long?'

'That will depend on you alone. For some the journey is short. For others it can take far longer.'

Now she watched the three small figures, following their progress until they were lost from view. With a pang of sadness, she realised that this might be the last she would ever see of them. All three were shadowed by death and, despite telling her how pleased they would be to see her again next year, all of them knew in their hearts that they would not visit Ansgar's Klyfta together again.

Sol had taken their advice and slept during the morning and now, sitting comfortably astride her horse, she felt ready. The memory of the terrible visions, brought on by the effects of the potion, had already faded to nothing more than an unpleasant nightmare. All Sol felt now was a burgeoning excitement; she had planned for this moment ever since Hanna had beguiled her with stories of her own rides to Blåkulla to delight in orgies and all other forms of sensual gratification.

Hands shaking, she prepared the balm. The sheep fat that she had brought with her in a small box had dried and turned slightly rancid; but it needed only rubbing and warming to bring it back to the right consistency. And then there were the three magic herbs – henbane, hemlock and black nightshade.

When the balm was smooth enough, Sol stretched out naked beneath the spreading canopy of a tree. Although the earth was warm, she had spread her saddle blanket under her. She rubbed the salve into her armpits and other parts of her body where the skin is thinnest. The pole with the dead robber's hair attached also received a thin coating before she placed it between her legs and pressed it firmly against the base of her abdomen.

This precious item was her sole means of travel to Blåkulla, she reflected. There was no other way to go. Grasping the pole more strongly with both hands, she relaxed – and waited.

While she lay anticipating what might now happen, she cast her mind back to the black nightshade. She had been given precise instructions on where by the river she could find more. She would take as much as she could to store and use in years to come – if this ride went well. Although excited and elated at all that had happened, Sol suddenly felt drowsy and she did not notice how listless she had become.

But suddenly she was under way and the ever-changing scenery immediately compelled her attention. There was beauty everywhere; colours became intense and spread, only to shatter in the light. The ground fell away from under her and she floated from side to side, up and down across Skåne's wonderful hills. Down there was Glimmingehus. Looking along its stepped gable, she wondered if Jacob would be outside – but it was empty, except for the storks that greeted her passing with squawks of protest.

Flying was wonderful! She rose and fell as though riding on invisible waves, following the dips in the undulating rich green countryside below. It was just like the Österlen landscape she had ridden through, except – surely the coastline should have been over there, and yet there was no sea. How peculiar, she thought.

Suddenly her grasp on the pole slipped and she nearly fell off. Frightened, she gripped it as tightly as she could and the effort made her hands hot and sweaty. Other figures were swishing through the air all around her. Among them she recognised the old witch from Ansgar's Klyfta swooping past and they waved cheerfully to each other.

And wasn't that the pastor's wife from back home at Gråstensholm? Sol was well aware that witches who had ridden to Blåkulla often denounced and exposed pastors' wives whom they had seen there – but surely not the pastor's wife from home? She, who had always been as virtuous and pure as any saint! Yet Sol was sure it *was* her, of that there could be no doubt.

But what was she doing here? She was riding astride a goat, which was proudly exposing its long pointed 'thing-we-don't-mention', as Silje used to say. Sol grinned – Silje could be such a prude – but just wait until she told them all about the pastor's wife!

Far away in the distance, Sol could see a dark blue mountain and as she drew closer to it, she was greeted by flurries of small demons soaring towards her. One of them settled on the pole behind her. First she felt him lift her and then enter her. Sol was ecstatic. This was how it should feel! This was a different experience altogether from Jacob's manly bear hug.

Then she realised they had arrived. All of them were there – men and women, famous and infamous, congregating with demons of every shape and form. The pastor's wife stood on the ground and with one swift movement she bent forward and raised her skirts, allowing the goat to mount her. Sol watched in amazement and the act of sheer wanton eroticism left her drained.

At that moment her own demon jumped from the pole to join in the manic whirling dance that all the others were performing around the edge of a large hole in the ground. Sol was not destined to join in the dance, however, because her pole, with the grey scalp flapping at its end, steered itself suddenly towards the very heart of the black hole at great speed.

She gasped in anticipation as she flew down into the void, which was much larger than it had at first appeared. The wind tugged at her and whistled through her streaming hair as she fell deeper and deeper. Then abruptly she came to a halt; setting the pole aside, she stood up among more gyrating, dancing hordes who were reaching out to draw her to them. Suddenly everyone stopped and became silent. From their midst rose the Evil One himself.

His gaze wandered slowly over the throng surrounding him. Then he looked directly at Sol and raised his hand, pointing a long finger straight at her. Without warning, the crowd had disappeared and Sol was alone with him in a small cave, where the air was hot and filled with the scent of carnal lust.

Satan looked at her and smiled – and because his appearance is created by the imagination of each person when they see him, he became the most wonderful, attractive and sensual man Sol had ever seen. He had cat-like yellow eyes like her own, which seemed to be on fire. His mouth was set in a wry grin, revealing white pointed teeth and his hair was a black flowing wavy mane. When she saw his naked, dark-skinned torso, her own body throbbed powerfully in every cell and she made no attempt to resist as he took her in his strong embrace. For over half an hour she was submerged in raptures of intense pleasure, each one more gratifying than the last. She could not have enough of him; she clung on tightly, refusing to let go, and all the time he was intent solely on pleasing her.

Only a hazy memory remained of their final act and the journey back. She could not even recall having flown through the air, when she regained her senses and found herself lying beneath the tree once more near Ansgar's Klyfta. She could feel that the insides of her thighs were sticky and damp and she had a headache, which she could only have brought back with her from another world – the slightest movement brought on a searing pain.

She could see that it was now late in the evening. Waves of nausea threatened to sweep over her each time she tried to move, so she lay still, relishing the continuing dull ache in her belly that told her she had been aroused for too long. Yet she still wished fervently that she could be so aroused all over again from the very beginning!

Ye gods, now I have something to teach Jacob, she thought, trembling. What we did was child's play, compared to this! Her mind throbbed with thoughts of passion. Oh, how she wanted to meet the man from Blåkulla, the Evil One, in person once more. If only it was possible to meet him here on earth.

Poor Jacob suddenly seemed boring and lifeless by comparison. She would have to teach him! Show him where she liked to be caressed and how she could be aroused – and now she knew more ways to excite him.

Suddenly she found she could not tolerate the awful pain in her head any longer. She realised it was the price she'd had to pay for her pleasure, but she decided she must try to rid herself of it. From her supply of herbs and potions, she took out a sleeping draught and prepared and swallowed it.

Eventually the merciful gods of slumber were kind to her and she slept through the whole night.

The following morning Sol felt well again, but was unsure whether she wanted to relive her experience very soon. In any event she wanted to find a way to guard against the after-effects in future. Also poor Meta would be waiting! With her guilty conscience egging her on, Sol rode quickly back through the woods of Linderödsåsen to the peaceful place by the river.

She arrived to find everything very quiet – too quiet and foreboding. The surface of the pool lay mirror-like, upset only by the little bubbling waterfall over by the rocks. The whole scene was bathed in shimmering sunshine – but there was no sign of life anywhere!

Sol turned icy cold. What if her selfishness had driven the girl away into a hostile wilderness – or if there really were wild boar or other predatory animals here?

'Meta!' she called, and listened to her voice echo from the rocks. 'Meta, it's me, Sol!'

On top of the rocks something moved. Then, from a crevice high up, a small figure emerged.

'Oh, thank God, Meta. You frightened me!' said Sol, her heart pounding, catching her breath. 'I thought you had got scared and run away.'

Very sensibly, the girl had taken shelter in the crevice, knife at the ready and she had gathered a supply of stones to hurl at any interloper. Now she climbed carefully down.

'Hello,' said Sol jumping from her horse. 'Silly thing – you might have fallen from up there! How have you been?'

Meta looked very pale. 'The woods were horrible at night. And the moon – it stared at me!'

'But are you not used to being alone?'

'Not so far away from people.'

'Have you any food left. I'm as hungry as a horse!'

Meta gave her a bashful look; she had eaten most of it. With a sigh, Sol took half of what remained and they set off once again.

'How far is it to Fulltofta?'

'Oh, a long way, over there.'

'That way?' said Sol with alarm. 'But that will mean going out of my way and I don't have time for that. I have to rejoin my – er – travelling companions and we're already late. Bosjökloster, then?'

'The same way, but even further.'

'Well it will have to be Vittskövle.'

Meta didn't answer, but sat quietly behind Sol, saying nothing as they rode on. Sol did not mind her being so close, since she had been washed clean and the lice had been combed out of her hair. Whenever Sol spoke to her, however, she answered with only one or two words. So they rode on in silence, until Sol could stand the atmosphere no longer.

'What's wrong with you?' she demanded sharply. 'Why are you so silent?'

The girl sniffed, shaken by Sol's tone. 'They say that the old Dowager of Vittskövle treats her servant girls very harshly,' she replied almost in a whisper. 'I'm afraid to go there, Mistress.'

'And who is this Dowager?'

'She is Görvel Faddersdotter. She has been wed three times and is now the widow of one of the noble Brahe family. It is said that she is the richest person in all of Skåne. Although over ninety years old, she still goes round checking everything with the eye of a hawk. Let me be your chambermaid instead, Mistress! I would do anything you ask.'

'My what?' stammered Sol, taken aback.

'Or something less, if I am not worthy of that position.

162

A servant – anything – as long as I can stay with you.'

Sol could not help giggling. Chambermaid! Where did the girl get her ideas?

Then she said quietly, 'Meta, listen to me! I am just a normal girl – well perhaps not truly normal – and not even of noble birth. I am never in one place long enough to take care of you. But you shall not go to Vittskövle. We shall find another situation for you.'

'It does not matter that you are not noble born and I do not ask for a wage. Can I not work for you to repay all the good you have done for me?'

Unexpectedly Sol felt irritated at being called good. Sometimes she enjoyed it, but at other times it annoyed her immensely.

'I did only what pleased me,' she said impatiently.

After a long silence, she heard Meta's tiny plaintive voice squeak again from behind her back. 'Please, Mistress!'

But Sol had already been thinking ahead. Perhaps Silje or Charlotte might help? They both stayed at home all the time and both had need of servants. Then again, to drag this young thing over countless hills and dales all the way to Norway? To take her from her Skåne homeland and her family – no, she had no family – but nonetheless, it could not be done.

'We'll have to see,' she answered.

Her mind in a quandary, Sol wondered how Jacob would react – and what about her own feelings? She wanted so much to see him once more.

As they reached Haväng, a short distance from Brösarps Backar, Sol saw a rider coming towards them along the shoreline. Before long, she could see that it was Jacob Skille. She reined in her horse.

'Hello,' she called. 'Are you here already?'

'Yes, I could wait no longer.'

He stopped as he saw Meta's worried eyes peering from behind Sol's back. His expression turned to one of disappointment.

'This is Meta,' said Sol quickly. 'She is a foundling. I shall try to place her with some kind people.'

He gave a sullen nod and turned his horse. How common he looks, thought Sol. He is strong and manly of course, but compared to the Prince of Darkness he is fairly insignificant. Still, it was good to see him again – there was still a lot they had to do together.

Jacob told her that they need not travel through Glimmingehus, but could take a shorter road straight across Skåne. 'It will be quicker and easier,' he added.

'And we must collect Jörgen as well?'

'Of course, it is on the way.'

They passed one or two large estates on their route, but in each case Meta managed to find a thousand reasons why she should not seek work on them: there are probably ghosts, she would say; or, no one lives there; or that house looks terribly dark – and so on. In spite of the fact that Sol knew full well that Meta could have no knowledge of these places, she said nothing to contradict the girl.

They stopped to pass the night in the barn of a deserted farmyard, far out in the countryside, unseen by anyone. Meta proved herself a nuisance, wanting always to hold Sol's hand because she was fearful that her heroine would disappear again. Jacob was greatly irritated by this and did nothing to hide his feelings.

The hay rustled at the slightest movement. In the half-light, Jacob had wriggled close to Sol and when he heard that Meta's breathing had become calm and deep he began to caress Sol's face.

'I have missed you greatly,' he whispered in her ear.

'Hush,' she whispered back.

'She is sleeping. Let us go outside.'

Sol sat up and at once Meta lifted her head.

'What is wrong? Where are you going, Mistress?' she asked.

'Nowhere,' said Sol, deflated. 'I was just getting comfortable.' She squeezed the girl's hand. 'I'll be here all the time.'

Meta fell asleep once more.

'I have looked forward to meeting you again,' whispered a very disappointed Jacob.

'I have also been gladdened by the thought,' she murmured.

'This will be our only chance, for tomorrow we meet up with Jörgen and then we shall have no time alone.'

'Jacob, I could do nothing else!'

'Well if you are going to adopt every ragamuffin …'

'There is something very special about Meta. I cannot explain it now. Try to sleep. We have far to ride tomorrow.'

'But I need to be alone with you now, Sol!'

'I know and I feel the same. Now goodnight!'

He placed his arm across her belly. She pushed it away gently, but firmly, then listened to him as he swore an unending series of oaths. In the end she resolutely turned her back to him and soon fell into a deep sleep.

* * * *

Sol did not wake until dawn was about to break. Then, feeling uneasy, she sat up immediately and looked about her.

'Jacob,' she shouted, 'Meta has gone!'

He turned over. 'Well, thank goodness! Now we can be alone.'

'No, how dare you be so selfish! We must find her again.'

'Why? Let her go, if that is what she wants. Girls like her have nine lives.'

'Not Meta, she is as frail as a newborn babe. When I found her, she was dressed only in worn-out rags, had not eaten for a week and a dozen big brave soldiers had tied her up and were in the act of raping her. From behind!'

'Dear God! Why did you say nothing of this?'

'And when should I have had time for that? She has been at my side the whole time. That was why I refused your attentions last night. I did not want to remind the girl of the soldiers.'

Sol stood up, suddenly pointing. 'Look, Jacob! The child has left a spray of flowers where she lay – violets, rosehips and almond blossom. It was her way of showing gratitude.'

'Yes, but why did she suddenly run off?'

'I don't know – but we must find her at once!'

'Yes,' said Jacob, 'we must – and then find some good folk who can take her in.'

'Thank you, Jacob!'

As they came to the entrance of the barn, Sol stopped and put her hands on his shoulders.

'You are a good person,' she whispered and then kissed him softly. Jacob pulled her roughly to him and kissed her with a hunger that showed the craving he had for her. Then they hurried out, taking everything with them, for they would not be returning to the barn. Sol tucked the spray of flowers into her horse's bridle and they set off at speed across the fields and through woods, back the way they had come. Neither of them thought Meta would travel further along the road ahead of them.

She had gone a long way, but eventually they caught up with her. She was a pathetic little figure, forlorn, sobbing and wandering from side to side down the path. Overcome with tears, she was barely able to see, and Jacob jumped quickly to the ground to murmur some words of comfort to her.

'Meta, whatever made you do this?' asked Sol.

The child turned away, unable to answer because of her tears.

'You frightened us both, you know,' she continued as Jacob lifted the girl up behind her.

'Tell us what it was,' said Jacob, trying to soften the tone of his voice.

'Thought it – was best,' sobbed Meta. 'So you could – be alone.'

'Damnation,' muttered Sol, exchanging a glance with Jacob. The child had obviously heard them.

But Jacob was gentler than she had thought he would be. 'You misunderstood us last night, Meta. We did not want to be rid of you! There was something that Sol and I needed to talk about in private, secret things that concern Denmark. But it can wait.'

Dear me, thought Sol amused, our embraces have now become matters of state!

'I did not mean to call you a ragamuffin,' he continued. 'I was tired and miserable. You know that people say things they do not mean when they are like that?'

Meta nodded and took a deep breath, her bottom lip quivering.

'Have you seen how fine the horse looks with your flowers behind his ear?' asked Sol. 'He said he is very proud of them!'

Meta gave a cautious shy giggle.

'And it is a pretty bunch of flowers, too. Violets, rosehips and almonds – all the colours of the Norwegian flag. It could not be better!'

Sol felt sure that the child had learned how to tie small bouquets to sell at the roadside at a very early age and wished to demonstrate one of her few skills to show her gratitude.

At that point, the path along which they were riding widened and Sol was able to ride up alongside Jacob.

'And I have something to tell you, Meta,' Sol said in a loud voice, looking at Jacob with a cheerful confident expression. 'I have discovered that I have no wish to be apart from you. We missed you so much, that I have decided to take you home to my kind and gentle Mama. In Norway! What do you say to that?'

'Oh, Mistress!' gasped Meta and hugged Sol so tightly that she could hardly breathe.

'But do you know where Norway is?'

'Ummm,' Meta considered this. 'Beyond those woods, perhaps?'

'In a way it is – and then across the sea, Meta! You must sail in a boat both day and night.'

'Oh! But that is dangerous!'

'Is it? What trolls are you afraid of there, then?'

'The great sea snake, Mistress. It will turn the boat over.'

'Not when I am aboard,' said Sol calmly. 'But of course – if you would prefer to stay here in Skåne …'

Sol could both feel and hear Meta swallow hard.

'No, Mistress, I will come with you.' There was a pause and then she whispered, 'Thank you, Mistress!'

Just as Sol had predicted, when they reached the farm where they had left Jörgen, it was almost impossible for him to tear himself away from the place – or more correctly from the farmer's daughter. However, now that he was in good health once more, Jacob Skille was merciless.

'You know you must return home to Ottilie,' he muttered.

'Which Ottilie? Oh, the pale-nosed prude! Well, perhaps I must. But I shall soon be back here!'

They gave him a little while to take farewell of the lass before they continued on their way westwards. Then they journeyed on without further incident until they reached the coast again and, in Helsingborg, Jacob found a ship bound for Norway on which the girls could book passage. Sol paid the skipper and then they went to spend their last night ashore in cheap lodgings that Jacob had found.

'That is perfect timing indeed,' he said. 'Half a day later and the boat would have sailed.'

There was no disguising the sadness and longing in his eyes when he looked at Sol. She however was strangely restless. In her mind she kept returning to her extraordinary meeting with the figure of Satan and she felt that she needed to be alone for a while. She found her friends' endless chatter disturbing, because she had an exquisite secret she could not share with anybody.

It was easier, however, for her leave the room in the lodgings now. Meta was sleeping soundly, exhausted and secure in the knowledge that she was going to Norway. After she slipped out, Sol found the moon was starting to wane, but still shone over the whole town. It bathed the vast fortress and its great tower, Kärnan, and Saint Maria's Church in its pale glow. But Sol knew what she wanted – she needed more than anything else to seek out her own world.

Jacob had told her about the ruins of the old dungeons, where the anger of restless souls could be heard at night – but he did not know exactly where they were. Raising the subject obliquely during the evening meal at the lodgings, she had gleaned more information and that was why she now made her way past the church of Saint Maria and across the square, heading towards the furthest outpost of the fortress. She did not look to see whether anyone was following her – but someone was indeed watching her as she hurried through the town to the ancient ruins.

When she had reached her destination, she stopped and looked around. Soon all this would be gone she thought; it would sink into the ground and disappear under the grassy mounds of earth on which new houses would be built. Dwellings had already begun to encroach on parts of the ruined walls and in a hundred years nobody would suspect they had ever existed.

Windblown trees guarded the entrance and Sol walked quietly down some steps into a passage leading between walls that had fallen down and were now overgrown with weeds. She came to an empty doorway and stopped – a simple broken hobbyhorse lay at the entrance, revealing that this was a place where children played. Stepping over it, she walked on through a maze of ruins, stopping briefly again to breathe in the air. After doing this, she was in no doubt about the particular direction she should follow. Climbing over heaps of fallen stones, she made her way round pools of rainwater, beneath large gaping holes in the roof, before finally reaching a crypt-like room where the atmosphere was thick with the past sufferings of the dead. This, she was certain, was the notorious dungeon.

Moonlight shone in through a large crack in the roof above her head and, by its glow, Sol was able to find a place to sit on a grass- and weed-covered pile of earth that probably concealed stones from the broken roof. She knew hardly anyone would ever come here – certainly not children – for she could see that bleached and shining shards of human bones lay half buried in the earth close to the old walls.

She sat very still with her eyes shut and listened to the chorus of voices from the dead, sighing as they slowly emerged from the past. She cared not whether they came from her imagination or were real – they were now part of her reality. She answered them, speaking softly, and sensed an invisible presence sitting beside her on the earth. Sol felt she was at one with all those unfortunate beings. She understood them and they understood her – regardless of whether or not they were the product of her fantasies. What did that matter?

'I am alone,' she whispered. 'Oh, so alone in this world that lacks imagination. It is wonderful, truly wonderful to be with you – you who already know what lies in worlds beyond.'

One by one they rose up out of the darkness, the shadows of individuals who long ago had been made to suffer and die; shadows that receptive folk could sometimes just glimpse out of the corner of their eye. This was Sol's world and she was at home in their company. She saw them, empathised with the hopelessness they had once felt as they endured the horrors of this cell, knowing there would be no salvation and that all they could expect was a slow agonising death.

Then suddenly, in the blink of an eye they were gone. The sound of heavy footfalls echoed down the passageways and, a moment later, Jacob Skille appeared in the doorway.

'So this is where you are!' he said harshly.

In an instant Sol took advantage of the situation. 'Yes, I heard you following me, so I decided to come down here. We will not be disturbed.'

He was not sensitive to the mood of the room.

'True,' he said. 'No one visits this place.'

She beckoned him to come close to her and they contrived to make love recklessly on the earth beneath the broken roof. Sol showed him all the new things she had learnt during her ride to Blåkulla. Jacob was willing to learn and soon felt he was quite an exceptional man.

Of course, he had no idea where these new sensual variations had come from and cheerfully thought that he was encouraging her to do his bidding. But he did everything she wanted, and to all intents and purposes they enjoyed a wonderful half-hour of intense pleasure – although he remained blissfully unaware that he was making love on a heaped pile of earth beneath which lay the scattered bones of the dead.

Eventually they returned to the lodgings, walking slowly side by side – but Sol's body felt numbed suddenly and she was quickly overcome by deep despair. She swore fiercely at her powerlessness, crying silently without tears. The passion and sexuality of this world, she told herself, were definitely not for her. This time, in the core of her being she had felt nothing, *nothing at all*. Far greater efforts would be needed now, if she were ever to be aroused again.

Chapter 9

The following morning, Sol and Meta left a deeply distraught Jacob Skille standing on the quayside at Helsingborg. He waved forlornly until their boat was out of sight and continued standing there, just staring out to sea, for a long time afterwards. For Sol and her young companion, the voyage was long and unpleasant, but they docked at last in Oslo, half a day before Dag was due to arrive, and disembarked around noon.

Meta had not been seasick on the crossing, but travelling in a boat no bigger than a nutshell across a sea full of imagined horrors had almost driven her out of her mind. She had held on tightly with both hands to handrails and bulkheads throughout the trip and couldn't get any sleep at all, because she had to make sure that unknown monsters of the deep were not lying in wait to throw themselves upon her beloved Mistress as soon as her back was turned. Once ashore, Sol took lodgings at an inn and instructed Meta to bolt the bedroom door and sleep until she returned; on no account, she told her, was she to open the door to anyone else.

'I want to visit my sister who lives here in town,' explained Sol. 'You cannot come with me because you are almost asleep on your feet. I shall not be away for long.'

Meta tried feebly to protest, but the welcoming bed won the day. Sol listened as she bolted the door and heard the girl fall at once onto the bed without undressing. Goodnight and sleep well, thought Sol, and set off briskly to find the Berenius household. On arrival there, she was taken aback by the sight of Liv, who at first just stood staring at her in disbelief.

'Come on, Liv,' laughed Sol, confused. 'It's me, Sol. Don't you recognise your incorrigible sister?'

'Sol? You – here? At this house? Oh, Sol!'

At last it dawned on her that she had a very special visitor and, once they were inside the house, Liv hugged her big sister very tightly, not wanting to let her go, overcome with joy.

'My dear child,' said Sol apprehensively as they drew apart, 'what do you look like? How you've changed. If it had not been for the colour of your hair, I should not have known you – and even that is matted and dull.'

Liv's hands were shaking, as she showed Sol into the best parlour. Anxiously she patted her hair, afraid her husband might find some reason to criticise it.

'Ch–changed? How h–how do you m–mean?'

Sol was astounded – Liv had never stammered before in her life!

'You are but half the weight you were – and your eyes! They are full of dread and have dark rings around them. I believed you to be well and living a good life. I read as much in letters from home. You have a wonderful big house and – are you here all alone?'

Her little sister nodded. 'Today is m–my – mother-in-law's gossip day. S–she is visiting the w–wife of Mister S–Samuelsen, the cloth merchant. Oh Sol, Sol – just to see

174

one of my own once m–more! T–to speak as I wish and know that y–you will not correct and question everything I s–say.'

Liv burst into a flood of tears and Sol took her sister into her strong vigorous embrace again. As she listened to the awful sobbing, she could tell that Liv's feelings of despair had been building up during many long months of loneliness. Eventually, when she had recovered sufficiently, Liv told Sol everything that had happened to her. The words poured out in a torrent and she obviously could not hold back the flood of tangled emotions any longer.

'I have tried to be loyal. I have no wish to speak about my husband behind his back, but …'

'Tell me everything,' said Sol. 'There are some things that must be told, even I can see that!'

'He is changing me, Sol! To fit in with his wish to have a docile, stupid slave of a wife. All that I have learnt at home is beneath his contempt and …'

'Is it?' Sol was enraged. 'No parents have been more worthy than ours!'

'No, and that is how I feel too; but Berenius despises them.'

'Must you keep calling him "Berenius"? It is ridiculous.'

'Oh, thank God, you think so as well. I thought I was the one going mad. And his mother …'

The whole story tumbled from her lips, while Sol sat speechless, full of indignation and dismay. To be refused visits from her family, not to be allowed to journey home, not to be allowed to draw and paint, not to be credited with even the slightest intelligence – this was barbaric, inhuman!

Broken lilies, thought Sol despondently. How extraordinary that she, Sol, the unyielding one who did not fit into any normal decent life, should have rescued two young girls who turned to her in the same week. To think that she was the strong one in all this! The situation was truly bizarre!

'And when it comes to the marriage bed …' began Liv, and then stopped. 'No! Forgive me!'

'Yes,' said Sol, 'you must tell me!'

'No, and please do not ask me to, Sol, for I am brought up not to discuss such intimate things with another.'

'As you wish. I will not ask again.'

'Sol, I am so unhappy! So – broken! Am I really so incapable of everything? I try and try, but nothing is ever right.'

'You have done nothing wrong. The fault lies with him – not with you.'

These words were pure salvation to her sister. All of the painful anxiety, the self-doubt and the loneliness of the months gone by continued to gush from her in an unending stream. Sol was astounded, but it was only when she caught sight of the scars on Liv's arm and learned they came from whippings with a riding crop that she finally lost her reserve and exploded with rage.

'This is completely unforgivable!' she exclaimed and burst into a tirade that would have seen the most hardened of men blanche. Not only did she spit out oaths and curses, but she also used words and phrases that would only have been uttered by stevedores down at the harbour. Liv, aghast, sat holding her breath. When she was finished Sol pulled her up from the sofa.

'Come on!' she said. 'Dag's ship should be arriving soon. We shall go down to the harbour and greet him.'

'Dag? Is Dag coming here?'

'Yes, we are to meet here in Oslo.'

'Dag,' murmured Liv, 'and shall Mistress Trolle be with him?'

'Which Mistress Trolle would that be? There has never been any such person for him.'

'But I thought …'

'It was nothing but gossip! Dag has had no time for anything but his studies. Maybe a drawing-room flirtation once or twice, perhaps, like everybody does.'

'But I cannot go out. I have not asked to.'

'Asked to? In our family there is no need to ask. You go where you will, when you will – accountable only to yourself.' For one fleeting moment, Sol wondered if she would be able to hold herself to account for some of the things *she* had done – but that wasn't important now. 'Come – and I will not hear you say "no"!'

One hour later, they watched as Dag's ship sailed slowly into the harbour. While they waited they had spoken of everything other than Liv's misfortunes and the younger girl had smiled for the first time in months. Nonetheless, she jumped at the slightest sound and looked about her furtively all the time, as though she was being watched by prying eyes. She was overcome with concern and worry about what her husband and his mother would have to say about this escapade.

'So blame me,' Sol had said. 'I can take it.'

While they were watching the few passengers come ashore, Sol secretly scrutinised her sister. Her extreme nervousness and unease were visible in every move and gesture. So when the old woman at Ansgar's Klyfta had told her, 'I only know that someone dear to you is suffering', it was Liv she had been referring to, thought Sol. Her eyelids closed a fraction and her brain started to mull things over. Then she saw a tall elegant-looking young man waving to them.

'There he is!' shouted Liv breathlessly. 'Oh, Sol, what a

wonderful day it is, meeting both of you at the same time! If only I could …' she broke off, her hand flying to her mouth.

'Come home with us?' said Sol, finishing her sentence for her. 'Is that what you'd like?'

'Oh, no! I did not mean that! I believe loyalty to be of utmost importance in a marriage – and I cannot help but be terribly ashamed that I have broken Berenius's trust today.'

'Thank goodness you revealed everything. And as for loyalty – well that applies to both parties, does it not?'

'But he is kind to me, has given me many things and never been unfaithful, even though he tells me it is his right, should he so wish. I should not have …' she broke off again as the tall young man approached them. 'Hello, Dag,' she said breathlessly. 'It's lovely to see you again!'

Dag hugged his sisters, first one then the other.

'So you managed to arrive before me, Sol. That was well done. I am to remember a great many people to you who never had the chance to say goodbye. You have been sorely missed, sister mine. Mostly by – umm – young lads! And good day to you, Liv, my little one, it's been too long! But my dear girl, you are so thin and pale! Is this man of yours not feeding you properly?'

These last words ended in laughter, but Sol touched his arm in an urgent serious gesture. 'The situation here is grave, Dag,' she said quietly. 'We must talk.'

'Sol,' said Liv dejectedly. 'You must not!'

'Yes, upon my soul I must! Dag, unless we do something that wretch will torment our sister to death!'

'No, Sol, please don't.'

'What is all this about?' asked Dag, deeply concerned. 'Tell me everything!'

As they walked away from the harbour, Dag listened to the whole story delivered by a fire-breathing Sol. When she had finished, he looked at them both in abject dismay.

'Liv is the most virtuous and best of all of us, isn't she Sol?' asked Dag. 'I know her better than anyone else, and there is no finer person. Who would dare to treat our sister so?'

Although neither he nor Sol were true blood relatives of Liv, when there was an assault on their family they stood more strongly united than many conventional families. Dag's expression showed his deep concern at the fact that Liv was so evidently overwrought and depressed.

'It is – not – so – bad really, Dag,' she stammered. 'Perhaps I – exaggerated.'

'Exaggerated?' exclaimed Sol. 'Just look at her arm, Dag! And as for that mother-in-law! Well, you heard what Liv said!'

'We have to travel home,' decided Dag bitterly. 'Tengel and Silje and Charlotte must be told of this – and Liv, you must come with us.'

'No, no,' she begged desperately. 'I cannot.'

'Yes,' insisted Dag. 'I will arrange transport at once. Are you ready to travel, Sol?'

'No, I must fetch my ... Oh, Lord! I've forgotten all about Meta again!'

'Meta?' repeated the other two simultaneously.

'Yes, but she has only herself to blame. It is as though she was born to be forgotten!'

Then she told them all about Meta. When she had finished, Dag shook his head in disbelief.

'You are a strange person, Sol! I have seen you, with a heart made of stone, do the most awful things to Tengel's patients – amputating legs with no regard for the screams;

draining putrid, stinking sores; picking up pieces of rotting corpses – all without batting an eyelid! Then some unfortunate young girl appears and you are full of compassion – but, of course, the poor thing must come with us to Linden Allée or Gråstensholm now. You did the right thing in bringing her.'

'Of course, I did! But Liv is right about her own future actions – it would not be right for our sister to travel home with us now. It would provoke her husband too much – and we do not want her beaten any more.'

'I intend to have words with this man,' said Dag sternly.

'No,' said Sol. 'that is the worst thing you could do. Now let me sort this out! Liv, you hurry home quickly before anyone returns – it's not far. Dag, you go and find us transport to Linden Allée, while I fetch Meta, child of misfortune that she is. It is some distance to the inn where she is waiting for me.' That last piece of information was a lie – the inn lay just round the corner, but Sol was hatching other plans. 'And then I will meet you at the town gates and bring misery with me.'

'What misery?'

'Meta, of course! Now Liv, you must carry on being the good-natured wife until we have spoken to our parents of this. Be placid and subdued like a lamb! I will see you soon.'

Sol hurried away and soon disappeared from sight round a corner. Liv and Dag continued walking slowly along the street together, taking their time. Liv felt so peaceful that she forgot she ought to be getting home as fast as she could.

'There is not much Father and Mother can do,' she said quietly.

'No, maybe not – but he must be taught a lesson.'

Liv gave a sigh. 'In the end I would suffer for it.'

'I know. That is what concerns me.'

Soon they were strolling hand in hand, as they had always done. Trying to sound cheerful, Dag told her of the life he had been leading in Copenhagen – but in his heart he felt only dull helpless despair. The master of the house and husband always had the law on his side. So was young Liv – the little sister who had been his reverential shadow throughout their childhood and beyond – now to be made to suffer for the rest of her life? Even though it was clearly absurd, there was one thought Dag could not put from his mind – it was that he was in some small part responsible for the sad circumstances in which Liv now found herself.

They walked on in silence for a few moments, before at last he asked, 'Where does he have his place of business?'

Liv stopped. 'You must not go there, Dag, I implore you. Please don't!' she begged him.

'I only want to tell him a few home truths – or to be more honest, beat him black and blue!'

'Dag, I beseech you!' There was desperation in her voice. 'Please don't do anything.'

He stopped and took her face in his hands. 'No, I shan't,' he promised. 'Let us see what Sol has come up with. She is usually quite inventive.'

Dag could sometimes be so naïve; but his distracted thoughts were elsewhere at that moment. For a long time he stood looking deeply into Liv's eyes – as they said goodbye, neither of them could ignore the look of sadness in the other's face. Dag promised her that she would soon receive news from home and then they reluctantly went their separate ways.

Liv stood watching him until he was out of sight. As she walked back to her fine house, although she felt buoyed up from seeing her siblings, she dreaded the thought of the retribution her husband would take if he ever found out that she had left the house.

* * * *

Meanwhile Sol had wasted no time. She had quickly hired the most elegant coach to be found in Oslo and ordered the driver to take her to the house of Samuelsen, the cloth-merchant. Seated in the coach, she adjusted her dress, so that she looked as refined as possible – not very difficult, as her best dress was one of Countess Strahlenhelm's cast-offs and very high fashion compared to the standard in Oslo. As she travelled, she searched through her occult possessions and put something in her pocket.

When they arrived, she instructed the driver to announce her as Countess Thott from Copenhagen – she knew there were so many Thotts that it would be impossible to keep a check on them all. The driver duly climbed the steps to the front door and in no time the 'countess' had been allowed in. Sol made a grand dramatic entrance, sweeping her skirts about her, looking very elegant in her stylish dress and a hat that reflected Copenhagen's current fashion.

The cloth merchant's wife, the more than amply proportioned Fru Samuelsen, curtseyed and scraped, and scraped and curtseyed for all she was worth, welcoming her aristocratic guest to her insignificant merchant's home. She explained that she was 'at home' to some friends – she was desperate to present the Countess to them – while at the same time trying to think what had brought about this visit.

Sol glided into the drawing room, her posture straight

and tall. With a patronising smile, she gazed in turn at each of the ladies assembled before her. In her best Danish accent – not perfect, but unlikely to be noticed – she bade her hostess introduce each of her worthy guests by name.

Fru Samuelsen was delighted to do so and Sol took special note of Fru Berenius, Liv's mother-in-law. They had never met, as Sol had not attended Liv's wedding, but on catching sight of her, Sol's first thought was, 'What an old hag!' So this was the creature that took such pleasure in persecuting one of the most loveable girls in Norway: this flesh mountain of a bitter old woman with a whining voice, sitting slumped in front of her. Oh, poor Liv, how you must have suffered! Still smiling, however, Sol turned her attention smoothly back to her hostess once more.

'Ah, yes! My dear Fru Samuelsen, I have come here straight from Court.' The sound of the assembled ladies all drawing breath at once was overwhelming. 'I was speaking with my dear friend, old Count Löwenbrander, and he asked me to call on you.'

Sol was able to say this in the certain knowledge that there was no such count. She had espied the name on the front of a lowly butcher's shop near her temporary home in Copenhagen. But the count's non-existence did nothing to stem her flow of invention and she continued blithely, 'He was telling me how in his youth he had fallen madly in love with you, but that family circumstances prohibited him from proposing marriage. Yet he has never forgotten you, Fru Samuelsen and he wished me to tell you! Ladies, is that not truly romantic?'

Sol treated them to one of her jubilant bursts of laughter and understandably the cloth merchant's wife was properly confused.

'No! But who can that be? Count Löwenbrander? I do not remember ...'

'No, of course not. He could not use his aristocratic name then, as you surely understand. Neither could he declare his feelings to you. But I'm sure you know who I mean, is that not so?'

The woman gave an uncertain chuckle that could have meant anything. Sol could see she was trying hard to remember. No matter – seeing the eyes of her friends wide with envy and disbelief made her a happy woman!

Without more ado, Sol sat down next to Liv's mother-in-law. She joined in conversation with the ladies and drew their attention to a picture hanging high on the wall while her hands moved swiftly over the table. Regretfully, a few moments later, she refused an offer of refreshment, saying that her coach was waiting and that she was on her way to visit other nobility; but she did not elaborate further.

Soon afterwards she made her gracious exit, accompanied by the good wishes of the many admiring ladies. Somewhat delayed, she arrived in due course with Meta in tow at the town gate, where Dag stood waiting beside a common horse-drawn wagon. Half an hour later, Liv's mother-in-law drew her last breath, following a very authentic heart attack.

No one thought to connect this with the wine she had drunk some time earlier – and certainly no one even considered it might have anything to do with the unexpected visit of the elegant lady from Copenhagen. Furthermore, as this happened while she was visiting others, Liv could not be accused of having anything to do with the death of her mother-in-law.

Sol wanted it that way. And Sol usually got what she wanted.

* * * *

Dag went first of all to Gråstensholm. He did this because it was his proper home and it was where his real mother lived. Charlotte was naturally overjoyed to see her handsome son once again and spent a lot of time wiping tears of delight from her eyes.

'We were not expecting you for a few days. We thought we might journey down to meet your boat. Anyway, how did they go?' she asked when she had calmed down and they sat together on the bay-window seat.

'How did what go?'

'Your exams, of course!'

Exams! He had forgotten all about them.

'Very well, thank you. Now that I have an excellent legal training, I will be able to take my pick of official positions. Without boasting, I can truly say that I came out best.'

'Of course, I knew you would,' beamed Charlotte. She found it impossible to stop gazing in wonderment at this grown man sitting beside her! 'I was sure you could do it. I'm not such a fool myself, you know, so you must take after me!'

'I know that. You have taught all of us, Mother, and you must take all credit and praise for that. But the years at university have been hard – a student is not valued very highly, especially when he belongs to one of the lower faculties. It seems being a priest or a deacon is the only worthwhile pursuit in this life. We were required to attend funerals and form a sort of guard of honour. The bigger the congregation the more distinguished was the corpse. All this took a great deal of our time when we should have been studying. But it all turned out well in the end.'

185

Dag then sat quietly for a long time, mulling things over. He listened to her distractedly as Charlotte told him all that had happened at Gråstensholm. But in mid-flow she stopped suddenly.

'What's wrong, Dag?' she asked with a worried frown. 'You look troubled.'

He sat up straight and sighed. 'Mother, I fear that in acting with the best of intentions you may have caused a terrible tragedy.'

Her cheeks coloured. 'I have? What do you mean?'

'Did you tell them at Linden Allée of Mistress Trolle, whom I had mentioned to you in passing?'

'Yes, I did,' she replied, perplexed. 'What happened with her?'

'Nothing, except that I thought she was pretty and that I was proud that she wanted to pass the time with me. But the fault is mine as well, for I should never have mentioned her name.'

'Fault? I do not understand.'

'All this occurred while Liv was being courted by that Berenius man, did it not? And he had been introduced to her here at Gråstensholm.'

Charlotte thought for a moment. 'Yes, I believe that is so. Why?'

Dag stood up and began to pace the room. 'The next thing I heard was that she was to wed. She had already agreed.'

His mother was becoming more and more bewildered. 'Yes, and it was an incredibly fine match for our young Liv.' Then she saw the profound look of distress on his face. She stared, waiting for him to speak.

'Mother, Liv is wedded to a wife-beater! A veritable tyrant!'

Charlotte sat motionless, lost for words, horrified. Dag began pacing again, then stopped and slammed his fist against the window frame.

'Oh, Mother! You should have seen her! She is a tiny frightened shadow! Her mother-in-law berates her from morning till night. She may not see her family, her husband chastises her and despises everything she has been taught – then whips her with a riding crop when she shows herself to be wiser than he is!'

'My dear boy, what are you saying?' cried Charlotte. 'What are we to do? Dear God, what can we do? Tengel ...'

'No, not Tengel! He will surely kill Laurents, and that must not happen – for Tengel's sake. We must keep this to ourselves, just you, Silje, Sol and me. Something must be done. Sol asked me to wait, but I had to talk about it with you.'

'Yes, yes, of course! Oh, my God, what have I done? But I could not know ... Oh please! Poor little child! Nobody on this earth is as caring and loving as Liv.'

'Amen. But say nothing of this at Linden Allée, at least not yet. Allow Sol and me to decide how things should go. Liv is terrified that there will be trouble.'

'I promise.'

Then they fell silent for a long time, sitting with their own thoughts. Eventually Charlotte turned to her son again. 'How did Sol get on in Copenhagen?'

'Sol? She's like a cat – always falls on her feet and has nine lives.'

'So she got herself into trouble?'

'She did that, even though she managed to charm herself out of it. Sol is so damned reckless!'

'You should not blaspheme,' she admonished gently.

'Ha! You should hear Sol explode when someone lights her fuse!'

187

'Yes, I can well imagine,' said an exhausted Charlotte.

* * * *

Sol had arrived at about the same time at Linden Allée and was welcomed ecstatically with open arms by Silje and Tengel. They embraced fervently for a long time and were still breathless when they finally broke apart.

'My dear Silje,' said Sol, looking her foster mother up and down in a pantomime-style show of surprise, 'you'll have to stop eating all those honey cakes!'

'It suits her to have some curves,' declared Tengel, putting an arm smilingly around Silje's waist.

'Yes, all right,' agreed Sol, smiling with deep affection. 'It does for now, I agree – but I have seen far too many overfed matrons recently. I would not want to have one at home!'

'That's easy to say,' laughed Silje, 'but you are quite right. I have it far too comfortable – and Tengel, if you see me eating one more cake, you must take it away and give it to the poor!'

Being the woman she was, Silje had been slightly hurt by Sol's unflattering comments and she vowed to herself that she would do everything possible to avoid attracting any similar remarks in future, so in a roundabout way, Sol had done her a service. But their great gladness at seeing Sol again far outweighed all other considerations for Silje and Tengel, and this teasing was instantly forgotten.

'Now who is this little girl you have brought with you, Sol?' asked Silje, peering at the newcomer.

Sol proceeded to introduce the embarrassed Meta and briefly recounted her story, leaving out the more brutal details for Meta's own sake. Silje and Tengel both showed truly heartfelt sympathy for the homeless orphan and quickly agreed to take her on as a maid.

In replying to their questions, Meta spoke all the time in a whisper, keeping her eyes focused firmly on the floor. She said she would prefer to work in the barn, if they needed her there, because this was obviously such a fine home and she felt her presence in it would not be fitting.

'But what were *you* doing in Skåne, Sol?' demanded Tengel suddenly in a suspicious voice. 'What took you there?'

'I was visiting friends,' she replied easily.

'Not at Brösarps Backar, then?'

Confound it, she thought, he knows! And did he know about the witches there, as well?

'No, why would you think that? To be precise, it was at Tollarp.'

'Were you in any difficulties there, Sol?'

'Difficulties? How do you mean?'

'I felt a – sudden affinity – with you one night. Silje and I tried to help you.'

Sol hastily began to rummage in her luggage.

'You did help,' she muttered, 'and I am very grateful. Thank you a thousand times!'

Tengel and Silje exchanged uneasy glances.

'And would you rather not speak of it?' enquired Tengel.

'I would prefer not to,' said Sol. 'I did a stupid thing that I will never do again. Of that you can be certain!'

'Perhaps one day you will confide in me,' said Tengel. 'For you see I found it very interesting. I received images of a – well, a creature that I am unwilling to speak of by name.'

Sol looked directly into his eyes for a long time. Tengel held her gaze steadily in return and at that moment she could feel how closely tied they were to each other by this unspoken bond that others would never understand. At last she nodded her head in assent.

'One day I shall tell you, I promise. But for now the memories are too fresh in my mind.'

Sensing something of the strong feelings passing between them, Silje interrupted quickly to change the subject.

'Oh look, here comes Are. Do you see, Are, who has come home at last? And this is little Meta – she is going to live with us. Meta, if there is anything you need to know about looking after the barn, then you can ask Are. He is in charge of all that.'

Meta stared shyly up at the tall, well built young man, who looked just like Tengel, but without the demonic expression.

'I understand. When shall I start?' she asked. 'I really want to do a lot of work.'

Are looked at her in shock.

'What did she say? I didn't understand a word!'

'Can you not understand me, Master?' whispered Meta in a dejected voice.

Are howled. 'Me – the Master? I am but fourteen years! And she cannot even speak properly!'

'My dear Are,' said Sol, 'Meta speaks the language of Skåne – a dialect all its own that is a cross between Danish and Swedish. You'll soon learn it.'

'Why should I learn it? Never! She must learn our ways!'

'Are, please take Meta out to the barn and show her your kingdom,' said Silje firmly, 'and make sure you are pleasant to her! We have things we must talk about.'

'Why can I not stay and join in.'

'You are not yet a man, that is why,' replied Silje.

'I am always treated like a child!'

'How will you have it, then?' asked Silje with a gentle smile. 'You refuse to be the Master and you do not wish to be a child! Now, take the girl and go.'

Muttering under his breath, Are turned and left and Meta, still feeling awkward, followed close on his heels.

'What on earth has come over him?' Sol wondered aloud. 'That is so unlike Are. He is usually the most friendly of souls.'

Silje smiled fondly at her. 'Have you forgotten how difficult it is at that age? Still a child, but with one foot in the world of grown-ups. I remember well how trying my own childhood was – and you were certainly no angel!'

Sol reflected on this for a moment. What had happened to her at fourteen years of age? Klaus, the bashful young stable boy – the sudden deaths of the verger and Master Johan – and one or two other unusual things.

'I have *never* been an angel,' Sol smirked. 'I expect it will pass for him as well. Anyway, I cannot stay long because I must ride to Tönsberg. I am on an errand for the family of a Danish noble. I shall leave tomorrow.'

'But you must not ride alone,' objected Silje.

'Silje, my dear, it is not even a full day's ride! I shall stay the night with them and return the following day. What can befall me while I am on horseback?'

'Let her ride,' said Tengel. 'She will take care of herself.'

'All right, but can you not delay a few days?' asked Silje. 'Poor Meta will be unhappy if you leave before she has found her feet here with us.'

Sol considered this for a moment. 'Very well, I'll wait,' she said quickly, then added. 'You're right.' But in the back of her mind she had found other reasons for agreeing.

'Good!' said Silje. 'And Sol, it was kind of you to take care of the girl.'

'Oh! If only you knew what she has been through! But I think I shall keep those things to myself for her sake.'

At that moment out in the barn a very disconsolate Are was showing Meta around. The poor girl traipsed obediently after him, nodding energetically whenever he explained something. Her wide eyes showed how impressed she was, but she said never a word.

Eventually Are yelled, 'Can you not at least answer one question?'

Meta gave a cough and her eyes brimmed with tears. 'I dare not, Master, for you do not like my language.'

'Master!' he repeated in a shout. 'Oh, dear Jesus, grant me patience!'

* * * *

In response to Sol's earnest request, Charlotte and Dag said nothing at Linden Allée about the suffering Liv was going through. Sol did not want an enraged Tengel to endanger her plans at this stage – so she set out as announced for 'Tönsberg'. That, however, was not where her plans were taking her.

Some time later, she stood concealed between a pair of houses close to the harbour in Oslo, opposite a large mercantile building that was the Berenius trading house. It was a long way from the home that Laurents shared with Liv.

Sol very deliberately took her time – throughout the day, from outside the building, she noted all that took place: the doings and the comings and goings of everyone. Several times she saw a youthful man with an air of authority whom she recognised as Laurents himself. He was an elegant type, but far too polished and arrogant for Sol's taste. She liked a man of power, that was true, but not his sort. She wanted someone who had been born with true authority, the kind that did not need to shout and threaten to be obeyed – a man in fact who effortlessly carried an aura of power within him.

Sol could not be sure what Berenius traded in, but she guessed it had something to do with timber. Later she had a vague recollection of cargoes of wood and lumber, but as she stood there all her concentration was focused on the people.

The gable wall of the Berenius building faced the street. High up in the wall was an open hatch, where she could see that some heavy-looking sacks were stacked, probably waiting to be hoisted down when they were needed. The hatch was directly above the entrance door – and Laurents, she noticed, spent a lot of time standing in the entrance talking with different people.

Sol returned early the following day and resumed hiding in a small gap between the houses. She had chosen that particular place, because a solitary bush hid her from the view of passers-by. It was very important that Laurents did not see her; she could have walked into the building unhindered and carried out her scheme more easily, but nothing, she told herself, must be allowed to link her plans to Liv. This was the thought that was always uppermost in her mind.

For many years, Sol had regularly practised her ability to move objects, using only her power of thought. During those early morning hours, she worked until sweat made her hair lay flat against her temples. Her heart was racing from the effort of moving one sack right to the edge of the opening and, although she had no idea what it contained, she dearly hoped it was something very heavy.

She had never tried anything like this before. She had moved small items across tables many times, but attempting to move something this large from so far away was proving difficult. After many attempts she reluctantly had to concede that it was almost certainly beyond her powers. For once Sol was forced to give in. This meant she would have to get inside the building – but how?

She had noticed a coal merchant's premises not far away and in the backyard she had seen old sacks and piles of rubbish. No windows at all faced onto the yard. This, she decided, ideally suited her purpose.

Half an hour later, what appeared to be a young boy trudged up to the entrance of the Berenius building. A sack full of bits and pieces was slung over his shoulder, a sooty cap pulled down over his dirt-streaked face and a large apron covered his breeches. (Sol, to achieve this effect, had tied her skirts up around her legs.) The filth on the 'boy's' bare legs and feet made it nearly impossible to see the colour of the skin beneath. Waiting for a suitable opportunity, when a lot of people were going in and out, he slipped in and made his way sure-footedly up the inside stairs.

Having reached the top floor, which seemed to be deserted, Sol left the sack near the hatch. She cast her eye over the large attic, where great beams formed a framework supporting the roof. It was dark and dusty, but at the other end she saw an open window. Very carefully she crept over to it. Looking down, she could see that about three cubits below the window was a lean-to roof. A few swift paces across this would bring her to the roof of the neighbouring house, from where she would be able, in stages, to reach another backyard further away.

There was someone on the stairs and Sol hurried back to her hiding-place behind the sacks. She dared not peer out, but after rummaging around for a few minutes, the person left. She could clearly hear the sound of people returning to the floor below her. Only one thing was bothering her: there had been no sign of Laurents Berenius all day.

As she pondered on this, a sudden thought sent a chill through her. What if this were the day of his mother's funeral? Of course, she had expected the woman to have a funeral, but she had heard nothing about it. She was not aware that a letter from Liv was already on its way to Linden Allée, in which Laurents had instructed her to say that no one from Liv's family need attend her mother-in-law's funeral. Liv did not write the truth – that Laurents was ashamed of her relatives and family, or that he refused to be associated with 'hopeless peasants', who had nothing in common with the merchant classes. Not even Charlotte or Dag were acceptable to him, because Laurents could not understand why any son-of-a-whore like Dag should be allowed to hold the title of baron. It made no difference that Laurents had himself been eager to experience the charms of countless women before he met Liv – and yet he saw no connection between that and the birth of a child outside wedlock. To him somebody like Charlotte was a woman to be despised.

As these reflections ran through her mind, Sol lay impatiently behind the sacks peering down at the street and the doorway below. The hours passed slowly, then finally, during the afternoon she saw Laurents Berenius arrive. He came by carriage and hurried into the building. All that remained was for him to come out and review his assets, which he invariably did from the strategically placed doorway.

Sol's wait seemed never ending. She could not stay away from home another day or they would begin to worry – neither did she want them to become suspicious of her. As she continued her vigil, she exerted all her inner strength to influence Laurents Berenius to come to the front door. She waited and waited, and had almost given up hope when she heard the faint noise of movement below and peered down.

There he was! His head was showing – but not quite enough. Then he moved forward a pace or two.

'Now stay just there!' said Sol slowly and deliberately to herself, at the same time willing the act silently inside her mind.

In preparation for the final move, she shifted her position slightly, but at that moment Laurents turned unexpectedly and walked away towards the harbour. For some time Sol could not see him from where she was hiding and didn't know what he was doing. As she waited, she realised that her fingernails were cutting deep into the palms of her hands with the tension. Then, almost immediately, he reappeared again, walking quickly back towards the building in the company of another man.

'Stop beneath the hatch!' she intoned to herself very slowly. 'Stop beneath the hatch!'

And this time they did – but when they halted, the wrong man stood in the right place. Another wait ensued.

'Change places! Change places!'

This time she whispered the command very softly. Even though she might not be able to move the sack using her powers, Sol felt sure she could at the very least get the two men to obey her suggestions. She could see that they were caught up in an avid discussion, both pointing and gesticulating in turn. From her hiding-place only the tops of their heads were visible – and she noticed absently that Berenius was beginning to go bald. But wait! They were moving again, and now he was in exactly the right spot!

'By all the powers that guide me, give me strength – and luck,' she muttered fiercely. 'The time has come!'

There was still a chance that he would move again, after the sack had started to fall, so she delivered one final incantation under her breath.

'Stand still, Laurents Berenius. Please stand very still!'

Using all her strength, Sol pushed the sack forwards. It toppled slowly, teetering for a long moment on the edge – then fell.

Laurents turned round, but did not look up. For a second, Sol stood motionless with panic; then, as she dared not stay a moment longer, she leapt across the attic, jumped down onto the roof below and then sped across the roof of the adjoining building, just as she had planned.

Moments later she was back out on the street, observing from a distance the great commotion outside the doorway of the Berenius building. Allowing herself a fleeting smile of satisfaction, she headed quietly away in the opposite direction and soon disappeared round the corner.

The sack had been very heavy – in fact much heavier than she had expected. It had partly burst open on impact, scattering some of its weighty contents in a heap in front of the building. As far as Sol could see, there was very little of Laurents Berenius still in one piece.

Chapter 10

Sol arrived back home at nightfall. Silje was the first to greet her and it was evident from the expression on her face that something was already disturbing the whole household.

'Sol, I'm so glad you're back,' said Silje in a worried tone. 'Charlotte and Dag are both here. We have had a letter from Liv telling us of the death of her mother-in-law from a heart attack. It seems she was visiting friends when it happened. Liv asks us not to go to the funeral, but I think we should travel down anyway. What do you think?'

Sol, who still had the death of Laurents fresh in her mind, did not answer immediately. She was still struggling to find a sensible reply when Dag appeared and cut in on their conversation.

'It is surely that husband of hers who has told her to write in that way,' he said. 'We should make up our own minds about whether we go or no.'

Silje turned to him, bewildered. 'Why so? What makes you say that?'

Sol changed the subject in a flash. 'When will the mother-in-law's funeral take place?'

'The day after tomorrow.'

Liv is all alone now, thought Sol; there is no one in the house but the dead.

'I think Liv needs us now,' she said gently. 'We should go to her, all of us who can.'

And so it was decided – but in the event they did not start their journey to Oslo. A new letter arrived late in the evening, before they had completed their preparations to leave the following morning. This time the letter came by messenger on horseback. It revealed that Laurents was also dead, killed in a tragic accident at work, and the mother's funeral was being delayed so that they could both be interred together.

'Oh, that *poor* girl,' declared Silje. 'To lose her wonderful husband after such a short time!'

Dag, Charlotte and Sol all exchanged blank glances; then Sol nodded meaningfully to Dag.

'I think it was the best thing that could have happened,' Dag announced gravely. Then in hushed tones he told the others everything they knew about Liv's unhappy marriage. While he listened, Tengel's face turned paler with every word.

'And why have you said nothing to us about this?' he demanded. 'My little girl!'

'We have only known the truth of it for barely a week,' replied Dag.

Silje burst into tears. 'So many times I have been saddened that she has not visited us or that she could not or would not have us visit her. I always so longed to see her – and all the time it was forbidden! Oh, Liv, my dear child!'

'Indeed, we too carry a great burden of blame for the marriage,' said Charlotte. 'I believe we talked her into it. She was led to understand that Laurents was the best choice for her.'

'I shall set out first thing tomorrow morning,' declared Silje. 'I shall stay with her until after the funeral and then bring her home.'

'And I shall go with you,' said Tengel.

'Yes, do that,' said Sol. 'And now I am hungry! I shall go and find someone to prepare food – and if they have gone to their beds, then I'll look after myself.'

'At this time of night?'

'What does that matter? Must one always follow custom?' she retorted, and left them.

After she had departed, the room fell silent. All those remaining sat and looked at each with wondering expressions.

'Sol is one of a kind,' piped up Are with a smile. 'She has never been one to follow custom.'

'I believe we have a lot to thank Sol for,' said Dag as he stared into the distance.

'Yes,' said Charlotte, her face thoughtful; memories were flooding back – the inn at Dovre – two assailants lying dead …

'She loves her family more than anything else on this earth,' added Silje, remembering how a little two-year-old Sol had induced Abalone's wretch of a son to cut himself with a knife after he had tormented Silje once too often. 'She will do anything for us.'

'True,' murmured Dag, while wondering just how Liv's mother-in-law had died so suddenly and so conveniently.

Tengel still said nothing. His eyes were focused on an unknown distant place. He knew much more than the others did. He had seen a verger staggering helplessly towards his church after Sol had used Hanna's poisoned barb on him – the same verger who had threatened to expose Tengel as a sorcerer.

'Sol asked us to wait a few days before telling you,' whispered Dag, mainly to himself.

None of them wanted to look the others in the eye. An unspoken pact now existed between them to avoid any more questions about Tönsberg. They all knew that although each of them held a fragment or two of the puzzle, only Sol could truly see the whole picture.

In the scullery, Sol was enjoying a large bite from a hunk of bread, but her mind was occupied with thoughts not unlike those of the rest of the family. She had arranged the passage of yet one more person to another life. It had all begun with a nasty playmate in the Valley of the Ice People – that is, of course, if you ignored her effect on Abelone's son, which was just something she thought of as practice. No one else was aware of the fate of the playmate who had tormented Dag and Liv in the high valley. Everyone had believed his death to be from natural causes.

Oh! The time she spent watching over her loved ones, so that nothing and nobody could harm them or speak ill of them! They were like children, vulnerable and ignorant of the evil in the world. So it fell to her to protect them, to make sure their lives were spent in peace and free from misery. But there were times when she saw how inept they all were and that was when she got quite angry with them.

Then there were the two thieves at the coach-house at Dovre – the ones who were trying to hurt nice Aunt Charlotte, the angel of the family. And there was the verger – now that one had really been fun! And Master Johan – that had been a little bit sad, but necessary – most definitely very necessary! And of course there had been some of Tengel's more sickly patients – but they didn't really count because they were half-dead already.

What about Copenhagen? She had behaved very well

there – or so she thought. There had also been the two highwaymen in Skåne. Ha! Self defence. No finesse at all – just crushed their skulls. She felt dissatisfied about those two, but there had been no time for anything else.

Liv's mother-in-law? Well, that was worthy of merit! Methodically planned by an incisive intelligence. And now Laurents – she thought she had done very well there too. The list was growing all the time – and many more names had been added recently. But what Sol did not know was that the ultimate prey was still out there – waiting.

* * * *

Liv stood in the centre of the best parlour in her home in Oslo. Her hands were pressed tightly together to stop them from shaking, but she could not prevent the tremors racking the rest of her body.

'He is dead,' she told herself, over and over again. 'He is dead and never coming back!'

But nothing would stop her from shaking – she was unable to think properly, her mind was in turmoil, her brain refused to function. When it did, she was plagued by images she would prefer not to see.

The thoughts had started when the news of her mother-in-law's death reached her, 'I must not feel relieved by this,' she had told herself. 'I must not think that it was because I wanted her dead. No, I have not wanted it, I have not! God, help me! Take pity on me! And now Laurents is also gone! But I must have no more of these thoughts, no more at all! My conscience can stand them no longer.'

She began pacing back and forth, wringing her hands. 'I

have no strength to oppose them!' she reflected. 'The funeral – how shall I get through it? Will no one come and talk to me about the practical matters and give me something else to occupy my mind? I am falling apart from within – torn apart by the enormity of the situation and by all that is happening around me.'

Then she realised someone was coming. She could hear voices she recognised – welcome cherished voices! Then Liv watched as the door flew open and Sol breezed into the room, followed by all those she loved. She was surrounded by concerned caring voices; held in caring arms. Mother was there, her eyes warm and brimming with tears, telling her she looked 'thin' and calling her 'dearest child'. Sol was chattering loudly, Dag was there too and Charlotte. All stared at her with worried looks, but she couldn't see them clearly for her tears.

Tengel had remained by the door. He stared at his daughter – the child he had carried in his arms, pacing back and forth across the floor, when she suffered from childhood ills. The little girl who had sat on his knee as she first struggled to learn her alphabet. The child who was always so gentle, so warm-hearted to everyone and everything. Now he hardly recognised her – the expressionless drawn face with deep grey shadows, the lifeless hair and bewildered eyes.

Tengel turned away, burying his face in his hands. Now he understood the meaning of pure hatred. Laurents Berenius and his mother could be thankful that their deaths had been fast and painless, because if he had but known, he would not have been responsible for his actions. Taking a deep breath, he wiped away his tears. So many times Silje and he had thought of coming to Oslo to visit Liv, despite her obvious wish for them not to do so. But their respect for her had decided them against it. She had asked them to wait a while until she had finished decorating the house, or Laurents was away and then she would so like to see them – could they wait until he returned? And so on and so forth.

Liv was surrounded by so many people, all wanting to hug her and take care of her, yet her face remained so lifeless that Tengel was very afraid for her. Eventually the others moved aside and she stood looking directly at him. At that moment Tengel walked over to her and she fell into his arms.

As fresh tears ran down his cheeks, he heard her quiet frightened whisper, 'Take me home, Father!'

'Yes, of course,' he said very softly, finding it hard to utter the words. 'You are coming home again where you will be made welcome and loved, my precious child!'

* * * *

Liv came back home, but she remained ashen-faced and terribly gaunt. She spent her time wandering quietly around the farm, sometimes going up to Gråstensholm and falling deep into quiet conversation with Dag, the person to whom she had always been closest. And all the time Charlotte was in the background, plying them with treats and being kind and considerate in every way.

One day Dag and Liv were walking across the fields and Dag stopped and took her gently by the shoulders, looking into her eyes.

'Dearest Liv! Why can't you tell me what is troubling you? I know there is something. We all realised there was when we came and fetched you home and you won't be well again until you have spoken of it openly. You have become a prisoner of some untold anxiety. They are both dead, Liv! What is it that you are in fear of?'

She lowered her gaze and squeezed her hands together tightly. 'I dare not speak of it aloud.'

'You have to! It is the only way you will release yourself from its grasp.'

Liv nodded. Yet still she said nothing as they moved on, making their way round a muddy patch of ground.

'Dag, I feel so guilty,' she said at last.

He took her hand. It felt like ice.

'What do you mean by that?'

'I don't mean that I deliberately wished Laurents dead, but I was constantly aware of the awful thought that I might never again be free of that degrading life. In many ways that was the same as wishing him dead, wasn't it?'

'No, I don't believe so. It seems more likely that you had resigned yourself to your situation.'

'Well, yes, I suppose I had.' Her voice was still heavy with doubt, yet she sounded a little relieved.

They had stopped walking again and once more Dag turned her towards him. 'Liv, my dearest friend, look upon this time as a challenge you cannot avoid. Use me as your confidant, as one who will always have the time and patience to listen, someone who will help you. Don't worry if you feel you need to repeat things many times. You have to rid yourself, body and soul alike, of all these horrors so that you can begin anew.'

'Oh, Dag,' she replied as she rested her head on his shoulder, 'I shall never be able to begin anew. I am more hurt than you will know.'

He placed an arm round her shoulders. 'Use time as your healer, Liv. He is your best friend at the moment. Now – come on – chin up!'

He held her slightly away from him and returned her despairing look with a friendly gaze. Then suddenly his soft smile died, as they were both engulfed by a deathly silence. Liv's eyes grew very wide and there was helplessness deep within them. Dag had stopped breathing – in that single moment of truth they both felt the same fear of the unknown.

Liv let out a little cry then turned and ran from him, faster than a fleeing hind, over the fields towards Linden Allée. Dag merely stood and watched, making no effort to follow her. Disturbed and confused, he walked back to Gråstensholm. When he arrived he found Charlotte standing beneath the salon window, pruning the rose bushes planted long ago by her mother. Seeing him approach, she smiled.

'Oh, are you on your own? I thought Liv was going to eat with us.'

Dag did not reply. He stood staring at the roses without seeing them. Charlotte put down the heavy shears she had been holding.

'What's the matter, Dag?'

There was a lump in his throat, making it impossible for him to speak and he swallowed hard.

'You don't need to explain,' she said softly and turned her attention back to the roses. 'I knew what was wrong as soon as you came home – that time when you spoke about complications with Mistress Trolle and Laurents's continual punishment of Liv. All those things.'

'Yes, that was my subconscious speaking out. It had already acknowledged that I was much too fond of her. But common sense told me that I could not tell her that – after all, she was a wedded woman. But today – just now ...'

His mother waited, willing him to speak out.

'I have never understood it until now – because we have

206

always been like brother and sister,' he said forcefully. 'But that is not what we are. I believe Liv feels the same way, despite being scared by the sudden discovery of the truth a little while ago.'

Charlotte nodded. 'I understand. When she heard about Mistress Trolle she was a little distraught, but she did not know the whole story. Perhaps because of that she succumbed to the pressure to wed Laurents Berenius. Liv is very easily influenced. Then of course you were in Copenhagen – you were resentful when you heard that she was about to be married and you saw no reason for it. Isn't that so?'

'Yes.'

He turned on his heel quickly, grinding the gravel underfoot. 'Why couldn't you have granted me the freedom to marry Liv?' he said in an aggressive tone. 'Was it because she is not of noble birth?'

'Dag, my dear, how can you say such a thing? Have you ever known me to be snobbish?'

'No, thank God, never.'

'Then just give her time, my boy! I think that you will have to tread very carefully. We none of us know the horrors of that marriage.'

'I can imagine some of them,' he sighed. 'Yes, I am afraid that this may take a lot of time. Perhaps I will never be able to reach her?'

Charlotte shrugged. 'You're right. She seems to be carrying a weight on her conscience, as though someone or something persists in making her feel guilty for everything she tries to do. And I am afraid that the possibility of love between two people who have grown up together as siblings might frighten her even more. Poor girl! We must give her all the care and help we can.'

Dag agreed with this completely, nodding his head repeatedly in response.

* * * *

A family gathering was held at Linden Allée and everyone seated themselves around a groaning table of delicious food. They bantered lightly with one another as they took their places and Sol shot a mischievous smile at Silje when she noticed that she was keeping well away from the cakes.

'Liv, you have to consider your future,' said Tengel seriously from his 'throne' chair at the head of the table, when things got properly under way. 'You are now the owner of an important timber-shipping business.'

'I don't want it!' she replied abruptly.

'Then you must sell it,' said Tengel. 'It cannot be allowed to drift with nobody at the helm.'

'Is it not a little foolish to sell it?' interrupted Are. 'As you know, Father, I want to work the forest here. Aunt Charlotte and I have been considering how it could be done. Now what could be better than our own business to transport and ship out everything?'

'A superb idea!' said Dag.

'But I know nothing of business,' objected Liv. 'Neither do I wish to live in that awful house with all its memories. I want to live here!'

'You can still do that,' said Dag, disappointed again that whenever he spoke to her she avoided his gaze. 'However I am a lawyer and I can help you to sort things out. You can count better than anyone I know, so you could keep the ledgers from here. I don't know what to do about the house, though. It would be a pity to sell it.'

'Then why not let me live there,' exclaimed Sol jauntily. 'Play at being the fine lady, holding court and such. Suitors will stand in line just drooling to get their hands on the exclusive house – and they'll get me into the bargain.'

'Don't talk nonsense,' said Tengel. 'You cannot live there alone.'

'Of course I can. I will hide in mystic seclusion behind dozens of servants. People will whisper – who is she, that beautiful woman with the sad eyes?'

'Sad eyes – you?' laughed Are. 'Your eyes are lusting for life and full of the Devil.'

'Are!' said Silje. 'How dare you blaspheme in this house!'

'It's not blasphemy – just an expression.'

Tengel sighed, but could not conceal a smile. 'Yet one more family meeting is starting to lose its way. We must talk seriously – you are all grown now except Are, but he is the only one who is settled. You older ones simply cannot stay here and waste your days. Dag, you have finished your education, but what will you do with that estimable qualification?'

'At the moment I don't know, Father. I have received two really good offers and there are several other possibilities.'

He had called Tengel 'Father' – this was something that greatly amused friends and relatives alike and they often teased Charlotte about it.

'So you stand like a mule surrounded by haystacks – unable to choose. Liv has inherited a fortune in the lumber business, but has not felt strong enough to deal with it,' Tengel paused and looked slowly around the table, 'and you, Sol – can you not come back and help me with the sick once more? Everyone misses you, most of all me.'

'I suppose I could,' she replied half-heartedly. What she did not say was that she had tasted freedom now, or to be more correct, her life had been changed beyond measure since the encounter with the Prince of Darkness. Nothing was as it had been. 'Yes I expect I can,' she continued guardedly. 'Perhaps just for a time, until I decide what I really wish to do with my life. It doesn't seem as though there are many suitors around here knocking at my door.'

'You've had plenty of suitors and you know it,' smiled Silje. 'About half of your male patients have asked for your hand. It is you who lack interest.'

'Well, I haven't found the right one yet,' she chirped gaily, and once more the discussion had lost its way.

* * * *

Harmony eventually settled again on the two farms. Sol helped Tengel with his sick patients, although she sometimes absent-mindedly gave them worthless medicines, while promising a swift return to good health and an earthly paradise as well. Occasionally the medicine worked and at other times it didn't, but this hardly mattered, because all the sick people loved her vibrant presence and visibly thrived when she visited.

Once or twice she went out into the woods to partake in a ride to Blåkulla, but the after-effects were so bad that all her thoughts were concentrated on reducing them. She often considered giving up the 'trips', but she knew in her heart that would be too difficult, because she was becoming ever more intrigued by the wonderful image of Satan who invariably met her at Blåkulla. Also after each experience she quickly found herself longing to see him again.

Although the scenery and activities at Blåkulla altered, 'he' was always the same – an appalling suggestive man with the demonic quality that Sol unfailingly sought. Maybe he grew slightly more handsome and more erotically attractive after each visit, or perhaps the distance between him and earthly men was disquietingly great. Whatever it was, she had met 'him' three times now and been taken to the heights of ecstasy and left with a bitter emptiness inside when she awoke from her trance. Several times her helplessness had nearly brought her to tears.

Furthermore she realised that, with each visit, her personality was becoming more divided. What she had come to think of as the 'abyss', the extraordinary depths of darkness into which she plunged herself willingly each time, was for her a boundary, a great dividing line. It was the passageway between her two worlds and she began to understand more and more clearly where her heart lay and where she longed to be. As this realisation started to dawn, it frightened her so much that she became, paradoxically, unwilling to admit it fully even to herself.

Meanwhile her little 'sister' Liv was very slowly becoming her old self again, but she still had a long way to go. Dag always showed her unending patience and had refrained from mentioning the near fatal moment when they both understood that they were definitely not brother and sister. Instead it was Liv who first brought up the subject.

They had been sitting at twilight in a window-seat up at Gråstensholm and were quite alone on this occasion. Charlotte was with Silje, discussing a recent visit to a neighbour and unusually for a time their conversation died to nothing. Then Liv sighed loudly and asked, 'What's to become of us, Dag?'

He shrugged uneasily 'What do you mean?'

'You know very well.'

'Yes,' he said after a long pause. 'You're right, I do. I simply have not had the courage to mention it.'

Liv waited. She had asked the question – now it was up to him.

'Do you want to, Liv?' he asked in a whisper. 'You know, do you want to marry me?'

She turned her face away from him, so he could not see her expression. 'It isn't so easy,' she replied softly. 'Wanting something is not the same as doing it.'

'Why not?'

She shook her head very decisively. 'I cannot talk about it, Dag. I cannot. It is just too – private.'

He gave her a long searching look, but she did not turn round towards him.

'Do you really want to?' he asked again, speaking very softly. 'Do you want to marry me?'

Now suddenly, to Dag's surprise, she nodded just as vigorously as she had shaken her head a few seconds earlier, but Dag did not continue to plague her with further questions about a subject that was obviously very hard for her. He turned instead to Sol, frank and forthright Sol, and asked her to see if she could very carefully find out what lay behind Liv's reluctance to marry him.

'First of all it's too soon after the death of her husband,' exclaimed Sol when she reported back to him. 'It does not seem that there has been a decent interval.'

'I realise that – but I can wait!'

Sol had recently decided once and for all not to carry on with the Blåkulla 'game', because it had caused such a disturbing imbalance in her life. For that reason alone, she was glad to have something else to occupy her mind.

'Of course you can wait! So I shall ask her, dearest brother of mine. Marrying you is the only thing that can liberate her. Why has it taken you so long to discover this, you oaf?'

'Did *you* discover it?'

'No, the thought honestly never occurred to me. We were all siblings as far as I was concerned.'

'It was the same for us – but we aren't, are we Sol?'

'No, thank God – for Liv's sake! I wish you good luck, little brother, and I shall find out the truth, mark my words.'

And so she did! Not long afterwards, in the bedroom she and Liv were sharing just as they used to do, Liv felt ready to speak about her terrible marriage. Sol lay quietly in the darkness and simply listened to her sister's soft voice.

'Our dear Mama had advised me to give him all the love I had, let him come to me and then receive him joyously. I should show him that I shared his – desire. I did all that, Sol – only to be harshly condemned for being unwomanly. I was told that I should remain passive from then on. He was the hunter, the conqueror. I was his woman, a chattel for him to be proud of and for him to use.'

'*Misuse*, don't you mean!' cried Sol, so loud that Liv had to hush her. 'I have never heard of anything so mean – or so wrong! You must not believe what he told you, Liv. Silje was right when she said that most men want a response to their advances and need to feel loved and wanted.'

'Do you think so?' asked her sister with hope in her voice.

'Think! I *know* they do!'

Liv was silent for a time. When she spoke again, her voice showed she was still too heartbroken to recognise that Sol had a great deal of experience in these matters.

'If only I had been strong enough to realise – but I was so cut off from everyone and so unsure of myself. I thought that the fault lay within me and that he was right to compare me with harlots and say all the other things that he did. That really broke me, Sol, and it was the cause of my humiliation, my shame and my feelings of guilt. Can you see how he crushed me? And, Sol … No, I can't say any more.'

'You must, please. Get it all off your chest now. Otherwise you will never rid yourself of all these thoughts. If you don't, then you will carry on worrying yourself with them. They will keep going round and round in your head.'

'No, it was just something that came to me.'

Sol waited; then, not being one of nature's most patient creatures, she muttered, 'Well?'

With an effort, Liv found the courage she needed. 'It may be a terrible thought, but I cannot free myself from the idea that … Well, you know, each time he used his whip on me or punished me in some other way he would afterwards become so caring and loving. Then he would – you know what I mean?'

Sol sat bolt upright in bed.

'Oh, what! No! No! What a pig of a man – how ghastly! Ugh!' Unable to find suitable words to express how she felt, Sol lay back down again. 'I would have killed him,' she muttered to herself, forgetful briefly of the fact that she already had.

'But that was just a distraction,' said Liv by way of excusing him. 'Worse was the constant pressure. Eyes were watching me all the time. I always had to make sure that I behaved properly. That is why I cannot marry Dag. I have nothing to offer him. I dare not show my feelings and I am always in fear …'

'In fear of what?'

'Being reprimanded.'

'By *Dag*?'

'Yes! He has always been such a stickler for being neat and tidy – he doesn't like things out of place and hates mistakes to be made.'

'True, but how can you compare that with being in love?'

'It's nearly the same thing.'

'Don't be silly,' said Sol.

They continued discussing this for a while, but Sol was not able to convince her sister of the truth. So the next day she went back to Dag and quickly told him the whole story.

'Your need for orderliness, Dag, frightens that part of her that craves spontaneity. There is no simple answer to it!'

Dag was sitting by the window, watching Liv help Meta with the chickens. He was deeply shocked by the way in which Laurents had gratuitously destroyed his own wife's happy and outgoing personality and, as Sol finished speaking, he turned angrily to face her.

'No, but at least she isn't in fear of me!' he exploded, although there was desperation in his voice. 'She knows me very well!'

'Yes, that is exactly the point.'

Words escaped him. 'But – but ...' He beat the palm of his hand against his forehead. 'How can she compare me to that beast?'

Sol looked at him steadily. 'I think you will find you have a very long road to travel, my dear brother,' she said slowly. 'And as well as long, it may also be a very *hard* road.'

Chapter 11

On a day when all four siblings and Meta were helping to harvest Are's turnips in a nearby field, they saw a distant rider on the road, heading for Linden Allée. There was a distinguishing military straightness in the man's posture as he rode and this compelled their attention. As the horse and rider drew nearer, they could see that he was indeed wearing military uniform.

'Who can that be?' wondered Liv.

Dag took a second look. 'That is the dragoon who escorted you to Skåne, isn't it, Sol?'

'Yes, so it is,' said Meta.

'Damnation,' hissed Sol. 'Forgive me, I didn't mean to swear. Jacob Skille – I wonder what business he has here?'

'I thought you liked him,' said Meta.

'Liked!' sniffed Sol. 'Maybe I did, but I'm finished with him!'

The others all gave her inquiring looks. By now, the rider had halted by the wayside and was seemingly rearranging his pack. He hadn't noticed them watching him.

Sol felt that she owed them an explanation. 'Well, we had a little – er – infatuation on the journey. It was

completely innocent and honourable, a trifle romantic –
but that is no reason for him to come here! Dag, couldn't
you be an angel and invite him up to Gråstensholm? I don't
want my past admirers tramping all over the house.'

'Yes, I'm sure I can,' he answered.

After the winter in Copenhagen, Dag knew his half-
sister better than the others. Wiping his muddy hands on
his working trousers, he started off towards the farmyard,
taking with him great clods of earth stuck to his boots.

'Oh, wait a second, it's best I come with you,' called Sol.
She did not want Jacob saying anything to her parents that
might compromise her situation. He was still some way
from the allée of linden trees, so Dag stopped and waited
for Sol.

'For God's sake!' she muttered, pulling so hard at one
last turnip that she fell over backwards. 'Why can't people
learn that when it's over, it's over?'

Are, who was watching the young peasant girl working
at his side, heaved a huge sigh of exasperation. 'No, Meta,
you've put it on the wrong pile again! The best ones go
there and the small and uneven ones over there. Can't you
see the difference?'

'I'm sorry,' panted Meta.

'Can't you do anything properly?'

Sol, already irritated by Jacob Skille's arrival, took
immediate exception to Are's impatience with Meta. 'Stop
going on at the poor child all the time, Are,' she hissed. 'She
rushes hither and thither just to try and please you, but you
completely ignore it. You only notice her mistakes.'

'When does she ever do anything else but make
mistakes? Look, she's standing there now, sniffing and
sobbing again. While she's doing that she puts the turnips
on the wrong heaps.'

'You make her nervous. She has never done this sort of work before. Can't you understand that?'

'No! Nobody should be that clumsy!'

Sol dropped the turnip from her hand and moved very close to Are, her eyes aflame. Because of his height, she had to lift her head to look her little brother straight in the eye.

'And how would you have behaved if you had been born of a harlot – a trollop without a man? Being there when she carried on her business with men, for as long as you can remember? Putting up with kicks and beatings from all and sundry because you didn't belong to a Christian community? Meta has lived in abject poverty, because no one wanted to take her and her mother into service. The only thing she had was a mother who, no matter how pitiful she was, tried to keep the girl from being immoral or turning to crime.

'Meta was so infested with lice, when I found her, that I could see them crawling on her. I had to bury her mother, who had been dead for three months, beneath a wretched hut, their only home, because Meta did not know how to take care of the dead! Since that time the girl has been alone and unprotected. When I found her she was bent double and bound to a fence by a dozen vulgar soldiers who were pleasuring themselves on the starving child – from behind! Judging from the marks on her legs, most of them had already indulged themselves before I came along and put a stop to it. And yes, I brought her back here with me! Why? Because I believed that this family would understand! It seems I was mistaken.'

Are was speechless. He had listened sombrely to everything Sol said and his silent expression betrayed the instant regret he felt over his total lack of sensitivity and understanding. Liv, the repressed and unfortunate one, had walked over to where Meta stood and held her close, circling one arm around her head and pressing her cheek against Meta's hair. In that moment an intimate bond was formed between the two young women – one which would be of great benefit to Liv. She saw in Meta another tragedy that almost overshadowed her own, and finding somebody to comfort and care for helped her forget her own troubles. Sol and Dag saw the beginning of this at once and it brought joy to their hearts.

'Why have you said nothing of this before?' asked Are softly. 'I had no idea.'

'I said nothing because Silje and Tengel accepted her without question – because I wanted Meta to be accepted as she is, not out of pity. And what's more, I thought you would be too young to understand such horrible things.'

'Well, you were wrong about that,' retorted Are and went back to his work.

Sol gave a start, suddenly remembering again the mounted solider on the track below. 'Dag, quick! We have to head off Jacob Skille! Come on, we must run! Dear God, how is anyone supposed to run with several pounds of mud stuck to their feet?'

They managed to stop Jacob before he reached the farmyard; or rather he caught sight of them and halted just beneath Sol's tree. It was a difficult moment for her and she was sure her welcoming smile resembled a rigid wolf-like grin, but Jacob gave no sign that he had noticed it. He was simply aglow with happiness at seeing her again and he gladly accepted Dag's offer to stay at Gråstensholm. Sol motioned to Dag to give them some space, and she walked with Jacob up to the house.

'And what brings you here, my friend?' she asked at last.

'I requested a transfer to Akershus,' he said with pride,

'and it was accepted. So now the two of us can be together, Sol. I have longed so much to feel your embrace. Now I am on my way to ask your father to allow me to make an honest woman of you!'

To her dismay, Sol realised that he was dressed in his finest uniform, straps and buckles highly polished, set off with a plumed helmet. He was clearly very serious about all this.

'You won't disgrace yourself by telling them that you've already made a dishonest woman of me, will you?' she hissed in his ear and her vehemence frightened him a little.

'I thought you had told them. Have you not spoken of us at all?'

'Why, yes! But I haven't gone into details. My parents are decent people who would have been very upset had they found out. Jacob, I beg you to wait before asking for my hand. Now is not a good time, for they are still distraught over my sister's tragedy, about which I shall tell you more later. My father needs me to help with his work through the winter.'

Well, well, thought Sol to herself. Perhaps caring for the sick has its uses after all – and, of course, the truth was she had been hoping to leave it all behind soon. Anyway, now that she had said it, a good purpose had perhaps been established.

Glancing quickly at Jacob, she continued smoothly, without pausing for breath, 'No matter, my parents will still make you very welcome. I have told them how well you looked after me in Skåne – but for the moment we can keep our love a secret, can't we? I will tell you as soon as the time is right.' Ugh! How hard it was for her to utter the word 'love'.

'But I have long dreamt of being together with you,' said Jacob plaintively.

'Meet me tomorrow by the river in the woods over there! After midday.'

He nodded his assent, a little disconcerted now that he had been forced to change his plans. Discreetly Sol waved to Dag, who had followed behind, to join them.

'And how long can you stay?' she asked Jacob.

'I do not report for duty for three weeks.'

Oh, God! Three weeks! How would she keep him at bay for that length of time?

When he met Silje and Tengel, who had not heard very much at all about Jacob Skille, they were very hospitable and thanked him for his escort duties in Skåne. Dag, however, knew that Sol was on tenterhooks and he quickly hurried Jacob away with him up to Gråstensholm. As they left, Sol heaved a big sigh of relief.

Later that day, Sol happened to glance through a window and saw Meta coming across from the barn carrying two pails. She met Are in the yard and he stopped to talk to her. Sol could not hear what he said, but she saw Meta raise her head and look at him with bewilderment. Sol could see Are's smile brighten and how his hand quickly brushed the girl's cheek. The he took one of the pails and walked with her into the house.

Sol moved away from the window with a satisfied smile – peace and harmony had been restored. She knew there was no question of Are acting out of sympathy alone; he had truly learned a lesson. Although for the moment it might be hidden by the trials and tribulations of puberty, there was untold warmth and humanity in the boy.

Meanwhile Liv had retold Meta's story to her parents, just as Dag had done for Charlotte. From then on everything was done on both farms to help the little girl from Skåne settle in and feel at home. She carried on working – everyone thought that would be best for her – but she was no longer treated merely as a servant girl and often regarded as part of the family. Nobody objected to this, because at Gråstensholm and Linden Allée, the everyday tasks and responsibilities were shared by all.

Sol met Jacob the following day, as they had agreed, in the woods beside the river. This was her secret place, where she used walk with her cat, which now had sadly departed for happier hunting grounds. Only Master Johan had ever discovered her at that spot and that was after searching through the woods like a madman. When they stopped, Jacob Skille sat down beside her in the soft warm grass.

'So how are things?' she asked.

'At Gråstensholm? Excellent, thank you. Dag's mother is a very fine and unusual lady. Pleasant to talk to.'

'Indeed, Aunt Charlotte is one of a kind. We all worship her.'

'I can see why. I have been doing some odd jobs for her. It's a big house to look after and Dag doesn't have the skills.'

'No and for the moment he is busy with our sister's problems. He is sorting out her husband's estate you see.'

Sol continued her hectic monologue in order to avoid any advances from Jacob, but as he listened to her his expression was sad. When at last she paused, he shook his head in a little involuntary gesture of confusion.

'Sol, why are you avoiding me?'

'Avoiding?' she laughed nervously. 'Do you call this avoiding? Meeting you here in the woods in secret!'

'Perhaps not. But your manner worries me. I have dreamt so much, Sol!'

'Oh, Jacob!'

She turned to look at him and he kissed her urgently and passionately.

When she managed to free herself, delicately and tenderly, she said, 'It may be that I have changed a little. In Skåne we were so free, so far from home, but here I must be respectful of my parent's wishes. Jacob dearest, will you think it strange if I do not ... want to be ... embraced by you – just yet? I want to feel pure and innocent until we belong to each other properly. Do you see?'

He was touched by what she had said. 'Of course I will respect your wishes. I can wait – forever if I must, my precious little dove.'

Dove! That's not what I'd call myself, she thought dryly.

Sol walked home, bearing the weight of the world's guiltiest conscience on her shoulders. How was she going to get out of this? She certainly didn't want to tell Jacob Skille to get back on the road from whence he came, although in all honesty that was what she truly wanted. But she had no reason to hurt his feelings – so what could she do? All the way home, in time with her footsteps and through clenched teeth, she whispered bemusedly to herself, 'Bloody Hell! Bloody Hell, Bloody Hell!'

* * * *

Dag stood uneasily in the large Berenius office building, down by Oslo harbour, and stared in disbelief at the farmer who had just arrived to deliver a load of timber. The man was twisting his cap in his hands uncomfortably as he looked back at Dag.

'You say you don't want anything for the timber, man? Why, then, have you brought it here?'

The farmer ran his fingers round the edge of his cap.

'Master Berenius, the sawmill owner, ordered me to bring it. It was needed by His Majesty the King – or so he told me.'

'What are you saying? It is quite true that the King shall receive a certain percentage and that he is due his taxes – but a full load? Has this happened before?'

'Ten loads a year, sire.'

'What? And the other farmers?'

'It is the same for them as well, sire.'

'Good heavens! No wonder Berenius was rich! But the other loads you bring – those that are not for the King – what do you get for them?'

The farmer told him. It was a ridiculously low price.

'No, I'm not having this. You will gather all those farmers who have delivered timber in the past year and ask them to come here one week from today. Here is a list of their names. You will all be paid what you are entitled to from this timber merchant for the year just gone. I cannot alter what Berenius paid in the previous years, but from now on you will have a proper agreement and be paid a reasonable wage for your work and your forests. Will that be satisfactory?'

The farmer was dumbstruck. He could do no more than nod, over and over. As he hurried away, Dag could see a delighted smile spreading across his face.

Dag turned to the foreman, who seemed completely confused.

'And what is it like for the workers here? What are their wages?'

'Wages?'

It appeared that they were paid in kind: bread or *brännvin*, a cheap distilled spirit similar to vodka. At Yuletide they were given one *daler*, a coin akin to the German *taler*. Dag closed his eyes and sighed.

'I will look through the books and see what I can pay them. I am ashamed! Ashamed on behalf of Berenius.'

As Dag began reorganising the business and putting matters in Oslo on a better footing, Liv's problems were also eventually solved, thanks to Meta. Nobody took so much care of the child as she did. Then, one day they came into the house together, dissolving into great bursts of laughter.

'Why, Liv!' said Silje surprised and delighted. 'You're smiling. Never have I seen a more welcome sight!'

'I don't know what it is,' answered Liv throwing her arms wide to embrace the world. 'Perhaps it's because Dag has done something truly inspired. He has sold that horrible house in Oslo and bought another one instead. It will be his office now that he is working in earnest. It will also be the family's Oslo home should any of us ever need to stay there.'

'That's wonderful news,' said Silje. 'But best of all is your happiness, Liv my little one – and Meta's of course.'

'What's more, Dag is changing completely the way they do business. He has given the foreman greater authority and made sure the workers have better conditions. The forestry farmers' financial standing has been improved by the new working agreements. They all worship him. The only issue is that the King should receive such a disgustingly large amount of timber – completely free!'

This was true, but the Crown was still only due a fraction of what Laurents Berenius had said. He had been pocketing the difference – an enormous hair-raising amount.

'Liv!' said Silje indignantly. 'You have no right to disparage His Majesty!'

'Yes, but what has he done to deserve all that timber?'

'Liv! The King is above criticism!'

Sol gave a derogatory laugh. 'Then you should have seen your beloved King, Silje, as I did at a banquet at the castle in Copenhagen – the flabby fat carcass they carried out, completely drunk! It took six men to lift him, while he babbled incoherently. King Christian IV's love of drink is surpassed only by that of his dear departed father, Frederick II, so they say. However, in his defence it must be said that his mind is crystal clear the morning after and no one can criticise the way he has ruled the country. But he should not have that tenth part of the farmers' timber – *and* the tax on what Liv sells – *and* the duties and tolls. He has now decreed new higher tolls for this year and *he* won't be the one losing out on them!'

Silje had been staring hard at Sol while her illusions were being shattered.

'You didn't need to say all that, Sol,' said Tengel. 'Dear Silje has always had a touching belief in the monarchy. We have tried to bring you up differently – we wanted you to be strong independent people, but that, in turn, means that you must have respect for the views and feelings of others. Is that understood, Sol?'

'Yes, forgive me.'

Tengel nodded. 'King Christian is a good man. The best Danish king we have had – and he does care about Norway. His father never did.'

Silje brightened up when she heard this.

'There is something else that troubles me,' said Are. 'There are those who disapprove of us mixing with Danes.'

'Are you referring to the fact that we are friends with Charlotte?' asked Tengel. 'They cannot be many.'

'I have heard nothing,' said Sol.

'And neither have I,' added Liv.

'I have,' said Silje. 'But as you said it is but a few.

Charlotte is a woman on her own and only fanatics could look askance at her.'

'Generally most people have accepted that there are now a lot of Danes in the country,' said Tengel. 'But if there are rebels against this, then I have the greatest understanding for them as well. Norway was once a great power, but through the machinations of several dynasties she became dominated by Denmark. A time of great tension may come, but hardly during Christian's reign.'

'What do you wish for?' asked Sol.

'I want a free Norway, of course, like we all do,' answered Tengel. 'But Charlotte is our dearest friend and I will *not* turn against her because of conjecture such as this. No, most people in these parts mix with Danes. So don't concern yourself with the odd ones, Are.'

'No, those I encountered who disapprove were just a couple of youngsters.'

Tengel nodded. 'Rebels in the making. We cannot afford to be involved. We must avoid attracting attention for Sol's sake.'

'For *my* sake?' echoed Sol. 'I can certainly look after myself!'

Tengel sounded sceptical. 'You must be exceptionally careful, Sol! One small step out of line could bring misfortune to us all – but especially to you!'

'Have I not been as meek as a lamb?'

'Yes, you have – but I can see the signs. You are becoming restless once more. Why only the other day you used magic on the shoemaker's wife, so that she made a miraculous recovery! It must stop. Use only herbs and potions, nothing more.'

Blithely Sol promised to be as virtuous as any angel.

* * * *

Sol lay in her bed, arms beneath her head, looking at the ceiling. She could tell Liv was asleep by her breathing. She was thinking to herself that it was high time to do something about Jacob Skille. He was still living at Gråstensholm and was due to leave in a few days time. Luckily he had not shown himself at Linden Allée for a whole week, probably because he was disappointed by her demeanour.

She was, however, starting to feel disquiet rise in her once again. It was the same disquiet that had driven her to take the rides to Blåkulla. She would not and should not go on another ride, as they only brought her disharmony and made her withdraw from the real world. Neither had she found anything to stop the terrible headaches and sickness that she suffered afterwards.

It had been raining for many days, but the ground was dry once more. What if she were to take Jacob into the forest and 'seduce' him? He would undoubtedly be pleased and would never notice that it was her intention from the start. She would ensure that they would be 'irresistibly drawn into each other's arms'. And that might help them find a solution. Having made that decision, Sol fell into a sound and contented sleep.

Dressed in loose flowing sensuous clothes, Sol went up to Gråstensholm the following day. When she arrived there, she found that the hall was looking very grand. Someone had obviously been at work here. There were drapes on the walls and a new fireplace had been built in the corner. Hearing voices from the salon, she walked over to the door.

Charlotte was laughing, a cheerful carefree laugh and,

without hesitating, Sol knocked and entered the room. As she did so, Jacob Skille and Charlotte moved quickly away from each other.

'Oh, Sol, it's you!' said the aristocratic lady, whose cheeks had turned bright crimson. 'Come in.'

Jacob Skille's face showed no emotion at first, but Sol began to see a silent plea, a desperate warning in his eyes. Don't betray me, they begged: please say nothing about us! Sol gazed steadily back at him and this seemed to calm him. She realised she had no desire to expose him – quite the contrary!

She couldn't later remember what they spoke about or what she had said – it was mostly banal chitchat. Charlotte delighted in showing her all the newly arranged furnishings and improvements, telling her repeatedly how wonderful it was to have a man about the house. Sol probably asked after Dag – yes, she had, although she knew very well that he was in Oslo. Then she had left a little later, confused and muddled, yet more than a little amused. So she, the irresistible Sol, was to be beaten to the post by a middle-aged and far from beautiful woman! Does Dag know about this, she wondered?

Still, she was very pleased that Charlotte had found romance. There had been precious little of that in her life! It was all the more satisfactory, as the two of them were closer in age than Jacob and Sol. So, although Sol preferred men with experience and authority, she was only too happy to let Charlotte have this one. However, she hoped Jacob was serious. Charlotte was *not* going to be hurt again! What would happen to Dag now? Were Jacob Skille's intentions honourable or was he after her gold and chattels?

No, she thought, absolutely not. Anyway, now she knew why he had not been down to Linden Allée for a few days!

She laughed heartily. She had been under no illusions about Jacob's love for her: it had never been anything other than a physical infatuation, just as hers had been curiosity and a desire for a little adventure. His feelings for Charlotte, on the other hand, were evidently entirely different. Indeed she felt she had sensed instantly, on entering the house, just how strong their feelings were for each other.

Quite unaccountably, in that moment Sol felt her emotions turn to a deep mood of melancholy. She was not sad about Jacob, far from it, but what was left for her? Was it impossible for her to love and be loved by a man in the way that Tengel and Silje loved one another? Or as the love between Liv and Dag was growing ever stronger, so that now it was plain for everyone to see? Was she unable to love anyone except one impossible ghostly character? Was any man ever going to want her for who she was and not simply desire her body, her beauty?

To her surprise, she found that she was trying hard to hold back a tear. She fumbled in the purse hanging on her belt and found she still had the small box of balm. Unused to the tears that misted her eyes, she left the path and ran headlong into the forest, until she came to a secret secluded place that no other soul knew about. She threw off her clothes and rubbed the ointment on herself, then she lay down with an improvised stick pressed hard between her loins. Half an hour later she fell into the 'abyss', into the depths of darkness on the special journey that invariably excited her and filled her with expectation. Oh, it had been such a long wait this time! She wanted it so much, so very much!

She met him once again, the Prince of Darkness, the only one who really loved and understood her. She knew this was true, even though their meetings were never more than episodes of tumultuous passionate sex. What was more, she knew that no worldly being could ever arouse her and satisfy her lust as he did. This was the only sort of love she craved.

It was as Tengel had said – Sol could not remain at home any longer, because deep and intense feelings of restlessness made her want to leave.

Everyone else seemed to be content with life on the farms. Are and some of the other farmers and woodsmen had begun to bring some organisation to their forestry, so he was often out in the vast woodlands for days on end. For her part, Charlotte was enjoying her new love, but for safety's sake she had drawn up a special will and testament in which Dag would receive almost everything if – and only if – she should happen to marry at any time. It had never crossed her mind that she, unpretentious Charlotte Meiden, would ever harbour such thoughts again! Life was so perplexing at times! But right now it was absolutely wonderful and delightful.

The colour had also returned to Liv's cheeks. She and Dag often disappeared on long thought-filled rambles over the farm, although they never strayed far out of sight of the house. As she was only recently widowed, Liv wanted everything to be done correctly and she still panicked like a startled deer at the slightest touch of Dag's hand. But she was certainly on the mend. It was incredible how much calmer her eyes had become and how easy it was for her to laugh once again. Little Meta, too, was also settling down well to her new life and every day would run endlessly to and fro between the barn and the house. She loved the work and the people among whom she lived and in all her short wretched life she had never been so happy as she was now.

With all these things falling successfully into place, Sol soon felt she was no longer needed. Autumn arrived and began to turn the canopies of leaves on the trees into swathes of yellow, red and brown. Seeing this, Sol asked to be allowed to stay in the house in Oslo for a while, just to help Liv with the decorating, as she put it. Tengel and Silje gave this a lot of thought, but they both knew their unruly foster daughter only too well and eventually they agreed to her request. As Tengel said, they could not hold onto her all her life; if they did, she would be impossible to live with.

Strangely they did not consider marrying her off, finding her a good husband and telling her, 'Here he is, now please take him and be done!' It would have been a simple task to find an unsuspecting man, for she had many admirers. However, if Tengel and Silje were really honest with themselves, they would have to admit that they would never have dared. Also Sol had never raised the subject either.

When her departure day arrived, it was with sadness that Tengel watched his beautiful niece ride away down the path from the farmyard under the glowing autumn colours of the linden trees. He was sad and disconsolate – and deeply anxious because she had not wanted any company on the journey, preferring to travel at her own pace.

Then later, on the road to Oslo, something extraordinary occurred – and it changed her life in a heartbeat. She had stopped at a roadside inn, where she knew they served good food, and as she sat down at a table and pulled off her gloves – it was cold riding this late in the autumn – her gaze fell on a man at a nearby table. As she looked at him, her heart missed a beat. This couldn't be true – she had to be mistaken! It felt as if her blood had rushed to her arms and legs and then drained from them again so quickly that she convulsed.

'It is *him*!' she thought, completely out of her wits – the Prince of Darkness from my rides to Blåkulla! But no, it surely cannot be him, that would be … But yes, yes, it is. He exists! He's come to this world of humans, just to meet me!

He wasn't exactly the same, though. This rendition was older – about the same age as Jacob Skille – and he had light brown hair, while Satan's hair, of course, was as black as coal. Neither was he quite so intensely demonic, she noted; he had in fact, a more human appearance.

But yes, of course, the Master, she reasoned excitedly, would naturally have disguised himself, so that folk would not realise who he was. Nonetheless there was a certain devilish prowess in his expression that gave him away. He was handsomely attired in velvet and silk – obviously a man of means – and at last when he turned his head in her direction, he instantly matched her gaze and his eyes lit up with triumphal recognition. Sol stared straight back at him and it was immediately clear to them both that they knew each other. She saw that he was accompanied by two men and seemed unable to free himself from them. Then as they all got up to leave, he came across to where she sat.

'We shall meet again, my beauty,' he whispered and hurried out.

Sol was bewitched. She had never seen such an attractive man in all her days – but then he was the Lord of the Night, the only one she could ever love – neither had she ever felt so aroused and, after he had gone, she felt she as though she was in the throes of a fever.

When at last her food arrived, she devoured it in no time. She had to wait to pay for the meal and when she left a little while later, the three men, of course, were gone. But Sol was certain in her heart that she would see him again. After all, had he not come from Blåkulla just to meet her?

Chapter 12

Relentlessly, every day Sol searched the length and breadth of Oslo's streets in pursuit of her lord and master from the underworld. She found she could not relax sufficiently to spend long hours in Liv's new house, no matter how much excitement she felt at getting it newly furnished and decorated. But although she went out every day to pursue her quest, she never caught so much as a glimpse of her quarry.

This, however, did not mean that everything else in her life proceeded smoothly; in fact she had only been in Oslo three days when she got herself into serious trouble. She had taken to walking among the city's many market stalls, partly to look for things to put in Liv's house, but also to find the fascinating man from the inn. That particular day, she stood at one of the stalls about to buy a beautifully tanned and decorated leather bedspread that would look perfect in the smallest bedchamber. A lot of the furniture and household goods had been sent from Linden Allée, but things were still needed. The tanner had just laid out the bedspread and Sol turned to him to pay for it when a lady of the *haute bourgeoisie* pushed in front and grabbed it.

'That's mine! I'll take it!'

Sol protested vehemently, 'No! Wait! Now look here ...'

The seller was a weak man, who refused to choose sides and he simply let the woman have her way. Sol became completely enraged, so angry that she didn't think about what happened next. She noticed that the lady wore a blouse and skirts, and the skirts were held around her waist with a knotted silver cord.

'May your skirts fall down, you old mare,' hissed Sol between gritted teeth. 'Then everyone will be able see that you are nothing more than rolls of ugly fat!'

So intense was her wish that, in front of all those around her, the knot in the cord untied itself and the heavy skirts fell to the ground. Precisely what the noble lady wore under her skirts and exactly what was visible will not be described here; but it is enough to say that great merriment ensued.

While she was panicking and attempting to regain her dignity, the woman screamed over and over, 'Get her! Get the witch with the evil eyes!'

Sol did not care. She was so embittered that she just hissed at her and let herself be taken prisoner. With a crowd of townsfolk following, she was marched between two burly men to the Mayor's office in a nearby building.

Sol felt as though none of this was to do with her. People, they were so paltry and small! Her guardian was far more powerful – he had even adopted human form in order to come and find her! Eventually they took her to a hall where several very important-looking gentlemen were seated, engaged in conversation. The crowd was made to stay outside while the two men led her in and bowed low.

One of them announced loudly, 'This woman has practised witchcraft in the street. It is beyond any shadow of doubt.'

As far as Sol could see, the Mayor himself was not in the room. These men, looking at her now with mild amusement, were his closest associates. As she looked back at them, she heard one of them sigh loudly.

'I'm sick and tired of this unending fuss about witchcraft!' he said in a world-weary voice. 'It's for the priests to deal with, not us!'

'Wait one minute,' said another, speaking slowly in Danish. 'We've seen this lady before, if I am not mistaken! By all the Gods, I do believe we might have quite a catch here!'

Sol looked at him questioningly, but did not recognise him.

'It is the woman with the yellow cat's eyes,' he said. 'She disappeared without trace from Copenhagen after causing quite a scandal. I think we should hold on to this one, Gentlemen! She knows a lot more than just her bedside prayers, so they say! After she had gone, there were rumours that she had made folk crawl across the floor like snakes – and much more besides.'

One of the more prominent men shook his head decisively, 'No, I don't care what you say. I want nothing to do with it. One of the Procurator's wagons stands waiting outside. Let us send this unfortunate woman to him. It is more of an issue for him to deal with than for us!'

The decision was taken and Sol was removed to the courtyard at the rear of the building, where a man-at-arms was assigned as her escort. As she walked over to the wagon, her situation started to become clear to her. She realised what she was being drawn into and it frightened her a little – not for her own sake, but for her family. She decided, there and then, she must not reveal her name to anyone.

The wagon driver, who had been fixing the harnesses,

turned to see whom he would be taking with him on his return journey. He was a stocky handsome-looking man with blond hair, yet he had a strange emptiness behind his eyes. When Sol heard him gasp in surprise, she took a closer look – and to her amazement she recognised him at once. It was Klaus – her very first conquest and Charlotte's former stable lad at home. She was about to shout a greeting, but stopped herself in the nick of time.

It had been seven years since they had met – but she could see immediately from his expression that he had never forgotten her. Of course! She remembered now that Charlotte had found him work in the Procurator's stables. She shot him a warning glance as she climbed onto the simple cart, followed by the man-at-arms. He carried a letter for the Procurator that would probably tell him everything about her. Sol decided in that moment that she would cut this journey short before they arrived at their destination – and Klaus was going to help her!

Her escort would pose no great problem, as long as she could find the right place. Klaus, having obviously recognised her wish for him to say silent, climbed onto the wagon without looking at her and they started out of the courtyard along a back street away from any crowds. They had soon left Oslo behind them and began heading west.

Before long the soldier leaned forwards over the driver's seat. 'We've got a real catch this time,' he told Klaus in an undertone. 'They say she's the worst witch in all the Nordic lands!'

'What, her?' asked Klaus with a quick frightened glance back at Sol.

'Oh, yes! It's straight to the rack and the wheel for this one, and then to the stake. I expect the Bishop will be there to watch the fun when this one burns!'

'But surely they won't burn her, will they?' asked Klaus his voice breaking with emotion.

'She's grand to look at, I'll grant you that! But they're always the worst ones.'

A muffled sound of distress came from Klaus and he seemed to shrink down into his seat. He continued to drive the wagon in silence, avoiding Sol's eyes and as they drove into a wood, the soldier rose from his seat and pushed past Sol with a vindictive grin to take up a position standing with his legs astride in the rear of the wagon.

This should be a good place, thought Sol, while still keeping outwardly calm and detached.

Then suddenly she let out a shrill piercing scream. It sounded exactly like the noise made by a bird of prey as it dived for the kill. At that same instant she picked up a strap that had lain on the floor of the wagon and threw it at the horse's rump. The sharp points of the buckle bit painfully into its flesh.

The terrified horse whinnied and bolted, violently jolting the wagon. The soldier lost his balance and tumbled backwards onto the road with a wild cry. The letter he had been holding fell from his hand into the back of the wagon and he ended up sprawled face down on the road, watching helplessly as the wagon careered faster and faster into the woods. The horse was running wild and it took all of Klaus and Sol's combined efforts to restrain and regain control of it. This task was made even more difficult because Klaus had himself been flung off his seat into the back of the cart as the horse sped off.

'You're crazy, Sol,' he gasped as he managed to resume his seat. 'What do you think the Procurator will say about this?'

'What do you think he'll say, if I simply let you take me

to him?' she replied doggedly, bracing her feet against the boards and grasping the reins. 'He will burn me at the stake – after he's tortured me and flayed my body to bare bones.'

'No! No, he mustn't do that! I've seen what they did with one witch – it was horrible!'

The horse was tiring, beginning to calm down and the wagon was moving more slowly now. They had both regained their breath and Sol smiled suddenly at Klaus.

'I think I'll get off here and you can carry on back to your stables.'

As she spoke, she reached into the back of the wagon and retrieved the letter that the soldier had dropped.

'No, I cannot arrive home without my prisoner – you know that! I'm going to come with you.'

'Then hurry, before someone see us.'

'What about the horse and the wagon?' asked Klaus anxiously.

'We can't take the wagon and there's no time to unhitch the horse. I don't know how the soldier is. He could be chasing after us.'

'No, he won't,' said Klaus bleakly. 'I don't think he'll ever run again.'

'Come on, let's go,' said Sol impatiently, far less concerned about the fate of the man-at-arms than he was.

Klaus gave the horse a sound slap on its rear. 'Home with you! Go back to the yard,' he said in a kindly voice.

With the empty wagon rattling along behind it, the horse walked off through the woods. The sound of its progress could be heard for a long time after Sol and Klaus left the road and headed off across a tract of marshland and bare rocks. At first they ran as fast as they could, but eventually they had to slow down because of the rough ground.

'Where are we?' asked Sol breathlessly.

They were standing on a ridge and below them in every direction they saw only forest. Far off to the south they caught a glimpse of water. It was the Oslo fjord.

'I don't know exactly where we are,' answered Klaus, breathing with difficulty. 'North of Akershus fortress, at any rate.'

I had worked that out for myself, she thought, giving him a shrewd glance. He was still simple and clumsy, but she could see why as a fourteen-year-old she had been so attracted to him – then as now it had been his rough strapping build, his innocent expression, his all too conspicuous masculinity.

Looking him up and down, she let out an amused chuckle. 'Well, Klaus my old friend! This is an unexpected meeting, wouldn't you say?'

He looked a little crestfallen. 'Bad luck follows you, Mistress. You aren't really a witch, are you?'

'What is it you want me to be?'

Klaus stared down at the mossy ground. 'My lass,' he said shyly.

'Then that is what I shall be!' said Sol in an unexpectedly gentle voice. 'But what are we to do now?'

It was obviously not easy for Klaus to follow more complicated thought processes and he dug absent-mindedly at the moss with the toe of his boot, staying silent.

'I cannot go home to Linden Allée again,' explained Sol. 'For the moment the authorities do not know my name and I want to protect my family. I cannot return to Oslo either, because they will recognise me by my eyes and I will be arrested at once.'

'And I can't go back to my stables,' said Klaus. 'Anyway I don't want to. It wasn't so good in the service of the Procurator.' Sol had noticed a number of scars on his cheek that may have been caused by a whip and he touched them distractedly with his hand as he continued. 'The only place where I had it good was at Gråstensholm. I wish I could go back there!'

'I don't think you can. I heard long afterwards that you were moved on to make sure that you and I were kept apart.'

From its perch in one of the few tall pines high overhead, a kite screeched. The noise echoed eerily in the silence and Sol looked up at it thoughtfully.

'They didn't succeed, though,' she muttered. 'We found each other this time, you and I.'

Klaus sighed as he savoured the memory. 'Ever since that time Sol I've had one great wish – to do it again!'

'Dear Klaus, have you not had other girls?'

'Yes, but they were as nothing. Like dead cows they were!'

Sol laughed out loud; she was flattered. 'Then we shall see. But where are we to go now?'

This time Klaus looked for inspiration in the heavens. 'I was just thinking …'

'Oh! Bravo!' thought Sol, but she said nothing.

'I was just thinking, we could go to my home.'

'To the Procurator's stables, you mean? That would be unusually foolish, I think.'

'No, no – I mean my home.'

Hmm! Well even he had to come from somewhere, concluded Sol. Perhaps she had always thought of him as a changeling, who had been dredged up from some troll-enchanted bog and left to plod unhappily around in the world of humans.

'But what will your family say?' she asked.

'I have none. Nobody lives there as far as I know.'

This news cheered Sol up. 'So why are we standing here waiting – is it far?'

'A bit of a way.'

It certainly was 'a bit of a way' and it was not until the next evening that they reached the wretched little hut, high up on the side of a mountain. Sol wanted to know what part of Norway they were in, but Klaus had no idea. All he could tell her was that his home was called Plassen. And all she could make out was that they were somewhere to the north and west of Oslo and Linden Allée – and at some good distance from them as well.

The timbers of the small building had stood up well, however, and they quickly began to clear it up and make it comfortable, tidy and warm. They lit a fire and, that evening, Klaus was able to relive his dream. When they became still again, he lay quietly with Sol in his arms, shedding silent tears of joy.

And Sol, to her surprise, was more than a little moved. Klaus was clearly still very fond of her in a down-to-earth sort of way. He asked nothing of her, accepted everything she did – and he was also physically very well endowed! If any man on earth was able to love Sol for herself, it was Klaus. Or was he also just attracted to her beauty? No, she would not doubt him – not Klaus!

Still, she reflected, Klaus would do for the time being. Realistically she had very little choice, now that she was too well known to show herself in public. Her desire for the man at the inn nevertheless continued to fill her thoughts. He was the real lover of her secret dreams – the Prince of the Underworld! And somehow she knew deep inside herself that she would one day see him again.

* * * *

No one at Linden Allée knew what had befallen Sol. She had quite simply disappeared from the new house. When they made enquiries among the household staff, they were told by a maid simply that she had gone out to make purchases and had not returned.

'Ah! Sol will always be Sol,' said Tengel, putting on a brave face, although they had all worried themselves half to death during the previous week. 'She's just got it into her head to set off somewhere.'

'I'm sure she has,' responded Dag, who had come to visit, bringing his mother and Jacob Skille. 'It would be just like her.'

After that, nothing more was said on the subject and minds turned to other things. Liv was quietly seated at Dag's side. She was not demonstrative in any way, but just looked up at him discreetly from time to time. Outwardly she had got over her depression, but she still carried all the guilt of the world inside her, planted there so cruelly by Laurents and his mother. Somehow a disastrous marriage always feels like a defeat, even for the innocent party, and it was not easy to hide this. Liv was one of the few religious members of the family and it could clearly be seen that she took her failure badly, although she was now sometimes able to smile at the world.

'I miss Sol,' she said absent-mindedly. 'I liked sharing a room with her; she was such good company – and she was always very concerned when I was awakened by evil dreams. Some nights she would comfort me, as a mother comforts her child. On others she would scold me for being so foolish as to believe their depraved lies. Now there is nobody who will comfort me – I wish I could die.'

The others stared at her in surprise.

'Do you suffer evil dreams, Liv?' asked Silje, aghast.

At that moment, Liv seemed to come out of her reverie. 'What? Oh, yes, I do. And now I shall not be able to sleep afterwards, because Sol is not here.'

'We can't allow this!' said Charlotte indignantly. 'Liv my dear, forgive me if I seem somewhat familiar, but I happen to know that Dag would like nothing more than to be wedded to you. Why not agree to it now?'

'Now?' said Liv, her eyes wide with surprise. 'It's much too soon.'

'But you desperately need someone to care for you.'

Liv looked at the floor. 'Or someone to care for,' she said quietly, 'so that I can forget my own woes.'

Dag smiled. 'You are very welcome to care for me.'

'But is that really wise, right now?' objected Silje who, in spite of everything, was the most conventional of all of them. 'I mean, won't folk shun you? It's so few months that have passed since Laurents's death.'

Charlotte looked at Silje for a long moment. 'I have never liked gossip and rumours,' she said speaking very slowly and putting her heart and soul into every word she uttered. 'On this occasion, however, I shall start some rumours of my own. I shall overwhelm our neighbours and friends with tales of how horrible Laurents and his mother really were. Then they will be predisposed to feeling sympathetic towards Liv – and Liv does deserve their sympathy! I shall make known the awful loneliness and the nightmares. I'll tell everyone how much love she has to share and how much Dag loves her.'

Silje nodded. 'Some folk will still talk – but I think most will understand. But what about the priest?'

'I will take care of the priest,' said Charlotte. 'After I donated that beautiful candelabrum to his church, he wouldn't dare object. Otherwise I'll take it back!'

'Mother, you are magnificent!' said Dag, laughing admiringly.

'It ought not to be a big wedding, though,' said Silje.

'Must you decide all this without asking me?' demanded Liv in a desperate whisper. 'Don't you understand – I cannot marry again! Not ever! I am good for nothing, useless and not worthy of anyone's love. I can't even be with child.'

'There, there!' said Tengel. 'You can't be certain of that – it could just as easily have been Laurents's fault.'

Dag butted in, 'And none of us thinks of you as useless or worthless. You know that!'

'There is nobody with so many skills as you, Liv,' said Charlotte. 'You keep house perfectly; you are artistic and very intelligent. And you are also very good with figures.'

'And you are filled with a great love of all living things,' said Tengel. 'You are always a ray of sunshine in all our lives. We are the ones who drove you into that awful marriage, Liv. Can you ever forgive us?'

Liv gazed at them with an unhappy, almost desperate look in her eyes. 'Nothing you can say will make any difference,' she said, her whole being strained like an over-wound spring. 'I can never marry again!'

Dag was saddened to hear this. 'Do you not want me, Liv? Is that what you are trying to say?'

Because she had been pushed too far, Liv burst into an almost uncontrollable convulsion of sobbing. 'There is nothing – nothing in the world – I want more. But he destroyed me. He destroyed … everything for me!'

Dag put his arms gently around her. 'Come, Liv!' he said gently. 'It will all come right in the end.' Turning to the others, he said quietly, 'I'll take Liv with me. We need to talk privately.'

All present nodded their agreement and smiled affectionately at them both, as they rose to leave. When they were alone outside the room, Dag said, 'Sol told me what Laurents had done to you. The way he had crushed your desire for physical love. I accept that, Liv. I understand that you will resist your feelings – or just be completely passive.'

'But that would not be *fair* – to you, Dag.'

He gave her a tender smile.

'Let's just say that it will be a challenge. You see I know how much warmth – fire even – there is within you. Give me a chance, Liv, that I may set it free again – even if it takes many years.'

She laughed, sniffing back her tears and pressed her forehead against his cheek. 'I cannot bear to be alone with my thoughts any longer, Dag. I need you close to me more than I can say.'

'That is exactly what everyone has been trying to tell you for a long time.'

'But how can I allow myself to be so selfish! What if I am never again as I was?'

'Liv, please listen to me,' Dag began earnestly. ' Please just listen …'

In the parlour, Silje was at that moment sighing loudly and shaking her head in bewilderment. 'I am beside myself with worry,' she said. 'Both our girls have such problems. It is awful that we cannot help them more.'

Are took a deep breath, stood up suddenly and announced, 'Tomorrow I shall ride to Oslo and try to find Sol.'

'No Are, not you,' said Tengel. 'You are needed here. I was about to say that I would go.'

At that moment Dag and Liv came back into the

parlour, walking hand in hand. Everybody turned to look at them with expectant expressions. For a moment there was a hush in the room.

'We're going to try!' said Dag. 'We will do our very best!'

Nobody spoke for a moment and Liv too remained silent, but she was no longer staring hopelessly at the floor and, in her eyes, they could all detect a faint glimmer of hope that cheered them beyond measure.

* * * *

Tengel travelled to Oslo, as he had promised, and looked high and low all over the city, but could find no trace of Sol – at least not before he happened to hear of the 'cat-eyed witch who had fled from her sinful life's final journey to the stake'. When he heard this, Tengel was seized by feelings of panic, but he dared not ask too many questions.

The elusive witch had, it seemed, made her escape and been swallowed up by the earth. It was hard enough for him to accept and it was not much to go on, but it seemed highly likely that the person referred to might have been Sol.

Although driven to distraction with anxiety, Tengel paused in a quiet part of the city and silently and prayerfully wished Sol well with all his heart. Then he set out on the ride back home, where he knew he would come face to face again with all the other worries that were waiting there.

First and foremost it was Dag who had problems – with the lumber business. He was bitterly disappointed by virtually everyone and everything. He had started with such good intentions, improving the lot of his workers and the farmers who came to sell their timber. So what exactly had happened?

Other farmers had heard of his business and his honesty. and consequently came to sell him their loads of timber for a decent price. But by then he had more wood than he needed and so they were forced in the end to sell again to their usual sawmills. This caused the owners of these mills to rail at Dag for his interference. The city's Timber Guild condemned him, workers stood and queued to be given a job by him and the authorities were not pleased by his criticism of the high taxes. So in a very short time young Dag had learnt swiftly and painfully that it is not always easy to do good for the underdogs in society.

At Linden Allée, Are was followed everywhere by the faithful Meta. She was there throughout the autumn, ploughing, helping with the calving, storing the winter feed and fodder, and raking up leaves with him in the yard as eagerly as though the leaves were valuable runaway chickens who had to be put back in the run. But although Are often groaned at her transparent eagerness to help, he never again scolded her.

* * * *

Sol found it amusing to live in Klaus's primitive little cottage – up to a point. They had very little in common, except at night. But Sol also took a certain daytime pleasure in sorting out the old hovel and making it pleasant for Klaus.

Each day he went out fishing and gathered frozen lingonberries. They did not have much to live on, but they survived. Sol, of course, knew that it could not last. Klaus was happy at that moment, but soon remorse and concern for the future would surely overcome him. Neither was Sol the most patient person in the world! She knew the old restlessness would begin to haunt her before long. She had already had enough of Klaus – he had nothing more left to give her. Nonetheless, a certain tenderness towards him made her stay on.

Meantime another problem had started to worry her. The first time she saw Klaus naked, she had been shocked to see how many scars were visible on his body. They bore terrible witness to the numerous cuts and blows that the poor boy had received since leaving Charlotte's employ. The worst of these was a nasty weeping sore across his buttocks and one thigh, where the flesh had become inflamed and swollen. In reply to her questions, he said that the scars came largely from a whipping he had been given for feeding a sick horse too much fodder. After that he had been forced to strip off and take his punishment in the most degrading way. It counted for nothing that the extra nourishment had helped the horse recover – there was to be no waste in those stables!

Sol attended to Klaus's wound as best she could. But the infection had gone deep and the wound continually oozed fresh yellow pus. Furthermore, the small supply of medicines from her pouch was almost all gone.

One morning, on waking, Klaus found he was unable to get up. He had a high fever and his leg was so badly swollen that he couldn't bend it. Sol gave him a real witch's brew, using nearly all the ingredients she had left. It helped for a few hours, but did not get to grips fully with the cause of the problem.

Then came the snow. Sol looked outside next morning

to see that everywhere was covered with a fresh layer of white. It looked about a cubit thick and it reflected the light so intensely that Sol was blinded for a few moments. They had eaten the last of the food two days earlier and she had thought of leaving Klaus on his own for a while to go fishing in the small lake. That, however, was impossible now.

Inside the hut, Klaus was nearly unconscious. Sol stood looking down at him for a long time, deep in thought. She still had the means to end his suffering and his wretched life. He meant nothing to her – had been no more than a distraction beneath the blankets of their bunk. Even that had not really done anything for her, because she knew there was only one who could awaken her lust, but she had to admit that Klaus had been quite amusing in their sleeping quarters while it lasted. He was uncouth, wild and powerfully built – and in love with her. That alone had meant a lot to her. But he was still only a vulnerable innocent soul, blindly treading this miserable earth!

She stood looking abstractedly around the cottage, which was little more than four walls and a roof. Then abruptly, memories of the man from the inn flooded into her mind again. Why did he not come to find her? No, she thought, he couldn't know that I am trapped here in this wilderness. He was bound to be waiting impatiently for her somewhere. Yes, but if he really was the Prince of Darkness and had come to seek her out, he would surely know where she was. That was obvious! So where was he?

Suddenly Sol got a grip on herself. What was she doing here with this wretch, Klaus? Why wasn't she out in the world? She took her small leather pouch of herbs and other mystical objects and contemplated them for a very long time, sitting beside the poor young man as he lay moaning with pain. Should she end his suffering? She asked herself the question very calmly, her gaze moving slowly back and forth from her pouch to him.

Then she made up her mind and was soon making her way down the mountain, moving resolutely back towards the world of people again. The path was almost vertical and the few trees that dared to grow there were clinging to the rocks with knotted roots – but she was not alone. Unable to find a proper sledge, she had turned one of the benches from the hut upside down and placed the limp form of Klaus between its upturned legs. Now she was pulling the inert figure and the crude sledge slowly down the steep track.

She had not given him anything to hasten his death – it had hardly seemed necessary. Nature would run its course either way. Somehow she just felt she could not leave him alone up there and if this was to be his final journey, he should at least have a Christian burial. She knew that he had a strong belief in God.

Yet she was not at all sure that this would be his final journey. It was true that he looked terrible, but although the poison had seemingly spread throughout his body, his young face was still smooth and handsome. The dumb sheep-like expression had taken on an immaculate, almost angelic hue and Sol felt herself moved by the sight. A tangle of words from the Bible came to her: 'Blessed are the meek for they shall see God', or something like that. The Bible had never been one of her stronger suits.

Now she had only one desire – to get Klaus to Tengel before it was too late. Not only did Tengel have the most powerful remedies, her own fundamental store of potions was there at Linden Allée. Just saying the name, Linden Allée, gave her a jolt. Why had she never been able to settle there? What was it in her that drove her further and further away? And now she would never be able to live there again

– she had forfeited that right in order that her family might live in peace.

Sol fought and cajoled the makeshift sledge, trying to get it down the path without hitting trees or running off the track into the void below. She dug her heels in and slithered long stretches, holding on to its sides for dear life. She swore when it almost collided with a stone and turned over; all the time she was worrying that Klaus was being thrown around so much.

Then at one critical point things went badly wrong. The bench rolled over and Klaus was tipped out, ending face down in the snow.

'You can't just lie there, you stupid clumsy oaf,' she muttered angrily, as she struggled with his arms and legs. 'Right! Now stay there, you fool!'

The journey continued, sometimes an inch at a time, sometimes quite swiftly so that she almost couldn't keep up with the makeshift sledge herself. In one steep downhill gully she simply sat on the bench with Klaus in her arms and let it run. Snow sprayed back into her face and it ended badly, when they both landed in the snow at the bottom and she had to begin the laborious task of putting him back in his place once more.

All the while Klaus was deeply unconscious – perhaps dead.

You're having a grim journey to your final resting-place, she thought, as she settled him properly. She had long since lost sight of the path and was now just heading in a general downhill direction. And then the inevitable happened – a giant ravine loomed before them.

While she would be able to climb down hand over hand, clinging to roots and rock, what would happen to the 'sledge'? She stood for long while considering her options.

'Oh, well! Kill or cure – at least he'll get down,' she mumbled quietly to herself.

After she gave the bench a gentle push, it began to slide downwards on its own over the ice and snow. So long as it remains the right way up, perhaps we'll be fine, she thought. But what if it turns side on?

In the event the old bench flew down. She stood and watched it bucking and slithering this way and that, tipping and righting itself by turns. Without her realising it, her fingernails were biting into deep her palms and her teeth were clenched as always happened in moments of tension.

'Stay where you are,' she begged Klaus, 'Stay still or you'll roll into the snow and I might not be able to reach you.'

Then he fell out – but he was already down on more level ground, where she could get to him. The bench continued careering down a long way until it finally came to rest against a tree on flat ground.

'Hooray!' yelled Sol at the top of her voice, waving her arms in triumph. 'We got down, Klaus, even if it wasn't by the prettiest route!'

* * * *

By dusk, she was trudging through a valley, heading for the home she had not seen for so long. But she knew she would not be there before dark and the night threatened to be very cold. She had taken a rope to pull the 'sledge', but being old and worn, it had snapped many times during the trip. It was now too short and consisted mostly of knots, so at times she had been forced to push from behind. There was no doubt she was exhausted and having had no food for several days did nothing to help.

Klaus had not moved at all. She had wrapped him up well and could not see his face – and she had no wish to see it, either! After checking again that he was securely positioned between the upturned legs of the bench, Sol straightened up and looked about her. To her relief she realised that she knew where she was.

She stood there for a long time. If they were to survive, they had to find shelter for the night – and soon. But would anyone welcome them? How far had the rumours of the witch with the yellow cat's eyes spread now? She could be making a fatal mistake – then a twinkle came to her eyes. There was one man she knew who would probably give them shelter for the night – and not denounce her.

Or would he? Did she dare? Would she not be walking right into the wolf's lair? Sol shuddered at the thought. She knew where he lived, the man that no one spoke to, the man that everyone avoided, the man without a friend – and by now it was not far to go.

He had come to Linden Allée one evening and stood in the shadows, waiting until all Tengel's patients had been given their potions and left the farm. Then he appeared, dark and awful to behold, still clad in his 'official' leather hood – he was the local headsman!

He had injured his hand and Tengel and Sol had tended to the wound, asking him to return the following night. He came the next night – and the next. Each time, he had sat watching Sol with a burning gaze while she dressed the hand. When she lifted her eyes to look at him, he turned his face away quickly, knowing only too well that nobody wanted to have anything to do with him. After that he never came back again.

The headsman – surely he, of all people, would not inform on her. Wasn't she his eventual prey, after all? All he had to do was wait patiently. Heaving a deep sigh, she took hold of the legs of the upturned bench and set off once more.

Chapter 13

Sol found the headman's cottage without too much difficulty. It was well off the beaten track, some way into the forest and there were no other settlements close by. Striding boldly up the front path, she banged hard on the door with icy hands.

'Open up, headsman!' she shouted. 'I am Sol, foster daughter of Tengel. I once treated a wound for you. Now I'm in need of help. My friend is hurt and we must have shelter for the night. Will you take us in?'

The door opened slowly, just enough for a burning torch to be thrust outwards. It lit up her face, but she could see nothing. Then the door opened wide.

'Can you help me with my friend?' she asked. 'He is lying in the sledge just here. I do not know if he is alive or dead.'

Without a word, the huge man took hold of Klaus and dragged him in, dropped him with a thump on the floor and closed the door.

'Is he your beloved?' inquired the executioner in a strained voice.

'Beloved?' said Sol. 'No, I have never had one – it is not in my nature. He is a dear friend and has suffered much because of me. Now I want to repay him.'

The man nodded; he appeared to have a hard face – the little that one was able to see of it. His eyes were fiery and dark and, as always, he wore the hood that covered his head and shoulders, except for slits that were let into it for his eyes and mouth. He wore a belt over his tunic and his trousers were tight fitting. It was impossible to tell whether he was young or old; he seemed to Sol to have been alive since the world began and had never changed.

They laid Klaus close to the hearth to thaw him out and the headsman brought ale and bread for Sol and himself. They had been eating for a while, without speaking, when Sol finally broke the long silence.

'How much do you know about me, headsman?'

He answered without looking up. 'I know more than anyone; I know who the cat-eyed witch is, the one the authorities are searching for. But I have not said your name.'

'Thank you,' said Sol.

'Your foster father is a good man. You and he helped me once without turning me away or insulting me.'

They said nothing more and when they had made Klaus comfortable – there was still some life in him as far as she could tell – she was shown a cot in a very small cubicle, the only other room in the cottage. Sol crawled under the covers, half-dead with exhaustion, aching in every joint.

The headsman came and lay with her, but she was indifferent. Several times during the night she realised that he was using her body, but she was too tired to object, and let him have his wish – he was a lonely man after all. Admittedly he gave off a variety of male odours, but he had helped her. Let this be her way, she thought, of showing him gratitude.

In the morning the headsman gave her a proper sled on which to transport Klaus and he kept the sturdy bench.

When they set off, he went with her, pulling the sled as far as he could. Very few words passed between them and they spoke only when it was absolutely necessary. At last they took leave of each other with just three words.

'Thanks,' said Sol.

'And you,' he replied. But he stood watching the two of them for a long time until they were out of sight.

It was dark when at last she pulled the sled up Tengel and Silje's linden-lined avenue. She had already faced unexpected difficulties, because the snow had melted during the day and it had not been so deep here on the lower ground. For most of the day, she had pulled the sled across grass, sand and bare rocks, her nerves jangling every time the runners squealed – and all the time Klaus lay pale and still.

Because it was late, the house was in darkness and seemed empty. First she tapped at Liv's window – her old room – but Liv was not there. Then she began to worry. She didn't know what might have happened at Linden Allée since she left. What if …?

But her second knock, at Are's window, proved successful. He came out quickly and let her into the hall. His face lit up when he saw her.

'Sol!' he whispered, 'Can it really be you?'

'Oh! Yes, dear Are, it's me all right – and it's wonderful to see you again! Can you wake Tengel? I have a sick man with me. Let Silje sleep, if you can.'

He nodded and left. Shortly afterwards a half-dressed Tengel appeared with Are in the dimly lit hallway. His face too was aglow with happiness at seeing her.

'Sol! My dearest child! Welcome home!' he said tenderly, putting his arms around her.

Without wasting any time, she told them about Klaus.

Immediately the two men went and lifted him off the sled and brought him inside.

'My God!' said Tengel in that warm reassuring voice she had longed to hear. 'This doesn't look good.'

'Is he alive?'

'If only I could tell! I shall take care of him. Go and get some sleep – you look worn out.'

'Yes, I am, but I have things to do now that I am home again.'

At that moment Silje came quietly down the stairs. There were more welcoming hugs and tears, and some time passed before they broke apart from their emotional embrace. When they had recovered their composure, Tengel turned enquiringly to Sol.

'Does it mean a lot to you if this man lives or dies?'

She thought before answering him. 'Not in the way you mean,' she said. 'But yes, it does. He has been kind to me and he has suffered cruelly at the hands of others.'

'Then I will do my best for him,' said Tengel, nodding. 'He will need it.'

Just then Silje caught a glimpse of Klaus's face.

'My God!' she exclaimed. 'It's the stable lad who served at Gråstensholm many years since!'

'Yes it is,' replied Sol. 'You tried to keep us apart, but fate takes its own path.'

Silje did not respond. She didn't dare. Instead they gave Sol something to eat and she sat in the homely kitchen between Silje and Are, who plied her with all kinds of questions. During this time Tengel was alone with Klaus in the special room he used for treating the sick. Silje was keen to hear everything that had happened to Sol and where she had been, but the answers were vague. Instead Sol wanted to know where Liv was.

'Don't you know? No, of course not. Dag and Liv have wed and are living at Gråstensholm now.'

'Upon my soul! That was quick! But well done – it's the best thing that could have happened to them.'

'It had to be – for Liv's sake. She was miserable, Sol, and tormented. That awful Laurents took every ounce of self-confidence from her. Thank God he died. I know that sounds terrible to say, but I mean it.'

Then my life hasn't been in vain, thought Sol. 'And how is Liv now?' she asked.

'She is better with each day. I believe she is getting over – well, you know.'

'Not having any feelings when she lies with men, do you mean?'

'Sol!' exclaimed Silje in a shocked voice. 'How can you be so blunt?'

'Dear Silje, it was I who told you about it! Sometimes I wonder if you still think the stork brings babies!'

'No, but it was because you said "men"! Not little Liv! No matter – you are so tired, my precious, that you really must get some sleep.'

'I will, but then I must leave again.'

'No! My darling child, why can't we keep you here with us?'

Sol was deeply moved by Silje's words and that she felt wanted.

'I'm sorry, but sooner or later one of Tengel's patients will be asked about the "cat-eyed witch". Then you will be drawn into everything. I have friends, Silje, to whom I can go – and I will be safe.'

Tengel had entered the room and heard the last part of the conversation.

'The bailiff's men have already been here, Sol,' he told

her calmly. 'We told them only what we knew – that we had not seen you for a long time.'

'Then I must be gone from here tonight.'

Tengel shook his head. 'Go now and sleep. Sleep for as long as you need! No man will harm you in my house!'

She didn't argue with him. She was grateful for all their compassion.

* * * *

Sol slept all that night and most of the following day. In the afternoon she met Liv, Dag, Charlotte and Jacob Skille, all of whom had come down from Gråstensholm to see her. They turned the whole day into a celebration of her return home.

At one point Sol said to Liv, 'It seems to be impossible for me to come to your wedding. Now I've missed two of them!' They hugged in silence for a long time and silent tears ran steadily down Liv's cheeks.

Little Meta was overjoyed to see Sol again and tears also coursed openly down her young face. Charlotte and Jacob had made their wedding plans too and this pleased Sol greatly. Dag was also very happy about this, because he knew how lonely his mother had been – and would continue to be if he accepted the magistrate's post he had been offered in Akershus. Jacob had asked to resign from the military in order to start managing Gråstensholm properly and he knew well how to work the farm. In the event, that evening with her family was one that Sol would never forget. Klaus was still alive, although unconscious, but no worse than before.

'If he should get well again,' Sol asked Charlotte, 'could he come and work for you? He spoke warmly of the short time he spent at Gråstensholm. He said it was the only place he had been treated well.'

'Of course he can. What say you others?'

Both Dag and Jacob nodded in agreement.

'But aren't they looking for him too?' asked Liv. 'You did say that he helped you to escape, didn't you?'

'I do not think they are too bothered about him. Anyway, he has to live somewhere – and he suffered so terribly at the hands of the Procurator. To be on the safe side, he can always stay hidden if the authorities make a visit.'

Everyone agreed with her.

'Can't you stay until Yule, Sol?' begged Silje.

A shake of the head was the only reply. Everyone understood that it was impossible and very early next morning, Tengel got up and woke Sol, as they had planned. For a while they sat together in the kitchen, as she ate one last meal. Then, she promised them, she would leave quietly and disappear once and for all from their lives.

'Where will you go?' he asked softly.

'To the Finnish woodsmen. There are folk like us among them, Father. I will be safe there.'

But for how long, he thought despairingly, the restlessness in your blood will soon call you away again. 'What are you really searching for, Sol?' he asked aloud. 'Do you know?'

'I didn't know before. But now I do know. It is a man – I have seen him no more than once – but he is a part of me. I cannot explain why.'

'Do you think your quest will end when you find him?'

'Yes.'

They sat again in silence for a while. Then Sol sighed a disheartened sigh.

'What's wrong?' he asked

She shivered. 'I am starting to lose control, Father.'

Tengel sat beside her on the kitchen couch and drew her to him.

'How do you mean?'

'Everything used to be such fun. I was always happy. I did exactly whatever I pleased. But now, although I am still free to do so, it feels like I'm walking in a field of mud.'

'These things happen,' he said patiently. 'Nobody can expect to live their life exactly as they wish.'

She took a deep breath. 'Why is there no one like you for me – of my own age?'

'Even if you had found someone, child, it would not have helped you. You are too badly smitten by our legacy.'

'Yes,' she whispered, 'I am. I feel like two separate beings, Father!'

Tengel was despondent. 'I have seen some of the Ice People imprisoned by their own evil. You are a prisoner of your divided temperament. You can't see it yourself, Sol, but your appearance has changed a lot.'

'In what way?' she asked at once.

'Don't worry, you are as beautiful as before. But your eyes – they have the wild look of a wolf and the frenzy of sorcery about them.'

She sat up straight. 'Then there is but one thing I can do; find that man. He will dominate and hold sway over me.'

'How do you know this?'

'Because ...'

No, she could not tell him about Blåkulla. It would all sound so absurd. 'I just know.'

Tengel stood up. 'Seek out the Finnish woodsmen, Sol! And if they cannot help, try Sweden. Your background is not known there.'

'But for how long? In no time I'll get the devil in me again and send someone to hell – or heaven – wherever they belong!'

Tengel shook her, gently. 'You must stop doing these things, Sol! Try to control yourself. Try to think first!'

'But that is just what I meant when I said I have lost control! I am completely indifferent to such things. What's more I have humiliated myself, Father, more than you can imagine.'

He smiled at her. 'And yet still you return home with poor unfortunate creatures you want to help! No, I understand what is in you, Sol, and if I could help you … But come home again when all is safe and this is forgotten – when you have peace in your soul – promise me that!'

'I promise. By the way, Father, I will need money.'

It was a relief for them both to change the subject to something so mundane.

'You shall have it.'

* * * *

The weather had turned very mild, almost balmy, as Sol set off once more from her home. She rode east towards Solör, expecting the journey to take three days. How she would find the Finns, deep in the forests, was another matter. She would have to ask her way – if there were folk to ask. Once she had skirted round Oslo and was travelling along the River Glomma, she began to feel safer. The stories of her eyes would hardly have spread this far.

On the evening of the second day, she decided to overnight at an inn. Next morning in the early sunshine, she took breakfast. Once again she was dressed very elegantly, glad to be rid of the rags she had worn these past months. Now, if she wanted to, she could look like a lady. Despite riding alone, something that was not very common for a woman, she had been well received by the innkeeper and the breakfast was excellent. After a quart pot of wine, the world looked much better and Sol began to regain her old self-confidence. In spite of everything, the world was full of new challenges and she suddenly felt sure many exciting experiences still lay before her.

Hardly had her reverie had time to take hold, when she jumped out of her seat and stared through the open upper half of the door to the inn. A rider had stopped outside and dismounted. He tied up his horse and made sure it was taken care of before he walked over to the inn.

It was *him* – the man she had been searching for! The Prince of Darkness had taken human form once again – was it just to meet her? Always at an inn! Why had she not thought of that earlier and avoided this long impatient wait?

His dress was not quite as resplendent this time, but it was elegant enough. Wide thigh boots and a lace collar showing over a laced elk-skin tunic. Now, without his hat, his beautiful blond hair caught the breeze.

Disguise again! For Satan was as black as night. Yet she knew him – oh, yes! She recognised him from her dreams – his expression and the demonic glint in his eye were things no one could ignore. He had entered the room, but Sol was no longer looking in his direction. She sat as though preoccupied with her glass of wine, examining the way the light shone through the pale yellow liquid. She sensed, rather than saw, the shadow that fell across her table.

'I knew we would meet again.'

The voice when it spoke was deep and full of promise. Sol tried to appear confused as she looked up at him. At first she pretended not to understand, but then a slow smile came to her.

'Yes. I believe we have met before.'

His hand made a questioning gesture towards the bench opposite hers and she nodded her assent. The innkeeper came over and the man asked for food and wine, without taking his eyes off Sol. When they were alone again, he spoke once more in that strangely thrilling voice.

'What is your name, my lovely? No, don't tell me. Ever since our last meeting I have thought of you as my Moon Goddess. Let me call you by that name!'

Sol laughed out loud. Ridiculous! Moon Goddess – when her given name meant 'Sun'!

'And you?' she teased. 'I see you as a disguised traveller riding the earth – but your true home is elsewhere.'

'I am no archangel.'

'And that was not what I meant, either.'

Sol felt a glow spreading slowly through her whole being. It was fun to sit and trade inferences about something they both understood so well. She was suddenly alive and happy as never before. At last she had found her equal: a man who could give her all that a woman craved.

'I know who you are,' he told her. 'I do not know your name, but you are called "the cat-eyed witch". Do not worry, I realise you are being hunted, but I have no desire to inform against you. You are known by another name as well.'

'Am I? And what is it?'

'The Yellow Spider.'

'Spider! Ugh! Why is that?'

'People are convinced that you lust after men and that you kill your lovers once you have embraced them.'

Sol was furious. 'That is not true! Absolutely not! First of all, I have only been with a few men, and both of them – all three of them – are alive!' She had nearly forgotten the headsman and had quickly corrected herself. 'And they are all well. I am not interested in ordinary temporal men.'

He smiled at her indignation for a moment – then quietly asked her where she was going.

'I am going to visit the Finnish woodsmen. They understand sorcery, so it is said.'

His eyes were sparkling as he listened and Sol sighed inwardly as she looked at him. Oh, how attractive he was!

'I could tell by your eyes that you were a witch, my little Moon Goddess.'

It did not matter to Sol that he spoke so openly. On the contrary, he of all men would surely understand such facts better than any other. Looking closer she saw that he was not a young man – but then the Prince of Darkness wouldn't be. He was a thousand years old at least – but in his kingdom, a thousand years was only a day. What would he be known as? Satan? Lucifer – the fallen angel who did battle with God and was cast down from heaven into hell? This must be the image of Lucifer as he had been soon after he was cast down. He was still beautiful, but already had something of the look of evil in his gaze.

The picture the world had created of the Evil One was not true. He was obviously beautiful, as beautiful as the Angel of the Lord had once been. Or was he able to transform himself into any likeness he chose? He appeared in so many guises – dragon, dog or snake. He could be everything and anything.

'Where have you been all this time, since we last met?'

she asked and was surprised to see him look a little embarrassed. 'No, forgive the question, it was foolish,' she added quickly and he seemed relieved. But she could not help wondering why he had waited this long to rise up from the 'depths of darkness' for a second time. That was what she was yearning to ask him – but truly it was of little importance. Perhaps he didn't want to talk about his other life.

'Little Moon Goddess, my journey will also take me to the east. Dare I suggest that we ride together? The roads are not safe for a lady on her own.'

Sol bowed her head graciously. 'I accept your offer, Sire, and you need use no title to address me – we *have* met before, have we not?'

She spoke with intentional ambivalence and his amused grin told her that he was also playing her game. Again she thought he was the most attractive man she had ever seen. Despite the deep lines of experience etched in his cheeks and the small creases at the corners of his mouth and under his eyes, he was almost unbearably beautiful. Those blue eyes twinkled and his golden hair layered itself in gentle waves. Perhaps there was a sign of grey at the temples, which begged the thought, what was his 'temporal' age? She thought it could be – well, forty maybe? How many thousand years he had really lived, no one would know.

She felt a tingling along her spine and the hairs at the nape of her neck stood on end. It was one thing to be with him on a ride to Blåkulla, dreamlike as that was and without any obligation. It was quite another to sit opposite him in a country inn and arrange to travel with him – with everything that journey might entail. Yet he was the only creature who completely understood her. So why did she feel nervous? She would have to admit to herself that the togetherness and belonging felt far greater during her secret rides to his kingdom. She was finding it hard to relate to him – as though they were fumbling around trying to weigh up each other.

* * * *

One hour later they were riding in single file along the banks of the Glomma in the hot autumn sunshine. The path was too narrow for them to hold a conversation, but Sol was conscious of his presence as he rode behind her. She could also sense that he was aware of her – both physically and mentally aware of her.

As she rode on, she was struck by a sudden insane thought – it was already obvious that this was the man for her, so perhaps she could settle down properly with him, here in this world? And make a home and have children? Could she then free herself of the sense of restless yearning that had always haunted her? For the first time in her life, she wanted to be like other women – know the comfort of a man and a home. But was this possible? Being together always, with one like him? Surely it wouldn't work – he was merely a visitor, a stranger in this world.

Nonetheless she intended to ask. By God, she would ask him – but not yet. First they must learn to know each other better. Sol had never desired anything so passionately as this and the idea of peaceful innocent happiness flowed through her like streams of crystal-clear water.

They rode for a long time before he called a halt. They had passed a settlement and were now in more barren countryside with isolated stands of birch and little or no cultivation. Her wandering knight pointed to a field shelter or small barn up in a clearing.

'Shall we rest there for a while?'

She nodded, her heart pounding with excitement. It was midday and the sun beat down on the walls of the barn, making it warm inside. He undressed her very slowly until she stood naked before him. For a long while he studied her and then began to arouse her passion with methodical practised expertise.

Never had Sol met such a skilful lover – although he was not as the Prince of Darkness in her journeys to the underworld; there he was more urgent. Here he seemed aware of precisely what a woman wanted and when he at last lay naked with her, her whole body quivered.

It was still not the same orgy that she had always enjoyed so much at Blåkulla. She did not know exactly what had changed – could not begin to explain it. In the 'depths of the darkness', she had never needed to be aroused, yet her body had always been on fire. Now, for the first time, a worldly embrace was arousing her. It gave her gratification, but not the aching ecstasy that demanded more and more. Yet of course it made her happy; she couldn't deny that!

As they lay panting and exhausted beside each other, she felt a warm sense of closeness to him growing within her. At last she had found a rock to build on – someone to live for. Softly she stroked the velvet-smooth skin on his chest.

This time I shall do nothing to stop being with child, she thought. If one is born from this I will welcome it with all my heart. The offspring of me, 'the cat-eyed witch' and Satan himself! I would love and cherish a child like that – if it were possible from such a union.

'You were very good,' he said in a voice still hoarse with passion.

'So were you.'

He obviously knew that already; after all this had not been his first time – but for Sol it had been different, in fact very different from her rides to Blåkulla. He was not as well endowed physically as he had been in the deep darkness of the abyss. No doubt that detail was part of his earthly disguise as well.

'We belong together now,' he whispered.

'Yes, but you know I'm no angel.'

'Neither am I,' he smiled.

'No, of course you aren't.'

He took hold of her mandrake. 'I want that,' he said softly.

'Why?'

'As a love token.'

Sol was reluctant. She could not easily part with her most revered treasure. But how could she deny him, when all mandrake rightfully belonged to Satan. With sorrow in her heart she let him take it. Then she got up and began to put on her clothes. He followed suit, slowly and leisurely.

'I have probably killed two or three people in my life,' she told him in a low voice, feeling that she could and should tell him everything. 'But I have decided to stop now. I want to start a new life with you – a better life.' She grinned at him. 'My foster parents have been urging me to make a new start for a long time, but until now I have been too wild and wilful to have regard for human life. Anyway all those I slaughtered have been evil people who tried to hurt my dear ones. I haven't killed anybody for any other reason.'

Sol's companion leered at her. He was very attractive to look at, standing naked against the wall. 'You don't need to apologise to me,' he smiled. 'I have destroyed a whole race of people!'

'Yes, you probably have,' she laughed. 'More than one I shouldn't wonder.'

'No! It's true!' He smirked boastfully at her. 'A whole population of witches and sorcerers.'

'What nonsense you talk!'

But even as she lightly scorned this claim, she began to realise somewhere deep inside herself the terrible significance of what he had just said. In that moment an icy force of great strength started to take hold of her. Rays of sunlight were flickering through the cracks in the walls and she stared at him, suddenly wide-eyed.

'Tell me, what is your real name?'

'Why?' He smiled unsuspectingly. 'You called me your wandering knight, didn't you?'

'No, I want to know what your real name is.'

'Why?'

Her world was suddenly tumbling and swaying around her, but she continued speaking calmly. 'I want to know, that's all.'

'Well, there's no harm in telling you. My name is Heming.'

The colour drained from Sol's face. 'Heming the Bailiff-killer?'

His grin vanished. 'How do you know me by that name? How the Devil do you know? No one this far south has heard that name!'

A burning rage of awful intensity began to rise within her and with it an overwhelming tidal wave of disappointment. The rage that began as a small involuntarily cry quickly grew into a loud and piercing scream of pain. Without any hesitation she grabbed a sharp-tined pitchfork that stood propped against the wall and, still screaming, she moved menacingly towards him, clutching it tightly in both hands.

'Stop!' he yelled. 'Have you gone mad?'

With all her strength, she hurled the pitchfork at Heming. He desperately tried to turn aside to avoid it, but Sol had moved with lightning speed. A split second later, the twin prongs struck him with terrible force, piercing his belly and skewering him to the wall. Heming's own primordial scream rent the air, just as Sol's died away. For a long moment she stood motionless, staring at him with the same unnerving look she had first given Abelone's son twenty years earlier.

'You are mad! You witch!' he managed to say with a violent gasp of breath.

Sol went and stood very close to him. 'Don't you recognise me? I am Sol of the Ice People, Tengel's foster daughter.'

Heming stared at her with a look of pure horror in his eyes. 'No!' he cried through his pain. 'You are dead! They are all dead!'

'No,' said Sol, calmer now, 'Tengel is alive; and so are Silje and Dag and Liv. All those you were searching for.'

'No! No!' he gasped again. 'It can't be true. Oh help me, please help me!' he whined. 'I am dying!'

'Yes, you are dying!' said Sol, spitting out her words with great venom. 'And I can't tell you how much that pleases me. For it was you who brought death to the Ice People. You killed Hanna! Thanks be to all the powers of darkness for granting me this chance to gain vengeance for Hanna, my teacher and my soul mate. I believe she knew this would happen. I think she predicted it.'

'Spider!' he yelled. 'Yellow Spider!'

Sol sat down quietly on a log to watch him die, utterly unmoved by his screams. When she spoke to him, her voice was a low monotone and he was forced to listen, although suffocating from fear and pain. Blood was coursing out of his body, running down his thighs; he tried to staunch the flow with his hands, but could barely lift them.

Sol's eyes were glowing fiercely, but her voice had lost almost all its vibrancy. 'So you are just an illusion! A vague memory of an unusually handsome man I met in my long forgotten childhood. Not a bit demonic!'

Naturally, he had no idea what she was talking about. He knew nothing of 'rides' to Blåkulla – simple, ignorant, unenlightened human that he was. He might have been able to beguile any woman, but he was no Satan. Sol had not understood that it was simply the balm she used that aroused her senses during her previous Blåkulla trances. Suddenly she felt deeply tired and confused – she didn't know what to do. All she was certain of was that she had never hated any man as much as she hated this one dying before her now.

'Help me please! Help me,' he whispered. 'I did nothing – it was the soldiers.'

'Silje suffered greatly because of you,' said Sol in the same lifeless monotone. 'And Tengel with her. I have done this for their sakes and for Hanna and Grimar, for your own father's sake and for the sake of all the many dead in the Valley of the Ice People. For all these people you will die, Heming the Bailiff-killer! And for all the children you cold-heartedly allowed to suffer the pain of death, so that you might keep your own miserable and worthless life!'

Heming could barely hear her any longer. Her voice was reaching him through a mist of pain and fear. There was a pounding in his ears; he tasted blood in his mouth and felt it run down his chin. He coughed and tried to shout – to beg for her help.

'For God's sake have pity on me!' he whimpered at last. 'Please have pity.'

'God has never stood by my side,' she said icily. 'Only the Devil, and now his heart is pleased. You have been hard to battle against, Heming Bailiff-killer. Have you done anything since you left the Valley of the Ice People except whore with women and deceive and defile? I suspect that your absence during the last months has been because you were in a dungeon and the men with you when we met at the first inn were your gaolers. Satan is pleased now, Heming. He is on my side, do you understand?'

The mist before him was thickening, but he could still see her hazily. Sol, for her part, sat perfectly still, hunched low on the log, watching him closely as he died. All the time there was a fierce yellow glow in her unforgiving eyes. Soon all Heming saw was those shimmering yellow eyes. Then suddenly they too were gone.

Sol rose to her feet and picked up the mandrake root from the floor, where it had fallen from his hand. She quickly restored it to its rightful place around her neck and without looking back walked quietly out of the hut. On horseback once more with Heming's empty steed following behind on its leading rein, Sol rode away towards the east to seek out the hidden settlement of the Finnish woodsmen.

Chapter 14

Winter came and went. The snows and the winds held Linden Allée and the farm fast in their icy embrace, as usual, and although the severity of the cold was nothing compared to that in the old high valley home of the Ice People, the warmer days of spring were still very welcome to everyone when they arrived.

Tengel and Silje often stood and looked down through the avenue of linden trees, from which their farm took its name, longing for the special moment that would announce the arrival of their foster daughter, Sol. Nothing had been heard of her at all since the late autumn day when she rode away. Secretly they had both inspected her special linden tree in the avenue several times – and as long as it remained healthy they were reassured. Summer returned, then gently gave way to another autumn as the seasons continued their ineluctable and majestic progress without pause.

At about that time Silje and Tengel's and Charlotte's first grandchild came into the world. Without any complications, Liv presented them with a strapping boy who was, at the suggestion of his very proud grandfather, to be named Tarald. He had staunchly refused their requests to allow the boy to be named Tengel, saying it was a name potentially filled with suffering.

Silje said nothing, but in her heart she hoped that her poor daughter had truly got over all her problems. In any event she had borne a child and she seemed to be so happy, calm and easygoing, now she was with Dag. Yet Hanna's haunting words still returned at times to nag her in quiet moments, 'All your children will bring great joy. Yet one will also bring you great sadness.'

Had she not suffered that sorrow already, after Liv's tragic first marriage and all the disquiet it caused? However when she mentioned this to Tengel, he turned away, saying nothing. He had obviously not wanted to answer.

But why was he like that, when Liv was seemingly so happy now? Perhaps he considered her happiness was still too short and unconfirmed to be really counted yet. Silje, however, had made up her mind to be positive about it and she trusted this would make it certain that no more harm could come to them.

Klaus, the former stable lad, had swiftly regained his health, thanks to Tengel's care and experience, and was happy working at Gråstensholm. He never uttered a word to anybody about his greatest yearning. There had never been anyone but Sol for him – and many times he too could be seen looking down through the two lines of linden trees.

Liv, as far as they all could see, was truly happy. Dag had made a pact never to reprimand her for something she may have overlooked in the house, or if things were not in their proper place. In any event, he never would have needed to criticise her, because a better housewife than Liv would have been very hard to find. Dag believed that Laurents Berenius's greatest fault lay in the fact that he had been driven by a burning desire to be the best and place himself above people and trample them into the ground, regardless of how good they were.

One winter evening, when Are had gone to bed, Tengel and Silje were seated in front of the fire, each quietly occupied with their own thoughts. They were listening to the wind whine outside and feeling grateful that they were well sheltered from the icy cold of the night outside. Then, unexpectedly, there was a loud knock at the front door and they both exchanged inquiring glances. Who would be out so late on such a freezing January night? It was moonless, very dark and there was still snow in the air. Tentatively Tengel got up and opened the door; outside stood an anonymous woman, swathed heavily in capes and shawls.

'Sol!' yelled Tengel after a moment, his voice a mixture of joy and pain. 'Come in! Come in, my dearest child!'

Evidently bewildered and exhausted, Sol came slowly into the warm comforting hallway. She did not speak immediately and her eyes strayed silently over the glazed mosaic window that Silje had been given long ago by Benedikt, the church painter. She scrutinised, too, the portraits hanging beside it. Painted by Silje herself, they showed the four children when they were still quite young. She had painted Liv and Dag twice, so that Charlotte would have a pair to hang in Gråstensholm. Sol recalled how restless she had been when sitting for Silje and how Silje had almost lost her temper. Nonetheless the pictures had turned out well.

Both her parents hugged her warmly and Silje's eyes filled quickly with tears. 'We have missed you so much, child,' she managed to say between her laughter and her joyful crying. 'You have come alone this time, then? Not another poor Klaus or Meta in tow?'

'No, I'm not alone,' said Sol almost out of breath. 'I do have someone with me. Can I bring ...'

'Yes, of course,' smiled Tengel. 'Fetch your waif! No one should be left to stand outside on a night like this!'

Sol went outside, returning a moment later with a small bundle that she nervously held out for them to see. 'This is Sunniva,' she said with a trembling smile. 'Will she be welcome here?'

Silje felt as though the ground had devoured her. 'Your child?' she whispered breathlessly.

'Yes. She would not let herself be done away with, Father. I tried with all the herbs I had, but she wanted to live.'

Silje swallowed hard. 'Of course, she is welcome,' she said, her voice shaky. 'Our second grandchild!'

'Second?'

'Yes, Liv and Dag have had a boy – about the same age, I expect.'

'Sunniva was born on the twenty-ninth of August,' said Sol at once.

'And Tarald on the twenty-fourth of August,' said Silje with a broad smile. 'And a terrible business it was too! The woman at Eikeby was due at the same time. But her child was not turned properly and Tengel had to ride back and forth between Eikeby and Gråstensholm.'

'What! At Eikeby? Giving birth is hardly news over there! She has a new one three times a year! What does the husband think he is – a buck-rabbit? So, was she all right?'

'Oh, yes. They had a weak little thing in the end – a girl. So you decided to call your little daughter Sunniva. That was a fine thing to do.'

'Yes, after my mother – and you too, Silje.'

'Thank you.' Silje was touched by this. 'And she's such a wonderful little pixie! Have you seen how pretty she is, Tengel? But who does she take after?'

'Her father,' said Sol adamantly.

'I just feel I know that face,' said Silje pensively. 'Where have I seen it before?'

'She is very beautiful.' Tengel had recovered from the shock. 'But who would have thought you would ever have a blond blue-eyed daughter, Sol? It's something I had never expected.'

'Can she stay here?' Sol asked quietly. 'I know of no place on earth where she will have a better upbringing – even if it hasn't worked on me! But then nobody would have expected it to work on me, would they?'

The others both looked questioningly at her. 'We don't need to stand here,' prompted Silje. 'Come in and sit by the fire. You must tell us everything!'

'Can she stay here?'

'You know that she can,' said Tengel. 'But now we want to know all that has happened to you.'

'May I eat first,' said Sol. 'I have almost forgotten what food tastes like.'

'Oh, goodness me!' Silje was appalled and ran at once to the kitchen. 'What does the little one eat?'

'Milk. Anything will do.'

Not before she had eaten her fill and her horse had been seen to, did Sol begin her tale. She lay relaxed against the sheepskin draped over the kitchen seat, and baby Sunniva, now well fed, slept soundly in Are's old cradle.

'They are looking for me right now,' she said in a voice that sounded very tired. 'I think they are trailing me. That is why I came here with the baby girl – I wanted first of all to be sure she would be looked after.'

Tengel's expression was inscrutable. 'If you could start from the beginning, perhaps?'

'Yes! When I last left here I met the man I had already told you about, Tengel. Do you remember?'

'Oh, yes, I remember – the only one able to bring you peace and happiness – or so you said.'

Sol gave a harsh hollow laugh. 'How true! Those were my words! Anyway, he is Sunniva's father – may he burn in the fires of hell!'

'So is he dead?' asked Tengel softly.

'Yes, I killed him. I watched him die a slow death. It was the most satisfying hatred I have ever felt, Father.'

'Sol!' said Silje aghast. 'You mustn't! He was still your child's father.'

Sol turned to her. 'Indeed, and thanks to him I can feel only a deep unbearable tenderness for my little girl – but I can never love her. And he is my sentence of death. Somebody found his corpse and others remembered seeing us together at an inn – they remembered the cat-eyed woman. The "cat-eyed witch" the bailiff had been hunting for so long.'

'But why did you kill him, Sol?' demanded Silje.

Sol answered sharply. 'Because the man I believed I could love bore the name I hated more than anything else in the world. His name was Heming the Bailiff-killer!'

'What!' cried Tengel, jumping to his feet.

Silje's hand flew to her mouth. 'Oh, no! Oh, no! Sol, say it isn't true!'

'It is true – by Satan!'

'Yes, I see it now! It is certain – she has Heming's looks. Oh, how terrible!'

Tengel was beside himself with anger. 'So that bastard returned to blight our lives once more and bring sorrow to our house. But Sol, he must not destroy you – you must not let him!' He pulled her to her feet and held her tightly. 'You are the daughter of my sister and I have loved you as I do my own children. Would you let the latest incarnation of the Ice People's evil spirit be your downfall? It must not be so, Sol!'

'No! I had not thought to go quietly into their trap,' she replied tearfully. 'I shall make for Sweden – but first I had to bring Sunniva to you.'

Silje tried to hide her forlorn feelings at the prospect of bringing up another child – especially now that the years were advancing. But she never for one moment considered refusing to do it.

'We shall care for Sunniva, don't worry about that,' she said. 'All of us here at Linden Allée and at Gråstensholm will look after her. But still you have not told us everything. Where have you been all this time?'

Sol sat down again. 'Well, when I had killed Heming, I resumed my search for the Finnish woodsmen. It took a long time and their settlements are spread over wide areas of the great forests. At first they were suspicious of me – we could not understand each other, for their language was not ours. But finally they accepted me and I lived among them. There I met the people of their clans who knew magic.'

Sol stood up and began pacing anxiously back and forth across the floor. She flexed her hands unconsciously as she walked, fighting feelings of deep unease. Past memories were seemingly distressing her.

'But they despised me for the child I was expecting and wanted me bound in the stocks. They were also fearful of my witch's craft, for I knew more than they did. Before long, I happened to cast a spell upon a man I didn't like. There were those who were not so intolerant, but they could not save me from the righteous ones. So I fled from there and lived alone with the child in a remote and empty woodsman's hut for a time. I survived on what nature provided, while the child took milk from me. Eventually, I realised I had no choice but to come back here, no matter how dangerous it might be. There was no fodder for the horse and I could not take the little one with me into Sweden.'

'No, certainly not,' muttered Silje.

'Then to the east of Oslo I went to a farm to beg some milk. I should not have done so, because they recognised me. I cannot hide my eyes,' she said emotionally. 'Later, when I had ridden away, they told the bailiff's soldiers, who set out after me – but I managed to fool them and so here I am. Soon enough they will discover where to find me. So I must leave first thing tomorrow.'

'Is there no cottage here where she can hide?' Silje asked Tengel.

He thought about this. 'No, all the farms are occupied and it is just a matter of time before rumours spread. Sweden is your only hope, Sol.'

'I know that. But I am so tired.'

They knew that she was not talking just about physical exhaustion. It was plain for all to see that her tiredness went much deeper than that.

* * * *

That night Sol went to bed to sleep at home for the first time in what had now seemed an eternity. In the darkness before sleep came, she lay thinking. Sweden? If she went to Sweden, what would she find there? New quarrels, new disappointments – nothing. There was nothing left on this earth for her any more – except perhaps one thing.

At first her rage towards Heming the Bailiff-killer had

been twofold, because he had also taken from her the thrill of her rides to Blåkulla. She had not dared to go again, because nothing would have been worse than to meet him there. She had spoken of this with an old Finnish woman, who was of the craft, and the woman had listened and heard her out, nodding understandingly.

Then talking Swedish in her singsong dialect, she told her, 'Try again! You will never see that man at Blåkulla now! The Prince of Darkness is never repulsive to those who seek him.'

Nevertheless Sol waited a long time before she dared try again. Finally, while living in the hut with the child, she had rubbed the witch's balm into herself one evening exactly as before. As it turned out, the woman was right. There was not a trace of Heming Bailiff-killer in the Satan who welcomed her and filled her night with lust. He had been demonic and beautiful and he was her own – not a twisted image of a childhood memory.

Sol never understood – or perhaps more accurately never wished or cared to understand – that it was the mixture of black nightshade, henbane and hemlock itself that produced these wild ecstatic dreams of a fantasy figure. In her eyes it was a magic substance, the key that unlocked the Underworld, the deepest darkness. She did not know that the herbs brought on hallucinations – nightshade the grotesque, nightmare scenes at Blåkulla; henbane the dizzy, swaying ride over land and sea.

Each of the three herbs was a deadly poison when swallowed, but rubbed into the skin in precise measures, they awoke incredible lust – followed by a merciless headache. Witches knew the perfect mixture. One ounce too much of an ingredient could result in a fearfully distorted dream – or even death!

None of this had entered Sol's mind while she lay in that remote hut, whimpering with blissful lust in a dream shared with a demon created from her own fantasies and desires. But suddenly, lying there at home again in her own bed, with the helpless infant slumbering at her side, she found a new enlightenment. Now she knew for certain what she wanted.

Sweden? Why should she go there? She would still not be able to stop herself killing or in some way injuring anyone who fell victim to her wrath – and then the cycle would begin again: fleeing, capture, poverty. She could only ever be really safe with one person – and that for all eternity! But how could she get there? Only through fire and brimstone could she reach eternal life in the Underworld. The only real answer was to be burnt at the stake as a witch.

Sol had never feared pain and the stake held no dread for her. On the contrary, just thinking about it brought on an intense feeling of ecstasy. Why had she been toiling so hard here on earth, only to suffer other peoples' foolishness and ignorance? It was so simple! Why had she not thought of it before? The Prince of Darkness was expecting her in the very image she desired.

With slow deliberation, she relived the blissful moments spent with him, not only during the throes of passion, but in the glorious understanding they shared afterwards as well. The smiling satanic eyes stared endlessly into hers; without any words they told her that they belonged together eternally. Suddenly the desire to be there overwhelmed her and she choked back a tear. Furthermore, if she were to remain there, she would have none of the after-effects she had experienced previously and her whole existence would be one unbounded burning rapture.

She slept soundly after these thoughts and when morning came she bade everyone farewell with a new sparkle of certainty in her eyes. She kept her goodbyes brief and unemotional in order to spare the others. She took the time to ride up to Gråstensholm to see the new infant and chatted happily with her unsuspecting friends. She even found time to exchange a few brief warm words with Klaus in the yard.

Tengel didn't understand why she only wanted a small amount of money for her journey; but she told him that she knew where she could get more on her travels. He was even more astonished when she handed over all her stock of medicinal and magical substances to him, including all the herbs she had inherited from Hanna. She even left the mandrake in his care.

'Just keep it until I return,' she told him. 'I don't want to be tempted to use it again.'

Tengel thought all this sounded wonderful and was very relieved – but he was still greatly surprised! He embraced her more than once before she left, his eyes moist and his expression tight with the intensity of his feelings. The weather had improved dramatically at dawn and when she finally rode away along the tree-lined avenue, the skies were clear and the sun was shining brightly.

* * * *

Then three days later, word reached them of Sol's fate. She had been captured not far away. In fact she had walked straight into the arms of the soldiers looking for her. There were no delays in the due processes either – the sentence was passed quickly. A pyre was built outside Akershus on which, following a day of torture, the worst witch they had known would be put to the flames.

Dag did what he could, speaking frantically to all the judges and lawyers he knew, but they all shook their heads. For his own sake and that of his family, they told him, he should not get involved. Nothing at all could be done to save this woman. Dag knew they were right and eventually abandoned his efforts.

Another person had prayed for her as well – the headsman. He went to speak to her personally, but seeing the strength of her resolve, he understood that he could do nothing either. Sol asked only that he did everything as quickly and humanely as possible. With a silent nod he pledged her his word.

Everyone had gathered back at Gråstensholm and Klaus was as upset as all the others. He remained immersed in a painful silence for a long time and obviously found it hard to speak. Then at last he found his tongue.

'I know where she is,' he told the others softly. 'She is in the Procurator's yard. They throw the worst witches in a hidden cellar where no one can get to them. But I know how to reach it!'

'Now you are contradicting yourself,' said Tengel, stressed and pale. 'How can you do that?'

'Not through the entrance – but at the back is a narrow passage between the cellar wall and the rampart. Down there is a small barred opening and inside that portal is where the condemned are held.'

'Then I shall go there.'

'No, that will not work. You are too big to enter the passage, as am I.'

'But I could?' asked Are.

'And I,' said Meta.

Klaus thought carefully, staring at them both. 'Meta, yes – and perhaps you, Master Are. I don't know.'

Are was worried. 'Can we leave the farm now? A storm is blowing up.'

'What damage can it do. It's the middle of winter,' said Silje.

Tengel prepared some strange things to take with him and then at twilight he set off on the road to Akershus with Klaus, Are and Meta. Liv and Dag had wanted to join them, but Tengel had advised against it. They would attract less attention, he said, if only a few went. As they journeyed, the storm whipped snow from the ground in huge flurries, so that it billowed around them like thick smoke. Tengel, with Meta sitting on his horse in front of him, pulled his hood tighter.

'Sol is not afraid of the stake, I am sure of that,' he shouted to Are, as they rode into the biting wind. 'Nor of the torture. But she does not know what it can do – how the instruments can crush a person's will, destroy their senses and their self-respect until they are no more. The stake will not break her, but we must save her from all those terrible instruments.'

'And it will take place tomorrow?'

'Yes, and the next day she will burn.'

'We must not allow it,' said a determined Are.

After a very hard journey, they arrived at about midnight. The Procurator's courtyard was dark and silent, except for the sounds of the storm howling in the trees and around the walls. They dismounted and Klaus led the way from the woods towards the back of the buildings.

The older men stopped at the rampart, while Are and Meta, after receiving strict instructions, crept into the narrow gap. It was a tight fit for Are, but they made it. Soon enough they reached the small opening and called Sol's name very quietly.

'Are?' they heard her whisper in astonishment. 'And Meta! What are you doing here?'

'We bring a message from Father. He and Klaus are nearby. He asks if you will accept his help. To be free from all this.' The young boy could barely hold back his tears as he spoke. 'We have potions with us.'

After a long silence they heard Sol's voice speaking softly again from below. 'Dearest baby brother! Tell Father that this punishment is what I desire. I do not want to evade it.'

Meta sobbed suddenly and Are hushed her. 'That was what we thought, Sol,' he said urgently. 'But father wanted us to ask anyway. No matter, we have cakes and wine from mother. They are not dangerous.'

In fact this was untrue. Tengel had anticipated Sol's answer and treated the cakes and the wine with a deadly poison. If she ate or drank only part them, she would quickly pass beyond further pain.

'They are very welcome,' said Sol. 'I have had neither food nor drink and it would be well to have strength for tomorrow.'

'And father sent you this box,' gasped Are, unable to speak clearly through his sobs. 'He thought you might need it to help shorten this night.'

'Witches balm!' she grasped it greedily. 'Yes, this threatens to be a very long night.'

'And I am to remember … everyone to you,' choked Are. 'They all love you, Sol. Mother Silje and Tengel, Dag and Liv. Dag is so upset that he was unable to save you. They all love you so much.'

'And me too,' sniffed Meta.

'And Klaus, and Aunt Charlotte and Jacob, and me. And all, yes all the servants on both the farms.'

'Goodness me!' Sol gave a hesitant chuckle. 'I truly do have many friends!'

For a long time Are found it impossible to speak.

'All of Linden Allée … and … Gråstensholm will miss you, Sol.'

'They must not,' she replied. 'Tell them all that I am happy now. They should understand this is what I wish for myself. I am not suited to your world. But Are …' she paused and waited a moment; she seemed surprised, almost overwhelmed by something. 'I feel as though – as if – at the moment I feel that I shall return in a different, more gentle incarnation. I cannot explain it. But Are, it is a wonderful feeling, please tell everyone! And please do take good care of Sunniva for me!'

'We shall all help,' he assured her. 'When Silje and Tengel are no longer able, then Liv and Dag will take over. She will be safe, Sol.'

'Then all will be well. Tell them all that they are the only people in the world that I love.'

'We know.'

He stretched his hand through the bars and held Sol's small hand in his. It was a long time before he could bring himself to let go, but eventually they left to set off on the quiet journey home.

As soon as they had gone Sol examined the things Tengel had sent her. Eagerly she rubbed the balm of henbane, hemlock and nightshade into her body. Then, without any hesitation, she drank the wine and ate the cakes, before she lay down on the wooden bunk. In the half-world of dreams into which she quickly sank, something was revealed to her with unexpected clarity: a very vivid memory.

'Now I know why Tengel the Evil One hated me so

much,' she whispered into the darkness. 'Now I know where I have seen him …'

But no one could hear her any more. She had already fallen into a deep trance and was no longer conscious of her surroundings. She was flying and she sped swiftly over the undulating countryside and across deep water until she reached 'His' mountain. There she turned to face the abyss for an instant and the next moment sped joyfully down into the depths of its pitch-black darkness, finally coming to rest in a field.

The Prince of Darkness came towards her, this time more fascinating then ever. His face resembled Tengel as a young man, although it was not him. This she knew with great certainty was her very own personal demon.

He reached out and embraced her very warmly. 'At last you are here, my beloved,' he whispered softly in her ear. 'Now we shall be together for eternity.'

His eyes were warm and filled with love – the true love for which she had always longed. Here was the desire, the sincerity and understanding that she had searched for all her life, but never been able to find. Now her love grew from deep within her – true love for 'Him' alone. She could find complete love with a man – she who had only known physical love until now and then only on her futile rides to Blåkulla. The kingdom of love was hers and, for the first time ever, Sol knew unbounded happiness.

Back at Gråstensholm at that moment they were all awake waiting anxiously and trying to control their troubled feelings. Not one of them had been able to sleep. Charlotte sat rigidly on the couch in front of the fire with Jacob Skille beside her. His sorrow was evidently no less than hers. Liv and Dag also sat on the other couch and she was crying uncontrollably in his arms.

Suddenly they all looked up. Above the sound of the storm they could hear a slow wrenching crash. It went on for a long time, then the high-pitched roar of the wind became the only sound again.

'What was that?' asked Charlotte in a shocked whisper.

Dag walked over to the window. 'It came from Linden Allée,' he told them. 'I think it was a tree.'

'In the avenue?'

'Yes.'

'Then it's all over,' murmured Liv with infinite sadness.

* * * *

A restless soul had at long last found peace. The end had come as Sol dreamed the most beautiful dream of love. Although physically confined in the wretched little cell, she was utterly unaware of this and she felt free and unfettered as never before.

At Linden Allée, a distraught Silje was waiting for the others to return and she heard the crash of the falling linden tree far more clearly, because it was near to the house. She was reminded immediately of the first time Tengel had seen the plague-sickened Sol. He had debated long and hard with himself then, uncertain whether it was worth saving the child's life.

But, yes! It had been a life worth saving! In spite of all her faults, Sol had shown them how to be unselfish – and loved them all. Thanks to her, everyone at Gråstensholm and Linden Allée had lived in peace over the years, free from all those who wished them evil.

Silje was sitting with little Sunniva safe in her arms,

pressing the baby close against her shoulder. Outside, the falling linden tree bowed slowly as it finally crashed to earth, having hung suspended for a while entwined in the branches of another tree. Silje's face showed no expression. She was shaking with cold, despite the warmth in the room, and in her memory Hanna's words were echoing persistently once again.

'Sol will not pass on our true inheritance! You and Tengel are the ones who will pass on the heritage of the Ice People.'

How she hated those words. Not for the first time, she wished with all her heart that she had never heard them. They seemed to torment and tantalise her unbearably now, as she looked down at the innocent-looking babe she was holding snugly and safely in her arms.

'What will become of you my child?' she whispered desperately. 'What will become of you?'

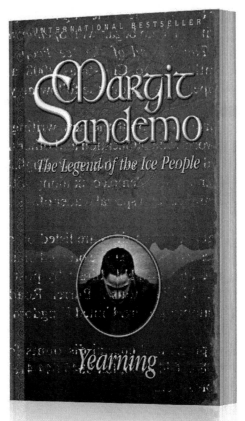

ISBN: 978-1-903571-81-1

Book 4 of The Legend of the Ice People series, Yearning, *is to be published on 2 October 2008*

Further Information

Publication for the first time in the English language of the novels of Margit Sandemo began with *Spellbound*. The first six novels of *The Legend of the Ice People* are being published monthly up to Christmas 2008 and further editions will appear throughout the following year.

The latest information about the new writing of Margit Sandemo and worldwide publication and other media plans are posted and updated on her new English-language website at www.margitsandemo.co.uk along with details of her public appearances and special reader offers and forums.

All current Tagman fiction titles are listed on our website www.tagmanpress.co.uk and can be ordered online. Tagman publications are also available direct by post from: The Tagman Press, Media House, Burrel Road, St Ives, Huntingdon, Cambridgeshire, United Kingdom PE27 3LE.

For details of prices and special discounts for multiple orders, phone 0845 644 4186, fax 0845 644 4187 or e-mail sales@tagmanpress.co.uk